WHAT COMES BEFORE DAWN

A MYNART MYSTERY THRILLER
BOOK 1

ADDISON MICHAEL

PAGES & PIE PUBLISHING
Author Version

2021 Pages & Pie Publishing

ISBN: 978-1-7359621-1-5

Library of Congress Cataloging-in-Publication Data

Michael, Addison.

What comes before dawn: a mynart mystery thriller / Addison Michael

Cover Design by Art by Karri

Editing by Tiffany Avery

While set in real places, this novel is a work of fiction. All characters, events, and police agencies portrayed are products of the author's imagination. Any resemblance to established practices or similarity that may depict actual people, either alive or deceased, are entirely fictional and purely coincidental.

www.addisonmichael.com

For my Family - Chris, Zoe, and Link
Thanks for letting me stay up past bedtime

WHAT COMES BEFORE DAWN

PROLOGUE
KRYSTA MYNART

Icy cold winter wind pushed its way through the window that was not supposed to be open. It wrapped its frozen fingers around her wrist, her face, and her neck. The chill settled in her heart. Krysta Mynart gasped loudly, coming awake from a deep, dark slumber.

She snuggled into her husband for warmth. His body always radiated heat but right now, nothing seemed to help. She was so very cold. Her brain was waking but her eyes refused to open as she processed one eerie fact. Her husband, Jason, woke religiously before the sun rose every single day.

"Jason?" Her voice came out in a hoarse but hopeful whisper. His arm was hanging over her body, limp and heavy, a dead weight across her stomach. She struggled to breathe as she felt hysteria rising inside of her. Something was wrong. She was afraid to open her eyes. She began to shiver and then shake from head to toe. Jason was always a light sleeper.

She could feel her head stuck in place to the pillow. She was so twisted in her sheets she could not move. Frozen air was blowing through the room. Senses suddenly heightened, Krysta noticed the sheets had wrapped her into a mummy-like cocoon as if she had tossed and turned violently. As if there had been a struggle. She gasped at the thought and tried to lift her head. She refused to open her eyes. Strands of hair pulled painfully. That wasn't the only thing that hurt. Her head throbbed, right at the temple. She was literally stuck. Stuck how? Her heart sank in her chest because the answer came to her with absolute clarity.

Krysta could smell a light, faint metallic odor. Not a foreign smell exactly, and she was able to place it instantly. She lay very still and finally opened her green eyes. She could no longer deny what her mind was telling her. There was no arguing the trails of brown-red she saw on her white sheets.

Jason was dead.

She sat up now, throwing the blankets and sheets up with her, ripping her blond hair off the pillow. Red blood matted her normally silky strands. Unearthing the tangle of sheets, she saw the horrific truth.

Jason was not just dead. He had been massacred. In his sleep. There was blood everywhere. Blood seeped from under the sheets, soaking through to the oversized comforter. Fresh pools of blood so vast it seemed no number of blankets would sop it all up.

Then she saw the knife. There was a knife laying at the foot of the bed. Her knife. Jason had given it to her as a wedding gift. She remembered it now as if it had happened yesterday, not seven years ago.

What in the world would I do with a knife? She had protested.

It's pretty. A souvenir… Consider it a wedding present? Jason had said. His eyes were full of mischief and he was amused. He had leaned forward and kissed the tip of her nose with his full, red lips. His beard tickled her.

You're lying! She had pushed his broad chest. She had gently touched the knife.

Okay, he had shrugged sheepishly. *You may need to defend yourself someday. Don't worry. I'll show you how to do it...*

Her mind worked quickly backwards through the night, but she had no explanation. Too shocked to cry, she stared into space. Why couldn't she remember anything?

She willed herself to remember but she knew it would not work. It was a thing she did. Chunks of time were missing from her life. One minute, she was in the moment, living life, the next, she was just... somewhere else. Always with the sensation that she had been teleported into a new scene in a movie. She just blacked out. And she knew, with absolute certainty, that she had done it again at the exact wrong moment. It had cost her husband his life. It was her fault that Jason was dead. No one would convince her otherwise.

"Jason?" she whimpered. "No!" She willed herself to cry. To take time to grieve for the loss of her beloved husband. But she couldn't. There was no time. She had to clean this mess up.

Forty-five minutes later, Krysta realized that the only blood she could clean up and make disappear was her own. All showered with a clean set of clothes on, she looked in the mirror. She had such a thin, long pixie face. Her blond hair fell just past her shoulders. Her big green eyes looked around as she said good-bye in her heart to her home. She packed a small bag. In the bag was a wad of cash, a few changes of clothes, and a passport with the name "Krysta Deffer."

Jason had told her this day would come. The day when she would have to run. She was prepared. She could grieve later. But for now, she needed to give herself as much time and distance as possible to get away. Once they found her husband's body, she would be the prime suspect. She had no alibi. None that she could remember anyway. For all she knew, she *had* killed him. Some witness she would be on the stand! She would only incriminate herself. The only thing she knew was she had been there when it happened. She was alive and he wasn't.

She could hear her mother's words floating in her head. The voice she had heard all the years of her childhood but tried to forget.

You're a wicked child, Krysta Suzanna, and one day the whole world will see you for who you are...

Now Krysta knew the truth. Her mother was right. All mothers are. She had no choice now but to believe her. Krysta was wicked. Soon, everyone would know as well.

Krysta opened the door to her home and paused. The sun was just creeping into the sky and a beautiful sunrise had dawned. She was struck by the evil that lurks in the night. *It's what comes before dawn,* she thought.

The ride to the airport took several hours from her rural home. Finding a plane ticket took even longer. Finally, at approximately 10:35 p.m., Krysta Mynart stepped off the plane in Canada and embraced a new identity, Krysta Deffer. No one ever questioned her.

The one thing Krysta hadn't counted on and had no plan for was her barely conceived embryo. Her daughter Paige would be born within the year and she would have to work hard to make sure Paige didn't turn out just like her. But that's all Krysta knew. The rest of the story would belong to Paige.

1

PAIGE

It was pitch black and I could see nothing. I had a blindfold tied tightly around my eyes. I took deep breaths in and out to calm my anxiety. I had learned that trick years ago. Never mind the fact that I was with a person I trusted. Though this was meant to be a good surprise, I could not stop the strange double jump I felt in my heart. In fact, this was probably the best surprise a girl could ask for in her life. I wasn't sure if my anxiety was due to not knowing what was happening or if it was from being quite certain of what was to come next. Was I ready to make such a big decision? What should I say and how should I react?

I pushed aside a stray piece of hair that had worked its way out of my blindfold. It never occurred to me that I should try harder with my hair. It's not like it was unkempt. Quite the opposite. It was thin, flat, and perpetually straight. Then there was the matter of make-up. I didn't have the slightest idea how to magnify my green eyes with make-up, so I didn't. On rare occasions, I wore mascara. Occasions like this one. But then wearing mascara and blindfolds don't go well together, I supposed.

Blindfolded with absolutely zero control over what was to

come next was extremely uncomfortable. Is this how mom felt when she had her blackouts? Was she in such a state of unawareness with her body still moving forward but seeing only blackness? Did she feel out of control too, or was her brain completely asleep while she continued moving on autopilot through half her life?

How strange that no one had ever heard of the condition mom suffered. Not even the therapist I had called the other day to make an appointment with had heard of mom's condition. Even I felt like it was a cop out! A way for mom to not have to own or remember anything that happened while she was blacked out.

I wondered if I would ever grow out of the resentment I felt towards mom. She had no excuse whatsoever! Yet she was constantly missing in action. Literally. It might not be so bad if I had other relatives around, but there was no one else. Because mom had these episodes so often, we didn't have any real friends or connections who were a regular part of my life. I had no clue how I managed to grow into a perfectly responsible adult.

I had also landed in a kind and loving relationship for the past six years, which was nothing short of a miracle. No thanks to mom! I mean, what did I really know about relationships? I certainly had never seen one modeled for me. The ones I watched growing up on TV seemed very unrealistic. I knew I didn't want to even try to copy those glamorized story lines. I had one friend in grade school whose parents seemed to really have it together. I supposed that was the example I was trying to follow. I guess it was working. But if I were really honest with myself, would I admit the discomfort I felt with my "healthy" relationship? I mean, the majority of our relationship had been spent on the phone while I was away at college. We said "goodnight" while I studied and worked on assignments and he went to bed. Did we really know each other?

Still, I had to smile when I remembered how Stephen and I first met.

My mother and I had arrived at a busy bookstore one afternoon with a list of books I needed for college in the fall. I was marveling at how fast time passes and that I was actually about to start college. But here I was. Though this was a mainstream bookstore, I had planned to get as many books as I could prior to my first semester in the fall. I even planned to read a few to get jumpstarted during the summer. I was beyond excited.

"Here, mom." I handed her half the book list so she could look with me. One minute, I was reading the back of a book, the next minute I looked up to scan the store for mom but she was gone. "Mom?" I said aloud, then sighed. *Here we go again*, I thought. Why couldn't mom just stay with me when we were in public?

Sometimes I found her quickly. Other times it took hours. That day I was frantically walking the aisles of the bookstore. I'd been up and down about five aisles of books when I noticed him. He was the type of man who would normally stop me in my tracks but my focus was on finding mom.

"Pardon me, miss. Are you looking for something? Are you lost?" he asked.

"Oh... yes." I continued my search. I was now standing on tiptoes to scan over bookshelves.

"Can I help you find whatever you're looking for?" he tried again.

Almost impatiently, I barely glanced in his direction. "My mother," I'd said. "I'm looking for my mother."

"Oh? What does she look like? Perhaps I can help you find her?"

"She does this all the time!" I said. I was so frustrated. "We can be in a grocery store, we can be at home, it really doesn't matter where we are. She just blacks out and wanders off."

"What does she look like?" he patiently asked again.

This was a huge waste of time. No doubt he had conjured up a picture of a little gray-haired lady with dementia. "She looks just like me, only older. My face is more oval. Hers is longer and thinner. Her hair is long and dark blond, much longer than mine and lighter – well, she has an ombre thing going – dark blond on top and lighter on the bottom, and her hair is a little thicker than mine. Same green eyes. I'm taller but we have the same nose. She's thin... too thin. She's wearing a white sweater and blue jeans."

For the next ten minutes, he helped me search the store.

A motion outside the window caught my eye. I glanced up, almost missing the bus that stopped by a bench where mom was sitting as though waiting to get out of town. I ran out of the store and barely blocked the entrance of the bus in time to stop mom from going who knew where *this* time.

"Mom. Stop!" I turned to the surprised bus driver who was waiting for mom to get on the bus. "She doesn't need a ride anywhere. She's with me."

The confused bus driver squinted his eyes at us, closed the door, and drove off.

"Mom. Snap out of it! Why do you always do this?" I felt tears in my eyes. Then I pulled mom into a hug. I felt, rather than saw, the handsome guy who had been helping me standing awkwardly nearby. In the moment, I had forgotten he was there.

His concerned eyes were a bold shade of blue and his nose was sharp and chiseled. His chin was angular and he had a slightly prominent Adam's apple. His profile was Romanesque. The blond disheveled curls on top of his head seemed a little on the long side. I noticed he was tall. Way taller than me, and that was saying something since I'm five foot eight. Was he six foot four?

"Handsome," I said out loud as I released my grip on mom. I was instantly mortified. "I'm so sorry," I tried to backpedal.

"Thank you! For helping me look for my mom. That was too kind."

"You're welcome," he chuckled. "I'm glad you found your mom."

"Yes. Me too. You go way above and beyond for your job. You're supposed to help me find books, not my mother." I could feel my face turn red at the failed attempt to joke. Was I flirting? To my surprise, he burst out laughing.

"I don't work here. I was looking for a book when you passed me and seemed so frantic. I couldn't help but wonder what you had lost. I had no idea."

I sighed and looked at mom. She was digging in her purse and didn't appear to be listening. Still, I hushed my voice. "This may seem very strange to you. But my mother does this thing where she completely blacks out and it appears that she's functioning and going about her day. When really, she won't remember any of this tomorrow." I was vaguely aware that I was repeating myself.

"Fascinating," he said. He paused, pondering my words. "How do you know when she's blacked out and when she's fully present?"

I shook my head. "That's just it. I never actually know."

"I can't imagine how difficult that must be for you. I'm Stephen, by the way." His eyes were inquisitive.

"Paige." As I grasped his hand in a shake, my breath caught in my chest. My heart beat faster and my stomach fluttered at the same time.

We'd been together ever since. Here we were six years later. He had stuck with me through a bachelor's degree and two years toward my doctorate degree. He understood my desire to be a vet someday. I was so close. Most of my classwork was done. I only had a couple of years of clinical rotations left.

"Paige?" Stephen's voice brought me back to the present.

"You're awfully quiet over there." He patted my leg and rested his hand on my bony knee.

I shifted around in my seat. My seatbelt was so uncomfortable. Were we going up? I had been noticing lately, ever since I finished my bachelor's degree and came back home, that Stephen was quickly becoming my everything. Was that even healthy? I supposed I should make a few other friends for balance. But the thought of bonding to another human being with my odd life circumstances sounded excruciating.

"Where are you taking me?" I could hear the way my voice sounded pitchy even though I tried to make it sound natural.

"It's a surprise," Stephen said lightly. "Just shut down your brain and enjoy the moment. I promise you will not be disappointed."

The silence seemed to last forever.

"We're here." When Stephen finally spoke, his voice was triumphant and excited.

I felt like I might throw up.

After what seemed like hours but was minutes, Stephen opened the car door. He took my hand, led me out of the car, and untied the blindfold. His bright blue eyes were lit up with excitement. I realized he might have gotten a haircut for this. His blond curls were tamer than normal. Stephen was so excited, but I was suddenly frozen to the spot. My breath caught in my chest. I was back to not breathing.

"I know, hon. Isn't it beautiful?" Stephen's eyes were on the view.

Everything was green. The drive that seemed to tilt upward made sense now. It all did. We were at the top of a steep hill and could see for miles. Green trees populated the neighboring hillsides. This area was known for the challenging hiking trails. In fact, I was never sure why we called them hills at all because they always seemed more like mountains to me. More than one hiker was rumored to have missed their footing or taken a selfie that ended with them going over an unexpected ledge.

I knew this hill in particular. It was the steepest hill around. I knew if I looked over the side, there would be a cliff that dropped straight into a twenty-foot drop with a river running below. I knew because I'd been here before. I'd watched a man go over the side.

2

NAMELESS

Allison was dead. She had been for years. He'd stayed by her side and watched her get sicker with every passing day. Through every cancer treatment, through every specialist, through every trip out of town, and through every single setback, he'd been there. He'd held his wife's hair back as she lost her lunch in the toilet, sometimes on the side of the road, and once or twice in a restaurant. Until, of course, she had started to lose her hair. It was tricky. The doctors wanted her to eat well so she could keep her strength up but often, the food just came right back up regardless. They told him she was strong in the beginning which might have been what prolonged her life. But Allison was doomed to die. It was her destiny.

His destiny became revenge. The only thing that made his wife's death worse was knowing that Krysta Mynart was alive out there somewhere. That blond-haired, green-eyed vixen. She was practically the devil! Allison never deserved to go this way. Cancer had sucked all the life out of her before she ever took her last breath. He had no desire to live his life without her. But he had one thing to do before he ended it all. Kill Krysta.

Only then would he be free. Only then would true justice be served.

Sure, the evidence stacked against Krysta from the crime scene would ensure that she served time in prison for the murder of her husband *if* the police ever found her. No one would take time to debate the overwhelming evidence at the scene of Jason's murder. He could appreciate that her fingerprints would be on the knife. *If* they ever found the knife. But even prison wouldn't be enough.

An eye for an eye, he thought. He needed to find her before the police did. The God of his understanding was a God of vengeance. That God would grant him the right moment in time to kill Krysta. She was evil and she didn't deserve to live. He was his wife's avenger. The only one who could get this job done.

He had people looking for her. It was only a matter of time before they found her, and he finished the job he had meant to finish all those years ago. No more surprises.

In the meantime, he had to be ready. Every morning he ran five miles. Late afternoons he lifted weights. Every Saturday he boxed with a friend. He was in the best shape he'd ever been in. His upper body was toned and muscular. His arms were noticeably bigger than when he was in his prime. His legs, while his thighs were bigger, were also stronger than ever.

He went to the gun range once a week, but he didn't plan to use a gun. He wanted to kill Krysta with his own bare hands. He'd look her in the eyes and watch the life drain out of them. He'd have the satisfaction of knowing he'd ridden the Earth of the Mynart stench. Only then would his calling on this Earth be complete. Then he could be released from this world to join his darling wife, Allison.

3

PAIGE

My eyes looked away from the view. I could not, however, look away from the burned down shack off to the corner of the hill.

"Paige?" Stephen asked. "What's happening in that beautiful mind of yours?"

I heard him but I couldn't respond. My mind was trapped in a memory.

The wood had once been light brown and heavy. It was a tiny two-room shack. And three people had been inside. Me, mom, and a man. I remembered raised voices, but only vaguely. I couldn't remember words, just the tones.

"Mama?" I could smell smoke. I tugged at mom's pant leg. How old was I? I had to look up to see mama.

"Not now, Paige." Mama's voice was tense and strained. I knew she wasn't angry at me. But I also knew better than to try again. The room was getting warm and smoky. Their voices were getting louder. I turned and ran. I ran hard and fast in the direction of the car. I could hear mama's voice, but I didn't stop.

"Paige?" Mama was frantic. I hid by the car. I was afraid. I peeked around the car but couldn't see much. I heard, and then saw, the scream of the man who was standing in front of mama, then was suddenly

14

falling off the cliff. His scream sounded farther and farther away as he fell.

"Paige?"

This time when I peeked out from my hands covering my eyes, I could see mama walking away from the shack with flames to her back. Large, angry, red and orange flames were coming out of the shack…!

Today was a bright beautiful day, but my mind only saw the shack on fire. Big, billowing flames that blew out the windows. I can still hear the sound the glass windows made as they broke.

My feet moved as if by themselves, taking me towards the remains of the building.

"Paige?" I could hear Stephen's voice behind me. He followed me. The sun was shining, but I felt so cold in my jeans and long-sleeved blouse. No doubt he was wondering why I didn't notice the blanket spread out on the ground with a small makeshift table in the middle. I saw it, it just wasn't important to me right now. Two wine glasses, a bottle of Moscato, and cheddar cheese sat on top of the table. I was walking in the *wrong* direction.

Stephen followed slowly. His body language showed uncertainty. He smoothed a sleeve of his button-down shirt. It was nice. It was blue to match his eyes with a white crisscross pattern. *Was it new?* I thought as I glanced at him following me.

I walked around the perimeter of the burned down shack as if in a trance.

"I used to have nightmares about fires. All the time, as a child. I dreamt there were fires in the house. I dreamt there were fires outside. One time, I even dreamt there was a fire on a dock between me and my mom and I couldn't get to her. I woke up screaming, all the time. My mom would comfort me, but she never explained why I had the dreams. She just held me and told me I'd be okay."

"Paige, I don't think I understand…"

I cut him off. "I've been here, Stephen. With my mom. I watched this shack burn down."

Stephen's mouth dropped open. He looked at me the way he sometimes did when I knew he was contemplating if I was showing signs of mom's strange disorder.

"Don't you see, Stephen, this is the place. I remember it all. I used to think it was all a part of those dreams. But it's real. My mom took me here."

Stephen pulled out his phone. I knew he was double checking my story. "Paige, this place burned down eighteen years ago. You would've been—"

"Five. I was five years old. Does it say anything about a man falling over the side of a cliff?" I asked.

"They called it the Hilltop Bar until it burned down, and it's been abandoned ever since the fire. They found Mike Polanski dead a few weeks after that smoke rose into the sky. He had been missing for a few weeks. Authorities suspected a connection but could not positively link the two occurrences."

I knew. He'd been here. With mom. With me.

"I need to talk to my mom."

"Now?" Stephen asked.

"Yes, *now*. Can we go?" I suddenly felt impatient. Stephen sighed and put his hand in his pocket. I assumed that's where the ring was.

Stephen ran a hand through his curly hair. "When will you let her go, Paige?"

"Go?" I asked. "She's my *mother*."

"She's a grown woman and so are you. Are you ever going to just let yourself live your life and do what makes you happy without having to check in with her all the time?"

"How dare you?" His words stunned me. They caught me off guard. This was important to me. How could he not see that?

"Do you even know what makes *you* happy?" Stephen's

voice was calm and direct. He searched my face as if looking to find some answer I was quite sure wasn't there.

"Where's this coming from?" I tried to defend myself. My voice sounded weak to me.

"You can't even answer the question, can you? What makes you happy, Paige?"

I ignored the question and took out my cell phone.

"Now's not the right time, Paige," Stephen commanded quietly.

I looked at Stephen. Before I hit send on my phone, it rang in my hand. I'd always known he thought he'd taken second place to my mom. But I'd never tried to stop that. Now was no different.

"Don't answer it." His voice was low.

I checked my screen. It was a number I didn't recognize. I decided not to answer.

Stephen turned away and started packing up the table, the blanket, and the Moscato. Clearly, there would be no proposal today. In fact, there might not be a proposal ever again.

Stephen's next words stopped me. "Do you love me, Paige?"

"What kind of question is that?" I could hear my sharp response.

"Just answer the question, Paige. It shouldn't be that hard. Do you love me?"

"Of course I love you," I snapped at him.

Stephen's phone started ringing.

We stood glaring at one another.

He let the phone go. Two seconds later my phone rang again.

Impatiently, I answered the phone. "What?" I barked.

"Paige Deffer?" An older man's voice was on the other line.

"Yes, this is Paige?" Who was this?

"Paige, this is Officer Stevenson. I need to talk to you."

"Okay, what's this about?" I asked.

"It's about your mother, Krysta Deffer."

"What's she done now?" I asked. My voice came out sharper than I intended.

There was a long pause on the other end.

"We believe she's dead, ma'am. We're going to need you to come ID her body."

4

PAIGE

"My mother was murdered." I thought about scrunching up my face and trying to look sad when I said the words, but I couldn't. I felt nothing.

Dr. Burnett sat quietly observing me with brown eyes that sat under giant, black-rimmed glasses. She was plain but attractive for someone I assumed was in her mid-forties. Her brown hair reached just below her shoulders. She sat still for what seemed to be an entire minute. When the shock of my statement wore off, her compassionate eyes settled on my face.

"Are you okay?" she asked me.

That's a stupid question. The hostility of my thoughts caught me off guard. "Well, I haven't cried about it. Isn't that weird?" I smoothed an imaginary wrinkle in my jeans and picked at a tiny hole I saw on my t-shirt. I had yet to take off the light-weight jacket that I'd bought at a thrift store. It was a black, vintage 80s jacket. I didn't take it off because I wasn't sure I wanted to stay. But now, I found it tight and confining.

"Some people have gotten so good at stuffing down emotions or shutting them off in childhood, they assume an emotionless state when a crisis occurs as an adult. It's a highly effective way of surviving the crisis and remaining a high-functioning human being. While it works for the moment, it's important to give yourself permission to grieve your loss. Everyone grieves differently. As I mentioned on the phone, I am trained in hypnosis. We can get into that if you would like?" She paused as she stared at me for a heartbeat. "But my hunch is, you're really here to talk about the topic you initially made this appointment to discuss. Ironically, you wanted to talk about your mother."

"Before she was murdered, I would have come in here and told you a very disturbing story about the day my boyfriend took me to propose. All I could do was remember a vivid memory of a traumatic event that happened in that exact spot as a five-year-old child with my mother."

"Sounds like it was important to you and you need to process that," Dr. Burnett said in a soothing voice. Her voice made everything that was so unsettled in my world seem like it could all fall right back into place. She tucked a stray piece of hair behind her ear.

"My boyfriend had laid out this blanket with all my favorites. It had that good specialty cheese and the best Moscato. The view was beautiful. But I didn't see any of it. It was like intense déjà vu. Only, I really had been there before with my mother. My mother was arguing with a man in a small bar. There was a fire. I was so little. I remember I tugged at my mom's pant leg, but she told me, *not now, Paige,* so I ran out of the bar. I hid by the car. I stood looking as the shack burned down, my mom walking away from it." I took a breath. I felt like I was coming up for air in a swimming pool.

"Go on," Dr. Burnett encouraged me. Her eyes were curious.

I realized this was a very dramatic introduction to my mom but then, I supposed there were a lot of moments like that.

"I could hear the sound of a man screaming. The man who had been arguing with my mom. The scream was loud at first, but it got quieter the closer he got to the ground and it stopped abruptly. He was dead." Even now, I could hear the voice.

"Thank you for sharing this memory with me, Paige. It helps me learn more about you."

I shifted uncomfortably in my chair. I really didn't make the appointment to talk about me. My right heel bounced against the ground, a sure sign of discomfort. I worked to keep the white Sperry slip-ons on my feet by firmly planting them on the ground.

"Paige, sometimes as kids, we make up stories in our own minds. And we believe them. Do you think this story is nothing more than an immature, childhood musing that kept your mind and imagination busy?" Dr. Burnett was peering over her glasses at me. "In fact, you clearly don't want to answer the question your boyfriend was about to ask. Is it possible you created this whole scenario in your mind and used it to buy you time so you can think about what your answer will be?"

"Absolutely not!" I protested. I didn't want to consider the logic in her words. "The memory seemed pretty real to me."

Coming here was a mistake. I wanted to ask what made this woman demean me and decide the memory was imaginary. I dismissed those thoughts. I wasn't here to talk about me anyway. I had only told her what happened as an example of a situation my mom put me in as a child. I needed answers now more than ever about mom, and I needed them now. Her death had brought some strange urgency. I was clinging to some shred of hope that I could find answers that would give me some sense of peace.

Dr. Burnett tapped the side of her face with her finger and looked thoughtful. "Should we switch gears and talk about the real problem here?"

"Yes." I sat up straighter.

"I've researched the symptoms you told me your mom has and have treated many people who fall into the list of possible disorders she might have suffered from. There are three categories of blackouts," Dr. Burnett paused and made air quotes with her fingers before she continued. "Disorder of circulation, called syncope, there's a disorder of the brain which is epilepsy, and a disorder of the psyche called psychogenic seizures."

"Okay, so which do you think my mom had?" I felt hope for the first time.

"It's not that easy, Paige. The problem is, in every case, with these possibilities, there's an actual seizure, and in many cases, the person goes unconscious. None of these disorders would cause her to keep functioning but remember nothing."

"No. That's not possible," I whispered. "There had to be an actual psychological or medical reason."

"Paige," Dr. Burnett's voice was kind but I thought she sounded patronizing. "There's another possibility."

My heart hardened. I'd heard it before but steadied myself for the inevitable judgement.

"Your mother's condition is not real."

"No." I shook my head. "I don't believe it. I've *seen* her do this. Over, and over again."

"Sometimes, we really want to believe the best of people. Especially our mothers. I – "

I interrupted her suddenly. "I want you to hypnotize me now."

Dr. Burnett paused to process my words. "I see. What are you hoping to get out of that?"

"I don't know. Maybe it will give me some idea about what my mom was doing before... leading up to her death. Something that will help this all make sense."

"Paige, I need to ask. Is it possible that you're in some danger here?"

"I don't know. I don't know what to think of any of this. That's why I'm here." *That, and Stephen thought it might help.*

"Okay, I can hypnotize you. But I'll only have time for that session today. We'll have to schedule another time to talk about results."

"I don't have much time. I need to figure this out right now."

"I understand." Dr. Burnett was maddeningly calm. "I have a session open on Friday afternoon. Is that soon enough to talk through this?"

"Friday is the day of the funeral. Not that I wanted a funeral at all. Stephen thought it would help me have closure." I stopped talking, uncomfortably aware that I was rambling. "Fine. Friday afternoon it is. How does this thing work?"

"Make yourself comfortable. You can choose anywhere in the room. Laying down, sitting cross-legged, or sitting right where you are. It doesn't matter. Just know you're going to be in this position for the next forty minutes."

I sat right where I was and closed my eyes. I heard Dr. Burnett's voice. As she counted backwards, I was aware of the soft, comfortable pillows that were propped beside me. I snuggled down into them, laid my head down, and I fell into a deep relaxed state until, quite suddenly, I awoke. I was confused and had to look around to get my bearings.

"We just finished a hypnosis therapy session, Paige. You're safe here." Dr. Burnett peered hard at my face. I stared back. I could see that Dr. Burnett was rattled. "I'll set up your next appointment for Friday. In the meantime, please Paige, be careful."

I walked slowly to the car where Stephen was waiting. It had seemed like a good idea for him to pick me up.

Stephen opened the door for me. When I was situated in the car, he turned to me with expectant eyes. "Well?"

"She thinks I'm in danger." I buckled my seatbelt.

"Why? Did you figure anything out that could be useful?"

"I don't know. I had her hypnotize me, but she didn't have time to discuss the session, only do the hypnosis. I'm going back Friday to talk through it. When I left, she looked at me weird and said, *be careful*."

"Man, would I have loved to hear that session." Stephen pulled his car onto the road. His smile was big enough to reveal his perfect white teeth and slight dimple on the right side of his cheek.

"Stephen! This is my life. Is this amusing to you?" I found nothing funny in this situation.

"No!" Stephen looked mortified. "I'm sorry. I just wonder what came up."

I sighed. "Me too."

"To switch the subject, Officer Stevenson called while you were in there. They've done all the tests they needed to do with the autopsy. It'll be a while before they get the toxicology report, but the cremation can move forward as planned. And we can have the funeral on Friday, as planned. Did you find a church?"

I nodded and cleared my throat. My mind was still processing his words. Why didn't his words evoke emotion? In the same way, I felt nothing when I had to view mom's body to positively ID her. I closed my eyes trying not to vividly see that moment. No matter how I tried, I could still see the strangle marks around mom's neck every time I blinked. While I knew struggling that way was a terrible way to die, I could not make myself feel anything. I simply nodded and tried to remove the image from my brain. I didn't want to remember her that way. But I hadn't decided how I did want to remember her.

"Yes, I found a church. Took forever. You know, the funeral homes were way too expensive. And a lot of churches in this town require that you be a member. I probably called twenty churches before I found this Baptist church who was willing. They asked for one hundred dollars for the services and the pastor to officiate."

"Can you text me the church info?" Stephen asked. "I would like to put out an obituary if you'll let me do that for you?"

"If you really want to. It doesn't matter, anyway. Not like we had any friends or family who will come."

"The obituary is a good idea for any friends or acquaintances you might not know about. The funeral is for you, Paige. You need closure. You need to be able to move on. You won't regret this. Trust me."

There was something in Stephen's eyes that I'd never seen before. When he said, "trust me," for the first time since we met, I didn't trust him. Not even a little.

5

NAMELESS

He sat on the front porch reading the newspaper the same way he did every morning since he'd lost his beautiful bride. He'd already been to the gym. As he'd slammed his fist into the punching bag, he thought his boxing buddy should be thankful that he'd gotten sick and had to cancel today. He'd had a dream about Krysta last night. He'd woken up angry.

He'd stood close to the punching bag and let his fists slam right into the place where her ribs would be. His anger connected to the bag through his arms, shoulders, and torso. He'd sent several private investigators throughout the years to find her. They each reported a lead or detail that helped him put together where she was. Then those investigators didn't come back. They'd all disappeared. Had Krysta learned how to defend herself? Did she snap the morning she woke up next to her butchered husband? He smiled at that thought. But he could not answer the question about how she'd made those trained PIs disappear over the years.

He would not underestimate her though. Never again. Something he should have learned the first time around. He frowned at the thought and subconsciously traced the light scar on his neck. Krysta had gotten lucky the night he showed up with a knife to kill her and her husband. The Mynart's were lousy thieves who had plans to take his money and run. It was pure, dumb luck that she'd grabbed the very knife that had killed her husband and fought back so ferociously. It put her prints all over the weapon. Her strength caught him off guard when she sliced his throat, narrowly missing the jugular. The amount of blood he was losing caused him to fall back. He had to find something to stop the bleeding. So, he'd ran out the back door, grabbing a kitchen towel on his way out. Which meant that Krysta got to live.

As luck would have it, she eventually fled the scene of the crime, making her look guilty. He'd searched for her for years. He'd even found her and made contact, but it all went sideways at the last minute. He had to regroup and think about a better plan. When he saw her again, she would not stand a chance.

He was tired of this life. Tired of living in a world where happiness did not exist. He just needed to kill Krysta to earn his way to the afterlife with his precious bride. Krysta had now eluded him twice. Next time, she would not be so lucky. Life would be better for everyone in this world if she was no longer in it. It was his final plan, his calling, before he left this Earth and reunited with his beloved wife. His heart felt pain and sorrow wash over him at the thought. Then anger coursed through his veins as he remembered those last days with his bride.

There had been an experimental procedure. Allison had been eligible. It took an entire year of gaming to save the money. Then his greedy partner had stolen his share and "lost it in one game," or so he said. One man's greed had killed his wife, Allison. Beautiful, sweet Allison, who died alone before he could even return home.

To have his best friend and partner in crime steal from him was one thing. But Krysta was an all-knowing accomplice. The way she took all the money and ran with a passport that must have been fake told him everything he needed to know. She had a premeditated plan. In fact, she might have been the reason Jason turned on him. She was an evil, conniving woman and she deserved to die.

He thumbed through the newspaper, his mind clearly elsewhere until he got to the obituaries. He gasped loudly. He read and re-read the name that jumped out at him.

"No!" he shouted. Not that anyone was around for miles to hear him. His home sat on seven acres and his nearest neighbor was behind him, just past the wooded tree line. He stared off into vast rolling acres of green grass, barely able to make out the gravel road that brought occasional travelers. All his plans. All his hard work. All for nothing.

Krysta Suzanna Deffer
February 25, 1963 - May 12, 2019
Krysta Deffer is survived by one daughter, Paige Deffer. Krysta was a resident of Little Rock, Arkansas. Funeral services will be held at 1st Baptist Church of Little Rock at 10 a.m. on Friday, May 17, 2019.

Her last name was different, but he knew that already. It was definitely her. Apparently, she'd had a child. This was news to him. Had she married, perhaps?

There was a picture. He studied it. Krysta had always been beautiful in a plain, elegant way. In this picture, her hair was darker than he remembered. She had been light blond when he knew her. Now her hair was dark blond, lighter on the ends and longer. Her thin lips were unsmiling. She used to smile easily. But he'd never forget her green eyes. They were hollow

28

and empty as they stared at the camera. Her smile never reached her eyes.

"How did she die?" he mused aloud. He read the short obituary one more time. A seed of doubt grew in his brain as he pulled out his phone to find more information.

What next? He made a quick decision.

"I've got to see it to believe it."

6

PAIGE

I'd been dreaming for days. Lost between what was real and what was not. I felt myself spiraling out of control, falling into a deep, dark abyss. Once I reached bottom, I knew there would be no way to get back out.

Then I heard a noise. A faint *pound, pound, pound* somewhere in the distance at first. Then it got a little louder. Was that in my head? I tried to turn my head toward the noise, but the fog around me held me in place. With each *pound, pound, pound*, my body and my heart ached as I felt myself coming into the present. I was waking but I still felt groggy, disoriented. I didn't even remember falling asleep. I knew I had spent hours at the precinct. *That* I remembered. When was that? Yesterday? Last week? They said they were still investigating the circumstances of mom's death. I was so confused.

"I'm sorry. I don't understand. How did she die?" I remember asking. It was all coming back to me. My body was shaking all over. I felt cold. I was on the thin side, so I always felt cold. This was different. This felt uncontrollable.

"We're still investigating the cause of death." Officer

Stevenson shut his folder. "All we know right now is that her body was found off I-40 in Little Rock. She'd been..." his voice trailed.

"Dumped? You think someone killed my mom and dumped her body off the highway? Tossed out of a car, perhaps?" In that moment, I'd felt so angry. "That's my *mother* you're talking about."

Stephen had placed a hand on my shoulder. "Paige..."

I jerked my shoulder away. I'd almost forgotten he was there. "NO! To *him*," I jerked my head toward the armed police officer, "my mother is just a body! Well, sir, she was my mother!" His insensitivity brought me to a level of rage I didn't remember ever feeling before.

"I'm sorry, ma'am. So deeply sorry. We'll notify you when we have new information."

"New information?" I had asked.

"A... toxicology report, did you say, officer?" Stephen stepped in. "How long does it take to do one of those?"

"It can take six weeks. Sometimes longer."

I remember taking a deep breath so I wouldn't yell again. "So, what's next?" I asked. I remember sounding stronger and braver than I felt.

"We just need you to identify the... her... your mother's body, ma'am."

"You mean, a trip to the morgue?" I didn't feel strong or brave anymore. Up to that point, there had been a small chance that they had her mixed up with someone else.

It was a nightmare. I'd only seen such things in movies but didn't know it really happened like this.

The morgue was cold. Of course it was cold. Nothing could have prepared me for the horror of seeing mom in that condition. Her face was not peaceful. Ugly purple marks bruised her neck. There was a bruise on her shoulder and her face. I wanted to look away, but I couldn't. I knew the memory of this would be forever burned in my brain.

"Yes," I said. "Yes, this is my mother."

Still, there were no tears. I felt nothing. Was I in shock? The last thing I remembered was agreeing to cremating mom's body after they released her. Somehow, Stephen had talked me into a funeral. Calling funeral homes and random churches to check costs for such things had been a surreal experience.

It was Stephen who suggested I go to the counseling appointment I had made. I had no desire to go. I didn't know why, but I couldn't remember if I had liked Dr. Burnett or not. Something was off. Did she hypnotize me? I thought so but couldn't remember what I'd found out.

After the appointment, I thought there was no way I'd sleep. I roamed around the apartment aimlessly for a few minutes. Mom's bedroom door was shut, the way it always was. She and I kept our own personal space and I wasn't planning to go in there uninvited today. I went to my room instead. I smiled at the purple curtains with tiny white flowers on them and the fat, fluffy bedspread that matched. It had been decorated this way since high school. My comfortable queen-sized bed was the only thing I thought could make me feel better. It turned out I was so tired, I kicked off my shoes and crawled right into bed with my clothes on and slept. Deeply. So deeply, in fact, I didn't know if I'd ever wake up until that nasty pounding started.

Pound pound pound. Louder this time, and I was finally awake enough to get out of bed.

I got up, disoriented, and went to the door. It was Stephen. I opened the door wide to allow entrance but said nothing.

"You're not ready," he said, more a statement than a question.

I flinched. It was the sound his voice made when he was

disappointed in me. "Ready for what?" I could not fathom what he meant.

"Paige, today is your mother's funeral. You look exhausted. Have you been sleeping?" Stephen's hair was freshly washed with every curl gelled nicely in place. He was wearing a black button-down shirt and black dress pants. He smelled like woods, maybe cedar, and the cinnamon gum that he was chewing. He looked and smelled so nice and for some reason, it annoyed me.

"No, it's not. It's tomorrow," I protested. I knew the date we'd chosen. Not that I'd even wanted a funeral in the first place. Stephen had insisted. How very selfish of him to push this on me in the first place. I glared at him feeling anger and resentment roll together. He said I needed the closure. I thought I just needed sleep.

He pulled out his phone and showed me the date. "The funeral is in an hour. Can you get dressed really quick?"

I stared at him, processing. That would mean I'd slept over twenty-four hours.

"Hey, are you wearing the same clothes you were wearing when I dropped you off the other day?" Stephen pointed at my rumpled button-down shirt and jeans. "That was two days ago! No wonder you didn't return my calls or texts…!"

I held up a hand to stop his talking and turned around. "Yeah, I was sleeping." I walked out of the room, vaguely aware that I was being rude. For some reason, I could not bring myself to care.

It took me less than fifteen minutes to get ready. I felt alarmed when I looked in the mirror. For a moment, I saw my mother's eyes staring back at me. I jumped a little, surprised by how much I suddenly thought I looked like her. While our eyes were the most common genetic attribute we shared, I decided it was the bags under my eyes that made me look the way she had started to look before she died. Like she had been looking more and more lately. Only her bags were because she didn't sleep and mine were because I had slept too much.

I quickly grabbed foundation cover-up out of my mom's makeup bag and smeared it under my eyes, patting it smooth with my fingers.

"Better," I whispered, satisfied that this had hidden some of the puffiness. On a whim, I also brushed on some mascara.

Then I got dressed. I didn't own much black, so I just put on what I had; a pair of black slacks and a black button-down shirt with low-black heels. Not like anyone would be there anyway.

I brushed my hair and sighed at the fly-away pieces of hair and static electricity in it. I pulled my hair into a braid. The effect was simple, and I looked put together.

Just like that, we were in the car, heading to the church. I didn't remember ever stepping foot in a church in my life. I wondered if it was this hard to find a church to attend on a regular basis too. Was that the reason I didn't go to church? I had no clue how I felt about God. Maybe I thought if he was real, then he was an absent God. A God I just didn't know. I'd never seen evidence of him. So, it was hard to believe God even existed.

"Did you write a eulogy?" Stephen asked.

"A eulogy?" I heard myself repeat the words dumbly. "No. It never occurred to me..."

Stephen patted my leg and his eyes seemed soft. "It's okay. You don't have to say anything unless you decide to when we get there. A lot of people go off the cuff."

"Yeah, I don't think I will."

"That's fine, hon. Here." Stephen pulled out a stick of gum and offered it to me. "You might have forgotten to brush your teeth."

He said the words kindly. In the past, I would have been

mortified, but right now, I didn't care. I took the cinnamon gum and popped it in my mouth. Shouldn't I feel embarrassment? Come to think of it, maybe I should feel sadness, or *something*? What I really felt as we pulled up to the church was how much I wanted and needed to get this over with.

7

PAIGE

"Not like anyone will be here." I grumbled and put my hands on my hips in the same defiant way I did when I was a kid. I stood staring at the church, remembering my argument against this.

"It's not for anyone else, it's for you, Paige. Trust me, I've had people I was close to pass away and I regretted not going to the funeral." Stephen's voice was patient, and he didn't appear to be taking "no" for an answer.

"Name two," I demanded. I was suddenly struck in that moment by how little I knew about Stephen.

"My cousin, John, and my brother, Greg."

For a moment, I was speechless. On one hand, I could ask him what had happened to them. On the other hand, I felt instant guilt and shame that this far into the relationship, I had no recollection that Stephen had lost any prominent members of his family.

I chose to say nothing and followed him up the stairs. Here we were, walking into this random church for a funeral where I was sure we would be the only two in attendance.

As it turned out, there were three people sitting in the

church when we got there. I turned around and went back out to the lobby and grabbed a program to confirm that this was, in fact, my mom's funeral.

At a young age, I'd played a game with myself. I called it "picture in my memory." When I felt a person had significance in my life, I'd stare hard at them to burn an image of them in my memory, so I'd never forget their face. The three people peppered around the sanctuary were not people I'd ever seen before. They had no significance to me. I stared hard at each of them as they turned to face me and Stephen as we entered. If this was important enough for them to attend mom's funeral, I needed to know them.

A man at the back of the sanctuary looked tall even from his sitting stature. He had dark hair with salt and pepper gray hairs sprinkled throughout his head. He was handsome and distinguished. His green eyes were serious and cold, emotionless. He wore a nice suit jacket and button-down shirt with jeans. He gave a brief nod as we passed.

A woman in the middle of the church hugged an aisle seat. She was wearing a light pink dress that appeared to be a size too small for her slim but tallish frame. Her long blond hair was tied back in a low ponytail. It was the only conservative thing about her. Her fingernails were neon pink and were newly manicured. Mascara streamed down her face with her tears. She blew her nose loudly into a tissue.

In the second row, closest to the urn that now held my mom, was a gray-haired gentleman who had a kind face and sad eyes. He wasn't crying, but he looked like he was going to any minute. He was a bit heavy with a stout frame. His brown eyes held depths of compassion and I liked him immediately.

We took our place in the front row just as the pastor rose from a chair on the stage and walked up to the pulpit. The pastor was short with jet black hair and kind brown eyes. How would he even know what to say? He'd never met me or mom, the only two people who made up our family. He opened his mouth and a loud, deep baritone voice began to sing "Amazing Grace." I could feel the reverberation of his voice deep in my soul. I felt warm and comforted to my core. Why had I never gone to church before? I searched my memory for a reason or a memory of mom expressing an "anti-God" viewpoint. I had nothing. All I knew was that Sundays were the day mom never got out of bed before noon. Church just wasn't a thing. In fact, I was a little mystified by church.

After the song, the pastor began to speak. "I rise before dawn and cry for help; I have put my hope in your word. Psalms 119:147." He paused and looked around the room. "I can't imagine how it must feel to lose a mother, a friend, a partner, and a daughter so early in life. I'm deeply sorry for your loss. These things don't make sense. I would encourage you during the times in your life that don't make sense to cry out to Jesus for help." He paused and shook a Bible in the air. "You can put your hope in God's word. Most Bibles have his words in red. Read this and look for his words. It's where I've found my hope during dark times." He paused again for emphasis and looked around. "Would anyone like to speak?"

"I would," called out an authoritative voice from the back of the church.

I turned around to see a short, petite, elderly version of mom walking down the aisle. My eyes widened in disbelief. *Who was she?* I wondered. Where did she come from? Clearly, she had slipped in after the pastor started talking.

I studied her perfectly pressed black dress and sensible high heels as she climbed the stairs to the podium. Her hair was chin-length and swung around her face in a bob. I imagine the woman would have gray hair if it weren't perfectly colored. Indeed, she was a shorter, thicker, version of mom with wrinkles around her eyes and lips.

"For those of you who don't know me," she looked pointedly, almost in disapproval, right at me before continuing. "I'm Krysta's mother, Margaret. And you can imagine my shock after not talking to Krysta in over twenty years to find out she had been murdered."

I could hear a gasp from the back of the room. Was it okay to mention the way mom died like that? I looked to Stephen who put a hand up that signaled me to hold my thoughts.

"Even as a child, trouble found Krysta. She had the best intentions and tried hard, but life just didn't seem to work to her advantage. I can only imagine that she tried to set out on a new path to reinvent herself and make a life for her child. And that took courage. If she were still alive, I would tell her I love her. And that I always have. That is all." Margaret lifted her chin and exited the stage as she had entered, regally, like a queen.

Did that mean I had family alive after all? Was she my grandmother? I shivered over how coldly she had looked at me. Weren't grandparents usually warm and loving?

"I didn't know your grandmother was around," Stephen whispered beside me. "You've never talked about her."

I was so lost in my thoughts, his sudden voice startled me. "I don't know her," was all I could think to say before the pastor was back at the pulpit.

"Thank you, Margaret. Anyone else?" he asked.

The nice-looking, gray-haired man sitting close to the front stood up. His walk was a lot heavier than Margaret's as he made his way to the podium. His face was red, a sure sign that he was either embarrassed or not comfortable speaking in public.

"Krysta was a loving and kind soul. She didn't deserve this. No one deserves to go this way." His deep voice broke. He paused, cleared his throat, and pointed to me. "She loved you. Her whole life revolved around you and doing right by you." He looked up at the ceiling and continued. "I'll love you forever, Krysta, God rest your soul." Then he sat back down.

I blinked in genuine surprise. "Who *are* these people?" I whispered.

The sound of the *swish, swish* of the tight dress captured my attention. Her ankles wobbled in each step of the pink barbie-like stilettos. It was the blond who stepped up to the podium next. Mascara marred her pretty face and stained her cheeks. Tears rolled unceasingly down her face. She tried to wipe them away with the back of her hand and smeared a line of black across her cheek.

"I'm Ashley…" she pulled out a napkin and blew her nose loudly into the microphone. "Krysta was my best friend…" The word "friend" trailed into a hysterical sob. Ashley took a moment to compose herself then spoke again. "She was the best listener. I always went to her with my problems… and I have a lot of problems. She always just listened. Then she'd hug me. And I knew everything would be okay. And it always was. I could always trust her with my stuff, ya know? She kept my secrets. She wasn't a gossip. And I'm gonna to miss her so much!" She quickly *swished* back to her seat as a new torrent of tears began.

I tried not to stare as she passed. I felt jealous of her tears.

The pastor hesitantly stepped back up. He looked at me inquisitively. Wasn't there one more person here? I turned around to see that the man in the back row was gone.

"Are you going to say anything?" Stephen poked my arm. The silence was becoming uncomfortable.

I emphatically shook my head. I didn't even know what I would say.

At my negative head shake, the pastor said a prayer and ended the service.

A recorded song track of sad hymns began to play in the

background. It occurred to me that I wouldn't even have known what music to choose as her favorites to play.

Stephen and I walked to the front of the church. We stood next to my mother's urn. The urn was plain and made of smooth bronze. The three attendees formed a line down the middle aisle to pay their respects.

Ashley approached first and hugged me. "Hang in there, kiddo... Man, did she love you! Here," she pressed a crumpled piece of paper in my hand, then she paused, gently stroked the urn, and walked away. I assumed I'd find a phone number on the paper and I quickly jammed it in my pocket.

The gray-haired gentleman with kind eyes approached next. He offered his hand.

"I'm so sorry to be meeting this way. Did Krysta ever mention me?"

I shook my head no.

He waved it off. "I understand. She didn't know how you'd feel about us. She just wanted to keep her life with you separate from her life with me. She didn't want to complicate things. But, wow, I never knew a mother who loved a daughter more than she loved you." He laughed sadly.

"I'm sorry, who are you?" I asked, feeling mystified. I had zero recollection of him.

He laughed again, this time louder. "I'm Matt. Matthew Cline. Your mom and I dated for over six years. She was supposed to be at my place the night she... went missing. I didn't think anything of it because, you know. She'd tell you she'd be somewhere and not show up... a lot. I'm sorry I didn't report it faster." His soft brown eyes teared up.

"Mr. Cline, it's nice to meet you. Thank you for coming. I'm sure you did what you could the minute you realized she was missing." I tried to be gracious, but I was starting to think I lived in some alternate universe. In fact, I was starting to wonder if it was my fault that I didn't know more about mom's life. Should I have tried to be closer to her? Should I have pushed my way in and made her tell me where she disappeared to all the time? I watched Mr. Cline leave. I felt nothing.

"My turn." Margaret stepped forward, peering critically at me. "Well, let me see you. Turn around."

"I beg your pardon?" I stared blankly at her, caught off guard. Was she serious?

"Come on, now." Margaret's put a finger in the air and drew a circle with one finger. "It's not like I asked you to do a dance, just turn around."

Why I agreed I'll never know. But suddenly, I was turning for her like I was five years old. What on earth made me want to obey this woman?

"How old are you?" Margaret demanded.

"Almost twenty-four," I answered.

"Hmm," Margaret tapped her foot, folded her arms, and looked at the ceiling, clearly doing math. "Well, then it's quite possible you *are* Jason's daughter."

"Who is Jason?" I asked.

"Perhaps your father," she said, raising her perfectly shaped eyebrows.

"I never knew my father. Where is he? Jason? Would he want to meet me?"

"Heaven's no, child," she snapped at me impatiently. "He's dead. Your mother killed him."

8

NAMELESS

Krysta was dead. Why wasn't that enough? He'd spent the past twenty-three years plotting and waiting for his moment. But when it finally happened, he realized it wasn't enough. He was deeply unsatisfied. Nothing had happened the way he planned. So, he went to the funeral. It was a pathetic sham of a funeral. Not even three other people were there when he showed up. He thought he had the wrong time. But that was Krysta for you. She was the most unlikeable, unfriendly woman he'd ever met. She was *nothing* like his darling Allison.

That's when he saw her. A beautiful, tall young woman with long, light brown hair and green eyes. She paused at the sanctuary. She immediately turned around but then came back in. There was a guy with her. They weren't well-dressed. They didn't look well-rested. Her face was pleasant and kind, but she reminded him of a timid field mouse. She looked right at him with big, green, inquisitive eyes. He wondered if he looked as shocked as he felt.

She was Krysta's daughter. There was no mistaking it. She was taller than her mother, if he recalled. Maybe thinner too but who knew as Krysta aged.

Until the other day, he had no idea Krysta had a child. Now he couldn't unsee the resemblance. His eyes bore into the back of Paige's head as she walked to her seat and all through the rest of the funeral. How old was she? Twenty, maybe? His heart beat fast in his chest. He did the math backwards in his head. There was one night. That stupid, careless night. But that was around twenty-four years ago. Was that innocent-looking girl older than she looked?

They were all drinking that night. He, Jason, and Krysta were all drinking while Allison lay in bed at home asleep. It was one of those nights when Allison begged him to get out and enjoy himself. As if that was *ever* possible. *To take his mind off things*, she'd insisted. Jason had passed out early. He and Krysta kept drinking. It seemed like she was purposely getting him drunk.

Suddenly, he was too drunk to drive home, so he decided to stay and sleep it off. True, he could walk home, but it was miles when he could just as easily stay here and sleep. Unfortunately, sleep didn't happen. Fortunately, Krysta had no recollection of it the next day. Well, it was one night. It meant nothing and no one was ever the wiser. That was a secret he was content to know died with Krysta.

The next morning, he had endured that long and god-awful walk of shame, from the car, to the garage, and into his home. Right before he'd found his sweet Allison dead, he'd remembered something Krysta had whispered in his ear the night before.

"I'm sorry, Ray. About the money. It's not personal. It's business. Someday, I hope you understand." She'd trailed her fingers from his cheek to his shoulder and let it rest there lightly for a second. It hit him about the same time he arrived home to find Allison dead. Jason hadn't lost the money. They had stolen it.

As he stood staring down at his dead darling bride, he knew.

They had stolen her chances to get better, his chances of paying off any leftover medical bills. They had stolen the last moments of her life on this Earth. They had taken everything from him. His devastation turned to anger. They deserved to die.

Except Krysta hadn't died. Until now.

As the funeral had continued, he studied Krysta's daughter. She looked innocent enough. But he knew better. He knew about generational sin. Theft, adultery, and murder were all legacies Krysta had passed on to her daughter. It was his responsibility, no, *his calling,* to take out this bloodline and terminate the sins of her mother.

He knew what he had to do. He was going to have to kill Paige, this daughter of Krysta's. He didn't need a reminder of the night he would regret for the rest of his life. Once the Earth was rid of the wicked Mynart women, he would be able to rest in peace. He quietly slipped out the door before the funeral ended. He had to make a new plan.

9

PAIGE

"Paige, welcome back," Dr. Burnett seemed a little warmer than I remembered. "Are you feeling okay after your mother's funeral?" Her brown hair was pulled back into a low ponytail at the base of her neck. She smoothed her skinny dress slacks that stopped at her ankles where her feet wore peep-toe black heels. Then she adjusted her matching blazer.

I nodded.

"I need to start today's session by apologizing for any doubt I had about your memories at the last session. I think the memories you have are quite real and speak to some dysfunction and traumatic circumstances from your childhood. I'm sorry you went through them."

Her words surprised me. "Did the session expose anything that could help understand my mother better?"

"Paige, I think the best thing you could do is learn more about you. Your mother is gone, and you are here now." Dr. Burnett spoke the words softly and kindly, but they didn't sting any less.

"Okay," I agreed. "Can you tell me what came up at that session?"

Dr. Burnett nodded. "I can. I transcribed the notes and I think it would be best for you to read your own story without me interjecting my opinions. Would that work?"

"Yes."

Dr. Burnett handed me the notes.

Hypnosis Session: Deffer, Paige
May 14, 2019

(Dr. Burnett) Paige, what memory are you thinking about, what do you see and how old are you?

Mama? I said. I was five years old and woke from a nightmare. Not just a bad dream. I even remember this nightmare because it wasn't the first time I'd dreamed it. It wouldn't be the last time, either. In fact, it was the same nightmare I'd had multiple times. The details only differed slightly. But it was always some variation of the same thing. This night, I swung my little legs over the twin bed and on to the floor.

(Dr. Burnett) Can you tell me about the dream?

In the dream, I found myself outside in the middle of the night. I must have been locked out of the house. I could feel heat on my back. When I turned, I could see large, angry flames burning bright orange and black and billowing out of a small shack of a house. I was so scared that for a minute, I could not move. I could hear the crack of the house collapsing and loud roar of fire crackling. Finally, I turned and ran.

Paige! Come on, baby, I'm here. I could hear my mama call

and saw that she stood at the end of a long dock with water at the end. Her arms were out. I ran to her.

Before I could get there, sudden fire erupted between me and mama. A wall of fire blocked my view of the one person in this life who could offer me safety. The dock was on fire and the fire from the home behind me was coming closer. I started to cough. I was suffocating with no way to escape.

(Dr. Burnett) Then what happened?

I woke up gasping and crying.

Mama? I asked. My feet were on the floor, moving, and feeling their way along the baseboards and my hands felt for the hallway wall to guide me to mama's room. Finally, I found the door. It was too dark to see so I walked forward until my hands found the bed. I crawled in, expecting to see mama but found no one. The bed was empty.

Mama? I whispered, but she didn't answer.

Mama? I said louder. The room was so dark and so empty.

The silence was overwhelming.

Mama? I screamed and began to cry. I slid out of mama's tall bed and turned on a light to get a better look. Mama was not in the room. She wasn't in the apartment. Mama was gone. Where had she gone? When would she be back? I didn't know. Then I remembered the nice people next door. Maybe they would help me find mama.

(Dr. Burnett) Did you go outside?

Yes, I had to stand on tiptoes to unlock the front door and then I used both hands to turn the doorknob. Then I was outside. We lived in what mama called apartments. Quickly, I went to the next door in the hallway and knocked. There was no answer. I knocked again. Still no answer. Finally, I knocked as hard as I could.

The door opened and the nice lady next door named "Mrs. Mona" looked at me with sleepy eyes.

Who is it, mommy? James asked as he poked his head out from behind Mrs. Mona. His black hair was messy. His blue eyes squinted at me in the dark.

(Dr. Burnett) Who is James?

James was my best friend.

Mrs. Mona? I asked her, trying to be brave. *Do you know where my mama is? She's not home.*

Child! Mrs. Mona gasped. *Do you know what time it is?* She immediately took my hand firmly and marched me back to my apartment. James followed her. Mrs. Mona knocked on the door before she opened it.

Krysta? She called. *Krysta, it's Mona. If you're in there, I'm coming in.*

Once inside, she called around the house a few more times. Then Mrs. Mona flipped on the rest of the lights to look around.

James held my hand. *Are you scared?* he whispered.

(Dr. Burnett) Were you scared?

Yes, I told James I was scared. His eyes were big and round. He looked like *he* was a little scared too.

Here, he told me as he dropped a shiny quarter in my hand. *This is my favorite quarter. It makes me feel better when I'm scared. You hold onto it.*

Thanks! I whispered.

Mama was not there.

Tell you what, Mrs. Mona leaned over to me, *why don't you go to bed, and I'll wait up for your mama.*

I don't want to go to bed, I whined but I felt so much better now that they were here. I was very sleepy, and it was nice that Mrs. Mona was going to stay.

Then why don't you crawl up here on the couch and we'll just wait until she comes home? said Mrs. Mona.

I nodded and climbed onto the couch. James sat beside me and patted my hand.

I must have slept for hours.

(Dr. Burnett) What happened when you woke up?

I woke up suddenly when I heard loud, angry voices. Who was yelling? I listened longer, afraid to open my eyes.

It was mama and Mrs. Mona. They were angry. Mrs. Mona told mama it wasn't okay to leave a five-year-old alone.

Uh-oh. I felt scared all over again. I was going to get in so much trouble for this! I shouldn't have gotten out of bed! Mama told Mrs. Mona it was none of her business. Mrs. Mona said she was going to call a social someone and mama got really quiet. Suddenly, Mama's voice got real calm. Scary calm.

Thank you for staying with Paige, Mona. You and your son need to leave now.

Bye, Paige, James whispered.

Bye. I peeked at him with one eye and whispered back. I held his shiny quarter so tight, it dug into my palm.

He leaned over and kissed my cheek. He slipped off the couch.

Mrs. Mona obeyed my mama. She took James and left. I watched the door shut.

(Dr. Burnett) Your voice sounds sad.

It was the last time I ever saw James.

Mama quickly went to the kitchen and came back with trash bags. She began stuffing every loose item around the house into bag after bag. I felt afraid. I was shaking! I got up.

Mama, why are you doing that? I asked.

Oh, Paige, darling! I didn't know you were awake! Well, since you are, you can help me. Take a few bags, she said and gave me two trash bags. *Run and put all your toys and clothes into these. We are going on a little adventure!*

(Dr. Burnett) Where were you going?

She said we were going to a place called America. Mama kept stuffing items in trash bags.

But I like Canada, it's my home! I started to cry. This was all my fault. If only I'd never gotten out of bed! Because of me, we had to move! *I'm sorry, mama. I'm sorry I got out of bed. I don't wanna move.* Suddenly, I was crying so hard, snot was running down my face. I wiped it, smearing it across my cheek.

Oh, Mama paused her frantic movements and looked at me. *Darling, we were going to have to move anyway. We could only stay in Canada four years on a temporary visa. You don't know what that means.* Mama paused to think of better words. *America is my home, and we have to go back to it now.*

(Dr. Burnett) What did you do?

I was stuck. I couldn't move for a minute. I wasn't American. I was Canadian.

Paige, mama's voice sounded different, nicer. *You go put your things away, or you won't have any things. We'll leave them here.*

NO!!! I ran to my room still sobbing. I put everything I could fit in two little trash bags. I was too afraid to ask for more. Maybe James could have the rest of my toys. He would like that. When I finished, I crawled into bed and fell asleep still sniffling.

(Dr. Burnett) I'm surprised you could sleep with all that going on!

I've always been a heavy sleeper. In fact, when I'm stressed, I sleep. When I'm angry, I sleep, Sad, happy, I can sleep...

(Dr. Burnett) Did you and your mother leave Canada?

When I woke up, it was morning, and I was in a moving car. Nothing would ever be the same again. I would miss our small place. I would miss James. I would miss my toys. I learned from that point on if mama was gone in the middle of the night, it was better for me to pretend not to know that and to just stay in bed.

Long after we got to America, a place called Arkansas, I learned that I'd *never* know where mama was going or when she'd be back. I learned how to be strong. I learned that nights during my childhood would be long hours filled with fear and loneliness. But I learned that I would make it through by myself just fine.

(Dr. Burnett) What else did this teach you?

I also learned not to ask questions. One day, I asked, *Mama, where were you?* Mama gave me a blank stare and didn't answer. I wondered if she heard me but then thought maybe she ignored me. Which was scarier than crawling into bed knowing I was completely and utterly alone with no way to defend myself from any monsters in the night.

I decided right then mama was sick. Sometimes mama's face would go blank and show no emotion, especially when she tried to remember things that happened the day before. Then mama would get incredibly sad and might even leave the room.

I lived for the times when mama would be happy, talking and laughing with me. Those were the times I liked best. Those were the times I knew mama was with me. I could pretend mama wasn't sick and didn't disappear for hours at a time into the night.

(Dr. Burnett) Do you know where she was going?

No. But mama was the only person I had, and I learned that I needed to take care of her. Maybe if I took very good care of her, I could keep her around for a long time. So, I decided not to ask mama anymore where she went at night and I wouldn't ask why she couldn't remember things like other mama's could. I would just take very good care of her and be the best Paige I could be.

"James," I mumbled. I looked up from reading the notes. "I forgot about James. She took him from me!" I felt anger. "She took me from my home. America is not my home! I was born in Canada!" I could feel my face flush and my heart beat with sudden rage I didn't know I possessed.

"When I hear this story, Paige, I see something else. I see a neglectful mother who had no right leaving such a young child at home alone. No matter if she thought you were asleep or not. That was dangerous."

I thought about her words.

"It's also concerning to me that you decided all of this was somehow your fault. Do you still believe this?" Dr. Burnett's eyes pierced into my soul.

I shifted uncomfortably. "I don't know."

"In fact, you would have every right to be angry at your mother. Have you ever considered that maybe you don't feel anything because you're angry and you think anger doesn't seem appropriate here?"

"I don't know."

Dr. Burnett was silent for what seemed like minutes. "It's okay, Paige. You're going through a lot. I just want to give you permission to think about this. Emotions aren't bad. It's okay to feel them and sometimes, the emotion you feel is appropriate, no matter how uncomfortable it is."

"Okay," I said. My voice sounded a little too upbeat in my own ears. I felt like time was running out to find my mom's killer. I knew there was something I was missing. "Thank you. Do we have time to do another hypnosis session?"

Dr. Burnett checked the time. "We do have about thirty-five minutes. Are you sure that's how you want to spend the rest of your time?"

"Yes, let's do this."

10

PAIGE

I was glad I had scheduled the counseling appointment right after the funeral because it gave me something to do. But I didn't like remembering the night we fled Canada. I certainly didn't want to stay home by myself. I was no stranger to being alone, no thanks to mom, but it was so quiet and empty here. I wondered what I was going to do with mom gone.

I felt so angry at Stephen for not taking the entire day off work. But he was out of vacation days. He didn't know this was going to happen. My mind made excuses for him because I didn't want to acknowledge what I felt to be true. Things were changing with me and Stephen. My life would never be the same. It made me wonder if he was going to fit into this different version of who I would be in the end.

It wasn't until I saw the mail sitting on the counter that it occurred to me, I was now on the hook for all the bills. The rent, food, water, heat, and air were all my responsibilities now. I thought about the veterinary tech position I had accepted. While I would draw a small salary, it would only be enough to get me through my last two years of school and clinical rotations for veterinary school. Then I would officially be a veterinarian.

The plan was to start working when the semester started back up. With all the chaos going on, I hadn't even thought about that. I'd never budgeted before. I had never needed to. I'd had small jobs to get me the few things I needed here and there, like gas and insurance, but at twenty-three, I didn't know if I could afford a place by myself.

I snapped my fingers. Stephen is a financial planner. Surely, he could help. Besides, it was way too quiet at the apartment to stay here by myself. As I grabbed my car keys, I knocked a letter off the countertop. It fell to the ground. As I picked it up, I noticed it was addressed to me from my mom's bank. It might be important. I grabbed it and threw it in my handbag. I didn't have the energy to open it up right now. I needed to get out of here. Not only was it too quiet and too empty, I felt the ghost of mom hovering. Everywhere I turned, I could see a memory of our life here together.

Once in my car, I opened up the phone tracking app Stephen had suggested we both install. I clicked on the dot that showed where Stephen and his phone were. It asked if I wanted directions. I tapped yes and started driving.

When I arrived at what I thought was Stephen's office, I glanced at my phone one more time and looked dubiously at the police station in front of me. I thought it was strange that Stephen had suggested we install tracking apps on our phones when we first met.

"Don't read into it, Paige," he'd said. "If anything ever happened to you and I couldn't find you, I couldn't live with myself. And you can see where I am, too. See..." he'd pointed at my phone. "That's the office and you'll see when I leave to meet my clients."

I had nodded. But I'd been so concerned, I went home and mentioned it to mom.

"It's sweet, Paige. That's how much he cares about you. You should be flattered. Besides, he didn't steal your phone and put a tracking device in it, he put an app on both of your phones. It goes both ways. He did ask your permission, you know. You could have said no. Maybe you should show up some day and take him to lunch."

I had agreed with her on that. Why didn't I say no? I couldn't ever seem to say no.

Now I sat looking at the exact spot the app pointed to as his office. I felt confused. Do financial planners share office space with police units? Maybe it was like when financial planners leased space from banks.

Once in the building, I'd be on my own. I'd have no idea where to find his suite. I was relieved to see a nice receptionist on the first floor as I walked into the lobby.

"May I help you?"

"Yes, I'm looking for Stephen Wilton's office. Can you point me in the right direction?"

The receptionist tilted her head and looked sideways at me. She picked up the phone and held up one finger.

"Oh, wait, I really wanted to surprise him. Can you just tell me what floor he's on? I'm his girlfriend."

"Oh! Okay, no problem." She winked at me. "Well, Stephen's on the third floor. Homicide." The receptionist pointed to the elevator.

"Thanks!" I smiled and turned to the elevator. *Homicide?* What did that mean? I was in the elevator and on the third floor before I could understand the answer.

The elevator opened to a team of busy people. Some in uniform, some in nice business casual wear. A woman who looked to be in her forties was clearly distressed as she sat talking to an officer at a desk. Her clothes were plain and her hair was rumpled. She didn't look like the type of client who would be in a financial planner's office.

I quickly spotted Stephen leaning against a doorway to an office, standing with his back to me. He had changed into jeans and black Converse tennis shoes but was still wearing the black button-down dress shirt he had worn at the funeral. I could see the outline of his back muscles under his shirt. I imagined his arms crossed in front of him since he stood that way a lot. He looked like he had casually stopped to chat with the guys inside the room who were actively working. I mustered up as much fake confidence as I could find and purposefully strode to the room.

As I approached Stephen and before he saw me, something else inside the room caught my attention. As I got closer to the door, I saw the wall. I stopped so suddenly, I almost tripped over my feet. My hands flew to my mouth. Forgetting Stephen or announcing myself, I walked further into the room in complete shock. There was a picture of mom right smack in the middle of the wall. There were five pictures in an octagon shape around mom's picture. I instantly recognized the pictures around mom as the people who'd been at the funeral. They all had names and ages tacked to them. Most shocking of all was the picture of me. I had made this board. Whatever this board was. There was a line of red yarn from mom's picture to a picture of me.

I moved forward feeling like I was in a trance. Could this nightmare get any worse? I walked further into the room, right past Stephen and the three other men who'd been talking in quiet voices. My presence sent them into a pandemonium.

"Hey!" said one.

"Whoa!!" shouted another.

"You can't…" I recognized the third one as Officer Stevenson.

I didn't care. I stood inches from the board. "Ray Lennon, fifty-two, Ashley Trieggar, thirty-six, Matt Cline, fifty, Margaret Terry, sixty-eight, and…" I'd been mumbling and playing my memorizing game until I got to my name. "Paige Deffer, A.K.A. Paige Mynart, twenty-five. I'm a suspect?" I felt Stephen's hand on my shoulder and whirled around. "I'm a SUSPECT? *Mynart*? Who is that? And I'm twenty-three!"

"Paige, hon, I can explain."

"No!" My hand sliced downward. "You think I killed my own mother?"

"You don't have an alibi for the night it happened…" Stephen looked sheepish and his face was pink.

"WHAT is this?" I took a step backwards and bumped the wall. "You're NOT a financial planner. You're a police officer? Are you on this case?"

Stephen put up his palms. "Paige, I can explain. Yes, I am an officer, well, a detective, actually. No, I'm not on *this* case. That would be a conflict of interest. I'm more like an advisor." Stephen's fingers made air quotes as he said *advisor*.

"What am I to you, exactly? Why would you lie to me about your career?"

"Paige, hon…"

"NO! I'm not your *hon*. This wasn't real. Nothing about us was true. We're over. Maybe we never really were." I turned to leave but quickly took out my phone. I took a picture of the wall with my phone.

"You can't do that," an officer in the room tried to stop me.

"This is part of a criminal investigation," the other officer said and came towards me.

"Officers," I said as I summoned my most authoritative voice. "Either I'm a suspect, or I'm in a lot of danger. Since I can no longer trust my local law enforcement to keep me safe, I'd like to educate myself on my mom's investigation." With that I turned and left. I could hear Stephen's voice behind me as he blocked the door with the other officers inside.

"Let her go," I heard Stephen advise them.

I had just hit the down button on the elevator when Stephen caught up to me.

"Paige, wait, I can explain everything."

"I have nothing to say to you. You lied to me." I refused to look at him as I pushed the "down" elevator button again impatiently.

"Yes."

"About everything."

"No."

"About who you were." I took at breath and corrected myself. "Who you are."

"Yes."

"And how we met." I threw back my head and groaned. "I can't believe I didn't see any signs. You didn't randomly meet us in a bookstore." I turned back to Stephen. "Were you stalking me? Waiting for a chance to jump into my life and play good boyfriend to get information about me and my mom?"

"Yes, but that makes it sound worse than it is."

The elevator opened and two officers stepped off, leaving it empty. Stephen followed me on.

"What could you possibly have to say for yourself?" I demanded.

"I fell in love with you. The minute that happened, I stepped off the case."

"I don't believe you," I said. "Why was there even a case opened back then anyway?" I didn't want an answer to that right now. Deep down, I knew why. I narrowed my eyes skeptically and I tried to sound as cruel as possible and switched the subject. "I don't love you. I don't even know you. I was nothing more than a game to you. What were you even looking for back then? Did you think someone was after my mom? Did it occur to you that maybe she was the one in danger?"

Stephen shook his head and shrugged.

"You can't even answer that because it's part of an *ongoing investigation.* Well, how do I move out of the suspect box?"

"Paige…" The elevator had opened and he stepped into the lobby with me. I walked through the doors and to my car. Stephen was still on my heels.

"Am I under arrest?" I demanded. I whirled around when I reached my car.

"No, but we might need you to answer some questions at some point."

"Well," I said as I opened my car door. "You know where to find me." I got in the car and drove away, leaving Stephen behind looking frustrated and confused.

It took exactly five miles of driving before I felt the anger whoosh out of me like a deflated balloon. I desperately tried to catch my breath and felt my heart skip a strange double beat. It didn't hurt exactly. I just couldn't breathe.

A myriad of emotions caught me all at once and I nearly doubled over in the car. My stomach revolted. I felt punched in the gut and pulled over just in time to stop the car and fling the door open. I leaned my head out and saw only the pavement before I closed my eyes and emptied my stomach. Funny, I didn't remember eating *anything* today and yet the contents of my stomach that were now on the ground made me realize otherwise. I sat up and grabbed a nearly empty water bottle and swished the water in my mouth.

I was so angry at Stephen! I would never forgive him. I was angry at mom for being so stupid to have gotten herself killed. How could she abandon me like that? But mostly, I felt angry at myself. How had I fallen for all of it? Those self-berating thoughts came to a halt as I noticed a red Cadillac parked behind me. Before I could process that I'd seen the exact same car pull out of the police station behind me, my passenger car door opened and slammed shut quickly. My mind zoomed in on the gun pointed in my direction.

"Drive."

11

STEPHEN

Stephen was rooted to the spot. He had watched her drive away, but he still couldn't move. He was actively trying to stop the panic that was welling up inside him. He loved her. She was his life. He didn't know how he would live without her. He certainly hadn't tried to fall in love with her. Quite the opposite, actually.

It had been his first case. They suspected this mother and daughter of murder. But they could never quite prove it. Stephen was brand new, just six months out of the police academy. He clearly remembered the day Lieutenant Roger Higgins called him into his office.

"Wilton? That's your name, right?" Lieutenant Higgins frowned in his direction. His thick eyebrows were furrowed into a serious straight line. He looked to be fifty, but to Stephen, anyone around his dad's age looked to be fifty.

Stephen's heart beat quickly in his chest. He remembered thinking, *Am I already fired?*

"I have a special assignment for you," Lieutenant Higgins told Stephen.

"Okay," Stephen breathed out in relief.

"We believe Krysta and Paige Deffer are a mother-daughter team who have committed murder on more than one occasion. We don't know the motive. It's a hunch based on a killing that occurred years ago at the bar where Krysta currently works. Here's where you come in. Paige Deffer, the daughter, is about your age and unattached. I want you to go undercover. Gain her trust and find the evidence we're looking for to close this thing." Lieutenant Higgins handed Stephen a manilla folder. "What do you think?"

"Absolutely!" Stephen was beyond excited to land such an important assignment so early in his career. He knew it had less to do with experience and more to do with age. But he was willing to let this be his career-defining moment.

Which is why he was so devastated the day he had to resign from the case. Most of their "dating" had been over the phone while she was away at college. It was easy to maintain distance. But then she had come home for a Christmas break. They were out walking to the car and she turned to smile at him. Her light brown hair flew over her shoulder. Her cheeks were pink with the cold. And her green eyes sparkled at him in a way that made his heart drop to his toes.

Her high-heeled black boots made her appear two inches taller that night. The boots came to the knee of her jeans, and she wore a bomber jacket that made her look like she'd stepped right out of the 80s. The 80s were his favorite era. His older brother had been a child of the 80s and felt it was his obligation to educate Stephen on what he would later believe was the best era there was. It was the only thing he had in common with his brother. They had decided women of the 80s were the most beautiful and authentic they'd ever seen. He knew his emotions were fully vested at that point.

He went to the lieutenant the next day and quit the undercover assignment. By that point, he had done a good enough job in the department that he was met with understanding and praised for his ethics. But Stephen wasn't naïve. He was well-aware that Paige and her mother continued to be under investigation. In his heart, he knew Paige was innocent, but he had not shared the same feeling about her mother.

Now, Stephen stood in the parking lot after she drove out of his life, feeling lost.

"Stephen," said a voice. Lieutenant Higgins was suddenly by his side. "I'm going to lunch. Why don't you come along? Unless you'd rather stand there all day."

Stephen agreed and walked with his boss to his car on autopilot.

As Lieutenant Higgins started the car, he broke the silence. "I heard what happened. Listen, we can't invite you back on the case exactly, but we can give you a new sort of assignment."

"What assignment is that?" Stephen asked flatly.

"What if you were an unofficial bodyguard?" Lieutenant Higgins suggested.

"I've lost all trust with her. You know what I know. I think I'm too emotional to work in that capacity. I'm pretty sure I'd take over the investigation."

"Look, Paige Deffer is either guilty or she's the next target. You could just follow her around, shadow her, and keep her safe."

"Is that ethical?" Stephen asked.

"Perfectly."

12

NAMELESS

He could have gone back home after that funeral. In fact, he wasn't sure why he didn't. Despite his best attempts, he could not find more information on Krysta's death. The media seemed to have locked it down. Which could mean only one thing. Krysta was murdered. Hearing Margaret confirm that during her eulogy made him even more curious. Who else wanted Krysta dead with enough passion to do it? Did she steal money from someone else and seduce him out of the last minute with his wife as well?

Whoever it was, he wanted to look that person in the eye and thank him. It would be an easy process of elimination. He actually felt confident he knew the answer and was about to "out" Krysta's murderer. As he watched the heavier-set man walk into the diner, he was feeling somewhat smug.

"It's you!" Matt Cline heaved his heavy frame into the booth in the corner of the small café. Matt's brown eyes were dark and accusatory. "I wouldn't have agreed to meet if I would've known it was you on the other end of the phone!"

"Fascinating," he said aloud as if talking to himself. He

could see the anger in Matt's eyes. For a moment, he wondered if Matt Cline might actually come at him.

It was 2 p.m., so the only other person in the café at the moment was the waitress. She looked annoyed, like they had disturbed her midday tasks. He drank his coffee calmly. His back was to the corner so he could see everything in the diner. It was an old trick his Army buddy had taught him. Always be able to see everyone in the room.

"You know, you have a lot of nerve demanding we meet, not even telling me who you were. I shouldn't have come! How'd you even get my number?" Matt Cline seemed like a trapped animal who was trying desperately to get out of his cage.

"Why did you?" he asked as he sipped his coffee calmly. He stared at Matt Cline.

"I thought you might have answers," Matt said slowly.

He signaled for the waitress to come.

"Can I get you something to eat? Drink? They have pie and coffee here." He was purposefully calm.

"What can I get you, sir?" The waitress asked.

Matt waived his hand. "Nothing."

The waitress turned away.

"I'm being rude. I'm Ray. Ray Lennon. And you are Matt Cline."

"You! You're the reason Krysta is dead!" Matt's eyes filled with tears and possibly regret.

"Am I?" Ray leaned forward. He clasped his hand together on the table. He wasn't as tall as Matt, nor did he have as much weight on him. Thanks to his daily workout regimen, Ray was in the best shape of his life. Ray had definition in his chest and forearms that he never had in his forties. He was better looking than Matt, too. *How had Krysta gotten mixed up with this guy?* Ray wondered as he sat studying him.

"Yes. You show up in town and she shows up dead. See the connection?"

"Hmm. That's not a strong connection if you ask me. In most cases, the strongest murder suspects end up being the husband or the boyfriend. I understand you were the latter?"

Matt leaned forward with a steel glint of hatred in his eyes. "You oughta do your homework *before* you go around sleeping with a woman committed elsewhere!"

Ray leaned his head back and laughed loudly. "Sleeping with her? Is that what you think?"

"Well, if not, what exactly *were* your intentions when she showed up to meet you at the bar that night?"

"I wasn't planning to sleep with her, that's for sure!" Ray smirked. "I was planning to kill her. I suppose I should thank you for doing that for me. Here's the deal. That was going to be my job. The last thing I had to do before I left this Earth. You jumped ahead of me and now you owe me."

"WHAT?" Matt's voice was so loud the waitress poked her head back out of the kitchen. He lowered his voice. "I owe you?" he hissed. "What makes you think *I* killed her?"

"The simple fact that I didn't. I figure you followed her to the bar that night, saw us talking, got jealous, confronted and killed her before she even made it home that night."

The two men looked at each other without blinking.

Ray finished his coffee. "I can prove it, too." He tossed Matt his business card. "Let that settle. I'll be calling you for that favor." Ray threw money on the table, got up, and left the diner leaving Matt Cline to ponder the "proof."

13

PAIGE

"Drive," she said again.

It was Margaret Terry, the woman who claimed to be my grandmother. "Don't try to pull anything, just drive." She was wearing a black hoodie pulled up over her shoulder-length dark hair. She tried to pull off a casual look by wearing jeans, but I caught a glance of her expensive Golden Goose sneakers with a flashy gold star.

My pulse beat erratically. I could feel my body flush hot and my senses heighten. I took a deep breath and a supernatural calm washed over me. Suddenly, my mind was clear and I felt in control. I took my hands off the steering wheel and held them up in the air.

"I said DRIVE!" Margaret's voice was strong and dominant.

"Where are we going?" I looked at Margaret.

"Doesn't matter. Just drive," Margaret Terry spat coldly a third time.

I put my hands back on the steering wheel. I shifted the car into drive and worked to remain calm.

"Is this how it ends with me, too?" My voice matched her

tone, and I wondered where this underlying calm was coming from. "Will you kill me like you killed my mom?"

"As if!" Margaret snorted. "I'll tell you what I told the officer – who looked a lot like your boyfriend, oddly enough – why would I kill my own daughter? I didn't know she was alive until… she wasn't. See?" Margaret reached into her purse and thrust a newspaper clipping at me.

"I can't read that, I'm driving!" I protested. "At gun point, no less."

"It's your mom's obituary. All this time, she was living a state away. I thought she left the country."

"Wait a minute. You saw an obituary a state away?"

"Yes, I live in Missouri."

I clenched my teeth. *Stephen.* I thought he was being so helpful asking if he could put an obituary out for me. He and his police friends must have figured out where she was originally from. Even *I* didn't know that!

"Krysta was a clever girl. A beautiful, clever, wicked girl. I bet you're just like her. Do you kill people too? Did you kill your mom?" Margaret's perfectly polished red fingernails were curled assuredly around a black gun.

"Of course not!" I felt indignant. "Why would a daughter kill her mother?" This had to be the most ridiculous conversation I'd ever had. "Will you just put that thing away? Do you know how to use that gun?"

"Well, yes, but I wasn't going to use it." Margaret put the gun in her purse. "You're the only family I have left, and I want answers." Margaret was determined.

"Same," I smarted off. "But we'll have to find a public but private place to talk. I don't trust you and we both know we can't go to the police."

"So, you're under investigation as well!" Margaret was triumphant.

"Trust me," I sneered, "you look way worse than I do and

you abducting me from the side of the road does *not* make me trust you more." I pulled my car into the most public, loudest place I could think of where no one heard, nor did they care, what you said, Coffee Villa downtown. I got out of the car and Margaret had no choice but to follow. We found a back-corner booth and sat down.

"To answer your question earlier," I began, "we did leave the country. For a while. I was born in Canada. Which makes me a dual citizen. Canada is my home, and I can't wait to get back there. Especially now."

"How long have you been back?" Margaret's eyes narrowed suspiciously.

"I don't know." I felt impatient. "Like twenty years... My turn for a question," I countered. "What I really want to know about is my dad."

"*If* he really was your dad." Margaret wagged her finger.

I desperately wanted to like this woman. As I watched her cross her arms over her chest, though I hated to admit it, what I wanted even more was for this woman to like me. She was the only family I had left and we'd just found each other.

Margaret waved her right hand as if dismissing a thought. "Well, if you didn't kill her and I didn't kill her, then who did?"

I rubbed my temples. There was that feeling in the pit of my stomach again. Was I about to be sick? "Can we talk about something else, please? And leave that other stuff to—"

"Your boyfriend?" Margaret interrupted her.

"*Ex*-boyfriend. I didn't know he was a cop."

"Oh, the plot thickens. Do tell!" Margaret clapped her hands together and leaned forward.

"Pardon me, but this is my life. I'm working through all that. Can you please tell me about my dad and why you think my mom killed him?"

"Think?" Margaret snorted. "She did. Anyone who sneaks out in the middle of the night and takes a plane out of the country leaving a dead husband in a pool of blood dripping off the sheets is very guilty. Your mom was 'America's Most Wanted' criminal of the year. Do you know that show?" Margaret answered her own question before I had a chance. "Of course not, you're too young. The police have been looking for her ever since. I'm surprised your boyfriend didn't figure it out."

"Oh, I think he knows more than he let on," I answered angrily. "Much more than me, apparently."

"Trust me. I saw this coming from childhood," Margaret said haughtily.

"My dad was murdered," I stated.

Margaret nodded.

"My mom was murdered."

"And?" Impatience laced Margaret's voice.

"Well don't you see? If they were both murdered, maybe the same person killed them both, but they had a harder time finding my mom?"

"Or your mom killed your dad and Karma came back to get her."

"I'm sorry, did you even love my mom?" I could hear the way my voice snapped. *Good*, I thought. I could feel a headache coming on and I wanted to go lie down.

"Of course I did, Paige." Margaret pouffed the back of her bobbed hair. "Unconditional love is what my mother used to tell me when she locked me in the closets for being bad. I refused to go that far, but maybe if I had, your mother might not have copied the same gene *my* mother carried. We women in this family have some bad genes. Let's just hope for yours and my sake that it skipped a generation." Margaret winked. "You can take me back to my car now."

"Yes, ma'am." I was happy to comply.

14

PAIGE

I woke up the next day to a loud pounding on my door. My stomach turned. My head hurt. I wasn't ready to be out of bed, let alone so abruptly. "Go away!" I yelled.

"Paige! It's Stephen. Please let me in."

"Ughhh!" I rolled over and grabbed my phone, which was beeping at me. I'd missed three calls from him the previous day and hadn't read any of his long text messages. But I supposed that he could just kick in the door since he was a cop. Or did he need a court order to do that? I didn't watch enough crime shows to know. Just in case, I rolled out of bed and met him at the door. I was wearing sweatpants and a t-shirt. I could feel the sleep still crusting my eyes and my hair was tangled. I couldn't care less what he thought of me now. He might be here to take me to prison for all I knew. I opened the door.

"Stephen!" I gasped. "How long have you been here?" Stephen's appearance was even more surprising than mine. I found him leaning against the wall in the hallway. He wore a wrinkled white t-shirt and jeans that looked very worn. His blond curly hair was going every which direction, and he looked like he had not been sleeping. Or perhaps he'd been sleeping in the apartment hallway? I held the door open for him to enter. He barely came through the door before he started groveling.

"Paige, please listen to me. You have to hear me out. I love you. I never meant to hurt you."

"That's it?" I put up a hand to stop his words. Then I waved my hand over him. "What is this? Your undercover look?"

"Please, Paige. I don't want to talk about that. I want… I need to talk about us."

He looked like he might cry. I envied him. No matter how much I'd tried, I still could not cry. "Why are you here, Stephen? Really?"

"I need to know if you love me. If you ever loved me?"

I thought about his question. At the moment, I felt nothing. No emotions at all. "Is this a trick question? If I answer the wrong way, do you put a note on the board next to my face?"

Stephen closed the gap between us and gently grasped my shoulders. I flinched. He dropped his hands as if my shoulders burned him and backed away.

"Stephen, I don't trust you. Surely you can understand that. All I need to know right now is if you are here to investigate me? Or take me in?"

"No. No. That's not why I'm here."

"Well, that's all we have to talk about right now. I would appreciate any updates on my mom's case. Other than that, I have nothing to say to you."

"Paige," Stephen's voice was utterly defeated. "It's not that easy."

"Why not? I'm one-hundred percent willing to cooperate and would be happy to turn over any evidence I might find on my end. Would that show the police that I'm less of a suspect?"

"Evidence? Are you saying there's evidence that you haven't turned over to the police?" Stephen's blue eyes took on a new intensity and they sparkled with excitement.

"Well, I can't say that it has anything to do with my mom's

murder. But I will say that I have a whole box of random things I collected that would show up after mom's black-out spells. They're things she could never quite explain where they came from…" I disappeared in my room for a second and came out with a large box. I set it in front of Stephen and opened it up.

"This shoe showed up one weekend when we were camping, and a hiker went missing… This shirt – see the blood stain here? My mom's friend went missing and a police officer came to the house to question us about it. This pocketknife. I don't know what this is from. My mom has always had it. This could be rust or blood. I'm not sure. But I know it's really old and it was sentimental to her."

Stephen perked up. His eyes got huge as he began to look through the stuff. "I'm going to need to take this in," he stated.

I shook my head. "Not without me to explain all the stories behind this stuff. Well, as much as I know, anyway."

"Paige, listen to me. I'll need dates if we can reconstruct that, dates and locations. I need you to tell me everything you know and then claim to everyone else that you know nothing. Say that you just found this stuff in the apartment when you were going through your mom's stuff. Otherwise, this could make you an accessory to murder, or multiple murders. You can't conceal evidence. It's illegal. But you didn't know what you were doing, right? You didn't know that this stuff could link to crimes your mom might have committed, right?"

"Right," I said slowly. I was lying. Of course I knew. I wasn't stupid. I just had never considered the full impact of my actions. Then I had a thought. It was a sudden, horrible thought. Had the other people died because I'd covered this up? Could my honesty have led to mom's arrest, which would have led to one less murder? Was mom a serial killer during her black outs? I had been so stupid to have ignored the possibilities I had been too scared to verbalize. Maybe mom would still be alive.

"Stephen, I'm scared," I whispered. "I think I might be in danger here."

Stephen pulled me into his arms and crushed me in a tight hug. "I've got you. I won't let anything happen to you."

"What time is it?" I pulled back abruptly. "I have a counseling appointment. I need to get dressed." I went in my room, shut and locked the door. I grabbed a t-shirt, threw it on, then pulled on a pair of jeans with holes in them, and slid my white canvas Sperry's onto my feet. I ran a brush through my hair and eyed my face critically. Today would not be a make-up day. I quickly brushed my teeth.

"I'll take you," Stephen offered when I reemerged.

I put a hand up. "No, I want to go alone."

"How can I protect you if you're by yourself?" he asked.

"Check the app you installed on my phone." I grabbed my jacket and car keys and went out the door.

I knew he'd follow me. As I got into my car and navigated into traffic, he made no secret that he was going to come along. I groaned. How long was he going to do this? I'd love to believe he was just protecting me and that he genuinely loved me, but I knew his interest in me revolved around solving this case.

I switched lanes. He switched lanes. Not like he couldn't just use the app to know where I was. I shook my head in disgust. That stupid app!

As I pulled my car into the counselor's parking lot, I parked the car and pulled out my phone. I quickly uninstalled the app and went into Dr. Burnett's office. I didn't even have time to sit down and wait before Dr. Burnett appeared and invited me back.

"Make yourself comfortable," she welcomed me. Her hair was straight today and she looked more comfortable in jeans and a nice, flowery blouse.

I plopped into a comfortable, overstuffed chair closest to the door. I liked the décor in the office. It was very calming. Gray and white tones with blue accents. The window slats were angled in a way that I could see a beautiful view of green trees and a sloping hill.

"How are you, Paige?"

"Okay, I guess."

"Is there anything you would like to talk about before you read your next hypnosis session transcription?"

"If it's okay with you, I'm in a bit of a time crunch. Can we jump right in?" I took the paper Dr. Burnett was holding out to me.

Hypnosis Session: Deffer, Paige
May 17, 2019

(Dr. Burnett) Paige, take me to the memory you've found. What do you remember?

Mom? Why didn't you come to my assembly today? I could feel the heat in my face as anger, and perhaps a sunburn, all mixed together. I was so mad that day! I clenched my dainty hands by my sides (people always commented on my small frame and tiny hands and feet). I felt my shoulders hunch up.

(Dr. Burnett) How old are you, Paige?

I was in the fifth grade by this point, but I'd had a lifetime of let downs already.

(Dr. Burnett) What did she say when you confronted her?

Paige, darling, I didn't know you had an assembly. Did you tell me? Mom reached for a long strand of my hair that had fallen out of my ponytail. In fact, I think my whole pony-tail was falling and my hair was a big mess, barely banded together in the back.

(Dr. Burnett) What did you say?

Yes, mom, we've been talking about it for the last couple days. I could hear my own voice rising. *EVERY other fifth grader's mom was there. Do you know how EMBARASSING it was? Not to mention, I had to WALK home. It's MILES from the school. And you were just sitting here? AT HOME? Do you even care about me at all?* I could feel the tears in my eyes.

(Dr. Burnett) And did she seem to care? How did she respond?

Don't be so hysterical, darling. I'm so sorry. Mom swiped my eyes. *You have such pretty green eyes… You must have told me during one of my episodes.* Mom's voice was calm and quiet.

(Dr. Burnett) And you said…?

That's another thing! No one's ever heard of your episodes. You should see the teachers when I try to explain. They all think I'm lying. It's so embarrassing! Can't you make yourself notes or something?

(Dr. Burnett) Do you think she understood you?

Yes, I think so. Mom put her palms up in surrender, her face sad. *You're right, Paige. I hate how spacey I am. I would've loved to have been at your assembly. I miss out on so much!*

(Dr. Burnett) An apology is nice. Did that make you feel better?

No. I felt so ashamed. Sudden shame hit me like a hot lash on my back and I could feel my face getting hot again. How could I have made mom feel so bad? Of course she would've come had she remembered. I was going to have to try harder to make sure mom got the message next time.

So I said, *I'm sorry I was mad, mom. I love you. Next time, I'll just put a note on the refrigerator.* I stopped talking.

(Dr. Burnett) What happened next?

Something caught my eye. I'm not sure. What was that on the floor? A dingy, rust-colored shirt? I'd never seen the shirt before. I walked over and picked it up. *What's this?* I turned to mom.

Mom had turned her back to finish washing dishes as she stared out the window. *What, Paige?*

I took a step toward mom when I felt the strange crunchy material. I flipped the shirt over and saw the dried, brown blood stained on the back. I gagged realizing I was touching a bloody shirt. What if mom saw me with... evidence?

(Dr. Burnett) Evidence of what?

I was asking myself the same thing. I had no idea. But it wasn't the first time mom had brought home something strange during her night prowls.

I had left the room by the time mom turned around.

Once in my room, I quickly shoved the shirt in with all the other things I'd collected over the years. I placed it in a box down in the floorboards under the carpet where I'd dropped a bowling ball some time ago and broke the floorboard. I'd put the carpet on top of it and no one knew it wasn't a part of the floor.

(Dr. Burnett) Where did you get a bowling ball?

I had found it one night just outside of mom's room and I just took it. I didn't even ask where she'd gotten it. I knew I needed to destroy these things. In fact, I had destroyed a lot of weird things over the years. But something had changed lately. Where I'd spent so much time protecting mom when she went off in these dazes, I was beginning to feel something different. Anger. Why did mom insist on pretending to forget everything? Why did she disappear every night and come home long after I'd left for school? Why did she pretend that even when she was physically present, she wasn't actually there and remembered nothing? What kind of a mother did that? Then I heard a loud knock at the front door.

(Dr. Burnett) Who was it?

I wasn't sure at first. *I'll get it*, I called. I ran to open the door, but not before looking out the peep hole. *Mom, it's the police.* I lowered my voice to a hiss.

Well, open it, darling, Mom said lightly. She stopped cleaning dishes and wiped her hands on a dishtowel.

I opened the door a crack, keeping the chain lock in place, and regarded the officer in silence.

(Dr. Burnett) What did the police want?

He said, *Hello, is your mom at home?*

I just shrugged. *Why do you want to know?*

(Dr. Burnett) What did your mom do?

Mom appeared out of nowhere. She shut the door, dropped the chain lock, and opened it back up.

Hello, officer, come in. Then she said, *Paige, it's okay. Policemen are here to protect us. How can I help you, sir?*

The uniformed man entered the house and stood seemingly ill at ease. *Are you Krysta Deffer?* he asked.

Yes, sir.

(Dr. Burnett) What did you do?

I watched mom's face. My heart raced with anxiety and I thought I might puke.

I'm not sure if you realize this, ma'am, but your co-worker, Alyssa Sky, has gone missing. The officer peered hard at mom.

Oh, no. Do you think she's okay? Mom's face scrunched up with concern.

I thought I'd pass out.

(Dr. Burnett) Why were you so anxious, Paige?

My mind went to the bloody shirt. Was it a woman's shirt? It seemed awful small... Then I thought, wait! Mom had a night job? Is that where she was every night?

That's what we're trying to figure out, ma'am, the officer said. *One of your co-workers saw you two arguing at the bar last night.*

Oh, is that all? Mom laughed a little. *We always snip at each other. We are both single mamas trying to make the bills. We're constantly trying to seat customers in our own sections. It's a first come, first served hustle mentality there. Sometimes people get crossways with each other. But we're like sisters. Ask me anything about her kids or past jobs... boyfriends...* Mom pushed her dark-blond hair out of her eyes.

I believed her and hoped the officer did too.

Well, what do you know about boyfriends? Was she seeing anybody? The officer was intense.

Yes... Mom's eyes shifted to me. *Paige, darling, why don't you go to your room?*

I obeyed. I shut the door but put my ear up to it. I listened for a minute. Apparently, this lady had a string of bad boyfriends. I tried to still my heart. Then I thought, what would the officer do if he saw the box I kept? The box! I turned and noticed I hadn't put the carpet back in place. I flew over and had just finished hiding it when my bedroom door opened.

(Dr. Burnett) At such a young age, you were covering up evidence for your mom?

Yes! And I did it just as mom popped her head in.

Darling, the officer is going to look around, okay? Be a good girl and stay out of his way?

I nodded and allowed the officer to look through my room. It wasn't until the officer had left the apartment that I noticed I'd been holding my breath. I exhaled and went back to my room. I leaned my weight into the door lest mom try to come in again. What if mom had killed that lady? If she hadn't, where did that bloody shirt come from? What if I asked mom and she killed me because I'd found the evidence?

(Dr. Burnett) How did that make you feel?

Chills worked through my body and didn't seem to settle. The thought that mom might do such a thing was the most ridiculous fantasy I could ever dream up. Wasn't it? I dared not pull out the other items I'd pilfered through the years after mom returned from fearful nights of emptiness and darkness. I could name every item by heart.

(Dr. Burnett) What were they, Paige?

A sticky set of car keys that didn't start mom's car. A hairbrush with mud caked on it. Multiple torn pieces of clothing I'd never seen mom wear. A paperback book with melted chocolate stuck in the pages. A pocketknife.... The knife was the worst item of all. It seemed to have brown blood on it. Not a lot, mind you. But it could be nothing else. It was old. A patch of rust on the blade scratched me when I picked it up. I kept this in the box. I dared not tell anyone or they might come take my mom away. What if the woman was dead because I didn't tell anyone? What if she was dead because of me?

I LOOKED UP FROM READING. Somehow the details of this in writing seemed way more real than the memory of when I had lived it.

"You covered that up your whole life," Dr. Burnett puzzled aloud. "Why?"

"She was the only family I had," I shrugged. "I didn't want anyone to take me away from her."

"This points to possible illegal and extremely dangerous activity."

"Yes."

"Before I go on, I need you to know, your boyfriend, Stephen, is a cop."

"I know." I dismissed this with an irritated hand wave. "Well, now I know. He lied and told me he was a financial planner. We aren't together anymore."

"Well, his office gave me a subpoena for your last hypnosis session. I had no choice but to release the files to them. He will likely ask for this one as well."

"Doesn't surprise me." I felt angry then immediately resigned. I was done feeling surprised. "I'm actually cooperating with him on my mom's investigation. I don't plan to hide anything. In fact, I'd like to do one more hypnosis session."

"One more?" Dr. Burnett asked. "Are you sure?"

I shrugged. "Well, I'm not sure how much longer I'll need to come."

"Okay, well get comfortable."

I did.

"Count backwards," Dr. Burnett ordered.

After what seemed like minutes, the session was done. As I started to gather my things, Dr. Burnett's words stopped me.

"Paige, I'm not in the habit of giving advice, I prefer to listen and guide, but I feel in my gut you might be in danger here. I get the impression that Stephen is not being honest. And it goes further than the deception of his profession. I think he was deeply jealous of your relationship with your mother. Paige, please, be careful with him."

"Thank you. I will," I said quietly. Chills ran up and down my arms and spine. One thought surfaced. *How jealous was he, exactly?*

"I'd also like to make one more recommendation."

"Sure."

"There's a group that meets every single day of the year in every city, multiple times a day. It focuses on co-dependency. I wrote a website on the back of my card here." Dr. Burnett handed me the card. "You can go to this website and find a group anywhere you go. I think this would be even more helpful than meeting with me. You can do both, but if you find yourself limited by one or the other, you'd probably do better with this."

"Thank you," I got up to leave. My mind was racing. Was Stephen dangerous? How was I going to get away from him? It wasn't going to be easy. I knew he was in the parking lot waiting for me. He had every intention of going where I went. And he wasn't making it a secret. I knew his car. I knew his plan. What I didn't know was how to get away from him.

15

PAIGE

I let myself into the hallway. My phone buzzed.

Margaret: *I'm sitting in Joyhouse Coffee Shop. Come meet me.*

"Grandma dearest," I whispered, but a plan started to form.

I walked quickly and got into my car. Stephen followed me in his car as I pulled out. I drove down the street. I jumped out of my car at the coffee shop. Stephen stayed in his car.

"Paige!" Margaret Terry was already there waiting for me. Her warm demeanor caught me off guard. I felt something was amiss. I went along with it though, curious to know her game.

She was pretty for her age. Some people would probably use the word attractive to describe her. Every hair was perfectly in place on her head. She wore her makeup dark, but it too was well-done. Her khakis were pressed and her short-sleeved sweater gave her a trim, put-together appearance.

"Hello, grandmother," I kissed her on the cheek and stood back. "Is that what I should call you?" I asked sweetly.

She waived a hand. "Whatever you want, dear. I have something to tell you." Her tone was sweet. A little too sweet.

"Oh?" I asked.

"I drink my coffee black, but I figured you were into that sugary stuff, so I ordered you a vanilla latte. I hope it's still hot." Margaret pushed a coffee cup with a lid on it toward me.

I tried to sit still. My knee bounced under the table.

"I've decided Jason must be your father."

"Oh?" I was only half interested. I watched the door out of the corner of my eye.

"You have his eyes and expressions," she said decisively.

"I thought I had my mother's eyes," I protested. "We both have green eyes."

"Well, yes, you both had green eyes. I'm talking about the shape," she said impatiently.

"Well, it's too bad I'll never meet him," I smarted to her.

"Yes. It is. But I might have the next best thing."

Now she had my full attention. I felt interested.

"Would you like to see where they lived together?"

My breath caught in my chest and I felt my eyes widen. *Would I!* "Yes. Yes, I actually would."

"Okay. I'll write the address down on this napkin." Margaret took a pen from her purse and jotted down the address.

"That's in Missouri!" My mind started calculating the amount of time it would take to get there.

"It's about two hours from here. There's not a lot I can give you and I don't know if she left you any money…?"

I shook my head. Suspicions crept into my brain. Is that what she was after?

"Well, it doesn't matter. It's an abandoned house. No one would buy it after… what happened. The bank foreclosed on it and it's been sitting there ever since. Anyway, it's a beautiful piece of land and you look like you could use some rest and relaxation. Or at the very least, a good drive." Her eyes were soft, and I believed her. I felt my guard coming down. Could I still form a relationship with this woman?

"Thank you." I took the napkin. I gently folded it into my pocket. "Hey, do you think you could give me a lift back to my apartment? My car's acting up and I plan to get it towed to the shop."

"Okay," she agreed as we got up to leave.

I put my hood up over my head. I followed her out the side door and slid into the passenger seat of her red caddy.

"Who are you ducking?"

"What makes you think –"

She held up a hand. I stopped talking.

"Your hood is up, and you just bent over to tie your shoe. I wasn't born yesterday. You're reminding me of your mom right now." I could hear the disgust in her tone. She put the car in drive as I told her the address.

After we turned a few roads I was convinced Stephen was still back at the coffee shop waiting for me to exit. I finally sat up straight. "So what? Why was my mom so bad, anyway?"

"There was always something really off about her," Margaret said softly, seemingly lost in memories.

"You mean how she blacked out?" I asked.

"No. What do you mean she blacked out?"

"You know. She seemed to be functioning, but I would always find out later that she wasn't really there. She never showed up for school functions because she could never recall any of the information because she wasn't *actually there*. You know, in the head."

"Weird. Really? Are you sure she wasn't just playing it?" Margaret wondered.

"Trust me, this was my life. I think I would've known."

"I meant that Krysta was just spooky. She could shut down her emotions and would have no reaction to things that would freak out other people," Margaret said with a shiver.

"Wait. Like what kind of things?" My heart stopped for a

minute. Was that what was wrong with me? Could I be doing the same thing?

"My husband, her dad, was horribly abusive. She saw some really terrible things."

"I'm sorry. I had no idea."

"Well, that's over. He died. Heart attack."

I pointed to the apartment building. She pulled in.

"Speaking of dangerous men, be careful with that boyfriend of yours. Don't ignore your instincts. Anyone you'd go to such lengths to avoid is worth avoiding."

"Thank you." I jumped out of the car. In the back of my mind was the realization that she now knew where I lived. I had no time to dwell on that. In fact, it could be a very short-lived problem.

It wouldn't take long before Stephen knew I'd tricked him. Once inside the apartment, I stuffed as many clothes into a backpack as I could.

"Toothbrush, toothpaste, make-up..." Mumbling out loud was forcing my mind to focus. I had to move quickly.

When I jammed my bag as full as I could, I paused and looked around. I grabbed a trash bag and began throwing more things in. I opened the Lyft app on my phone. The nearest one was ten minutes away. It would have to work. I selected the ride.

I walked through the apartment. My mind memorized every detail of my soon-to-be former home. This had been my home since we left Canada. So many memories played in my head. There was one problem. All of them had my mom in them. This wasn't my home anymore. It never was mine. It had only been ours. Without mom, I didn't want to be here. I pushed open the door of her bedroom. I sat on the edge of her bed. Nothing had changed since the day she died. The bed was messy. There was a small pile of dirty clothes in the corner of the room. It looked like she might be back.

"Mom, I really wish I would've known you better," I whispered as if I was afraid to utter the words out loud. Sudden chills touched my arm and a loud thump sounded on the floor at my feet. I looked down. A journal? I picked up the book. Had it fallen from the bed when I sat down? Indeed, my mom's handwriting filled about twenty pages. The dates were sporadic. There were blank pages in between writings. Some were neat, and some were sloppy and hard to read.

"Thanks, mom." I whispered that too. Of course, I didn't believe in ghosts. Nor do I think my luck was that good. I simply had uttered the words that came to my mind. There was no time to read now. I grabbed the journal, left the room, and stuffed it into my already jammed backpack. As I finished re-zipping, a fist hit my front door. I gasped and jumped up. Stephen must have discovered I wasn't at the coffee shop.

I threw the backpack over my shoulder. Then I threw the trash bag out the window. I quickly checked the Lyft app. The ride was now three minutes away. I moved the trashcan near the living room window. An empty beer bottle rolled out from behind the trashcan.

"Weird," I said quietly. But I turned my attention back to the window. I'd used this window once before. Only back then, it was because mom had locked us out. I wasn't leaving from the inside then.

I opened the window and knocked out the screen. I realized as I hoisted myself up and attempted to go head-first that I wasn't as small now as I was the first time I'd gone through this window. The fist was now pounding on the door.

"Paige, I know you're in there!" Stephen yelled.

"Hurry, hurry, hurry," I whispered. "I hope this holds me." I climbed on the trashcan. It teetered dangerously underneath me. I put a foot on the sofa to balance but it was too low to get my body up and through the window. I got my balance, leaned over and grabbed the windowsill. I pushed off the couch and put more weight on the trashcan. Using the trashcan like a springboard, I got one leg through the window. The trashcan fell noisily to the floor. I caught my breath as I sat straddling the window, one foot in and one foot out. I swung my other leg around which landed me on my stomach.

The air whooshed out of me. I let out a small *oomph*. I caught my breath for half a second. Adrenaline pumping now, I noticed the pounding had stopped. Had he heard me? I jumped to the ground. It was way further than it looked. My ankle twisted underneath me. Pain registered but there was no time for that. The Lyft app made a *ping* on my phone. I ignored my ankle, picked up my trash bag, adjusted my backpack, and ran to the black Civic.

"Where to?" the Lyft driver asked.

"Joyhouse Coffee Shop. Go!" I got in the car and ducked down in the back seat.

The driver hit the gas. "You in trouble, miss? Need me to call someone?"

"What? Me? No. What makes you think that?" I'd always known I was a terrible liar.

"You're ducking down."

"Tying my shoe."

"Well, there's a guy looking out the window you just jumped through."

"Oh. Did he see me?"

"Not sure."

I said nothing more. I had the jump on Stephen for now. Time was on my side. But only by minutes. I pulled out the napkin with the address. I programmed it into my GPS. Keys in hand, I jumped out when the driver stopped. I thrust a twenty-dollar bill at him.

"Keep the change." It was only a ten-dollar car ride, but I

didn't care. I didn't have time for change. I was going to run out of money soon. I didn't care about that either. I limped to my car and drove to the highway.

16

PAIGE

I hit the highway. After twenty miles became fifty, I started feeling quite confident that I didn't have a tail on me. My ankle still smarted but it was better. I rolled down the windows to enjoy the sunshine. I cranked up the radio and belted out the first song I recognized. The wind whipped in from the windows as I started to sing at the top of my lungs to hear myself. I smiled. For the first time in years, I felt a smile that could heal my heart. I felt free.

I watched the green trees that lined the highway and noticed the way the road climbed hills, some tall and some small. The road curved in sharp and then subtle bends. The warm air from the wind whipped around me and made me believe, even if only for this moment, I was going to be fine.

I made a stop at a quicky mart gas station not too far off the highway. I couldn't risk the time of getting taken off course. I grabbed a few supplies I thought I might need to get me through the rest of the afternoon and even into the night. A 24-pack of water, beef jerky, a few bananas, and a bag of Doritos.

"That'll be $15.24," the cashier popped her gum at me.

"Okay." I reached in my handbag to grab my wallet when

the corner of the white envelope I'd grabbed the other day poked me. I finished paying and jumped back in the car. Before I pulled out of the highway, I grabbed the envelope and opened it. It was from my mom's bank.

"That's odd…" I read aloud.

Attention, Ms. Deffer,

It has come to our attention that your mother, Krysta Deffer, passed away unexpectedly. First, we would like to offer our sincerest condolences. Second, we extend our gratitude for her many years as a valued client. Finally, we would like to notify you that according to her will, her account is payable on death to you. We can transfer the money into the account you have with us here or send you a check. Please call us so we know how to best accommodate you in this situation.

I read on. Mom's account held $17,142!

I checked the time. It was 4:24 p.m. I made a quick call to the bank. A nice female answered the phone with a professional voice. I felt instant relief wash over me as they agreed to transfer my mom's money to my account.

"Will there be anything else?" she asked.

"No," I said but changed my mind. "Oh yeah, can you change my address? I have a new one." I rattled off the address of where I was heading. It was a spontaneous decision to give them that address. I didn't know anything about the house I was running to. All I knew is I didn't plan to go back to the apartment. Ever. I guessed I'd figure the rest out later.

"I can but I'll need a signature on some paperwork. Can I send it to your new address?" She asked me kindly.

"Absolutely," I agreed. I hung up after assuring her there was nothing else she could do for me. I started my car to leave but hesitated.

"On second thought…" I said quietly. I went back in the gas station and looked around more. At the back of the store, I found more supplies I figured I would need once I got where I was going.

I paid for my things a second time and loaded them into my trunk. Feeling prepared, I pulled my car back onto the highway. Even if for today, I knew I was going to be okay.

Another hour lapsed as I crossed the state line to Missouri. The sun was starting to set when I pulled off the highway, following the GPS. The more I drove, the less highway I saw and the more open land. The houses became more sparsely populated and spread across miles of green acres. Some acres were surrounded by thick green trees that seemed to block the sun from the home. Other homes just sat on wide open spaces with few trees. Still others had fenced in properties with animals such as cows, sheep, donkeys, and goats. There were even a few ducks on a pond.

"I'm in the country now," I said. It seemed so still and peaceful. The country road continued to wind another few miles.

When the GPS finally said, *You have arrived,* I slowed my car. Was I already here? It seemed so fast. Did I even remember the ride?

I could see a solid single-story cabin style home in front of me. Tall grass surrounded the abandoned structure. The house sat on a quarter acre of land that sloped into dense, overgrown woods that started at the back of the house. It was impossible to tell how much of this belonged to the home. I figured it would be no problem to break in. Fate had brought me this far. Now fate could bring me home.

I parked my car in the gravel driveway and waded through the tall grass. I came to the back door and tried the knob. I should have known this wasn't going to be that easy. It didn't budge. I grabbed an old debit card from my wallet and worked it through the door. After what seemed like an eternity, the door clicked and opened. Cautiously, I entered.

The smell of strong wood and dust made me sneeze. While not putrid, it was a distinct oak smell that over-whelmed my senses. I lifted my chin. Nothing a little fresh air wouldn't fix. I left the door opened and immediately tried to open the windows but had no luck. The windows would not budge. I opened the front door to get a breeze going. As I did, a letter that was stuck in the door fluttered to the ground. It was a square card with my name and address on the front. I was instantly alarmed. No one knew I was here. There was a post-it note stuck to the top with a handwritten note.

There hasn't been mail here for years. Your mailbox is broken so I put it in the door. If this name is correct, please contact the post office. Thanks!

I opened it quickly. It was a card from Margaret Terry that said *Welcome Home*. I froze for a moment. Was she so sure I would say "yes" to coming here that she put postage on an envelope and mailed it to this address? What was she up to? I supposed I should just take it as a nice gesture, but I knew better. I wondered what she was planning. I shoved the card back in the envelope. I mindlessly held onto the envelope as I walked through the rest of the house.

The inside of the home was quaint. It was small but homey and I instantly felt comfortable. The kitchen and living room were an open floor plan. There were two bedrooms and one bathroom. One bedroom was clearly the master. I hesitated at the door and took a deep breath. I don't know what I expected, but it was an empty room. There was no sign that anything like a gruesome murder had happened here. I searched the floor and walls for blood. I saw nothing. I felt no fear.

I went to the car and grabbed my trash bag full of clothes and the backpack I had packed. I threw Margaret's note on the floor, then I hauled in a pillow, an air mattress, snacks, fruits, and a flashlight.

I went through the kitchen and opened a door that led to the garage. There was a garage door button on the wall by the door. I clicked from inside the house, and nothing happened. I walked into the dark garage. I used my flashlight and disengaged the release lever on both sides of the garage door, enabling me to manually lift open the door. It was heavy. Then I pulled my car in and closed the garage door. I had no idea what tomorrow would hold but for today, all was well.

I didn't anticipate the inconvenience of no electricity and no running water, but I was sure I could make it through the night. Good thing I had been charging my phone in the car on the way here! I used a pump to air up the mattress, made the bed, and laid down. I took out my mom's journal and opened it up. It was just getting dark enough that I needed a flashlight to see the words. I flipped through to the beginning.

February 16, 1996
It's been a long day. Worst day of my life. Jason is dead. I woke
up to blood everywhere. But I have no recollection of what
happened. None. I just woke up in the middle of all this blood. I
wasn't sure who it was coming from. Until Jason didn't wake up.
It was so very icy cold in the room. I'm not sure why. All I know
is that he is dead and I'm alive. Now what? My mom always said
one day I would get what was coming to me. I guess she was
right. Why am I alive? What happened? I should feel devastated,
but I feel… numb. I found something on the bed. It was the knife
Jason gave me as a wedding present. It had blood practically drip-
ping off it. I keep trying to remember why he gave it to me as a
gift. He told me he was a gambler. He did it as a hobby, but he
always had a contingency plan in case we had to get out of town.
In fact, he got us both fake passports. Did I use the knife on him?
I'm on a plane to Canada as we speak. If he's dead and I'm alive,

I'm the prime suspect. Which means I needed to get out of town. Fast. I only grabbed as much money as I needed for now and could carry without looking suspicious. The rest is still hidden in the floorboards. That's another thing… if someone did this for the money, they would've taken everything. Wouldn't they? Maybe someday I'll know. Maybe. I miss him. Jason was my soul-mate. I felt so happy with him. Now he's gone.

I put the book down and stared at the ceiling. I clicked off the flashlight. The bright moonlight shined in the window. There was no window covering but I felt oddly at peace. I could hear cicadas clicking a rhythm that was comforting.

I'd set up the air mattress in the living room. I couldn't quite bring myself to take a bedroom. I did wonder vaguely if the second bedroom would have been mine if my dad were alive today. Somewhere in the middle of my thoughts while staring at the ceiling, I fell asleep for what must have been hours.

Bang!

17

PAIGE

I woke suddenly. I stiffened and squinted desperately in the dark when I heard it again.

Bang!

This time I could tell the direction. The front door was wide open. The door banged against the house in the wind. I could hear rain sprinkling on the roof. Then it came in louder and louder. The rain was coming down so hard it sounded like the roof might collapse. Shivers ran up my spine and the hair on my arms stood on edge.

What was I thinking anyway? The roof could cave in for all I knew. Here I was alone and unprotected in the dark, in the middle of nowhere, with no one to care if anything happened to me.

"What do you want?" I whispered. I rose to stand at the door but didn't close it. The peace I felt earlier slipped away like the river of emotions I so desperately tried to feel. The silence was unsettling. The loud torrent of rain was my only answer.

I stood at the open door and peered into the darkness. The rain flew sideways. I did not get wet. What had made the door open? I had locked that door. The wind and rain flew the opposite direction of which the door had flown.

I took a step forward into the rain. Staring hard through the precipitation hitting my face, I felt, rather than saw, a force beckoning me. I followed the force. Rain pelted my skin hard. I blinked the water from my eyelids. I was looking for what or who threw that door open.

Suddenly, I saw her. Lightning lit up the sky. Just for a moment, the sideways rain revealed a silhouette of my mom.

"Mom!" I ran out further into the rain. "Mom! I miss you!"

As quickly as the image formed, it whipped around. I fell back in a puddle of muddy water. I could see her reaching out her hands as if to stop me from coming after her. Her eyes looked at me, wide and scared. She pointed at something far off in the distance, but I dared not take my eyes off her silhouette.

Danger… I heard the word audibly and as quickly as a flash of lightning strike, she was gone.

Slanted rain pelted me hard as I sat in that puddle of mud and water. My mind didn't register the way the rain soaked my clothes clear to my skin. My heart felt only pain. Pain of loss, pain of sadness, pain of all the things I never said. Pain that I never really knew my mom and never would.

"Mom?" I heard my voice barely audible in my own ears. "No! Don't leave me again! I don't know what to do without you!" Finally, the tears came. Not just a few dainty tears. Pain-filled, gut-wrenching torrents of tears that rivaled the rain. It started deep in the core of my soul and rose through my chest, into my heart, which I felt would surely explode. They pushed through my eyes. It was impossible to distinguish between the rain and the fluid that poured from my eyes and streamed down my face.

The rain and I were one. I sobbed for what seemed like hours. In fact, I was afraid I'd never stop. I was alone. Truly alone. No parents, no siblings, no relatives. I had just taken over an old house where my father had been murdered. Most likely by my own mother.

They say the mind is a strong force that has the ability to will things into action. Had I willed my mom here? As quickly as I had the thought, I realized the answer. She had come to give me a message.

The urgency of the word hit me like a stack of books falling off a bookcase. *Danger.*

Get up! My mind yelled. *You're in danger and all you can do is wallow in self-pity in a puddle of mud?* Suddenly I realized I was soaking. It was the kind of bone-chilling wet that makes one wonder if clothes had merely become another layer of skin.

I scrambled to my feet and peered hard into the darkness. In one more streak of lightning, I could only see trees swaying with the whipping wind and the torrent of the rain. I hurried inside with a sense of urgency and locked the door. Everywhere I walked, water pooled off me into a small river that moved me through the house with every step.

As I changed from wet clothes and dried myself off with a shirt I'd packed, I reflected on the fact that I didn't feel scared. I just felt sad and lonely. I began to shake from head to toe. I noticed a small wet piece of paper peeking out of my wet jeans. I pulled out the soggy business card and flipped it over.

The scribbled website was still legible on the back and it reminded me of the last conversation I had with Dr. Burnett. Was that less than twenty-four hours ago? It was before I left, *after* she handed me the card and told me about group therapy. *Just take it one day at a time*, she'd said.

"I can do that," I said out loud to the empty house. "I can do that." All dry for now, I found my air mattress, crawled in my warm makeshift bed, and fell back to sleep.

18

PAIGE

I didn't want to go. Group therapy sounded awful, not helpful at all. It just sounded stressful. Much to my surprise, Dr. Burnett was right. When I looked it up on my phone, I found that even in this small country town, there was a group that met.

In fact, I was unsure what made me walk through the door. I guessed it was because it's not logical to think that I can be alone forever. The short amount of time I had found myself alone had proven to be horribly uncomfortable. I'd lived my whole life around my mom, watching over my mom, thinking about my mom, protecting my mom. Now that she was gone, I didn't know what to do. I felt so lost, I didn't even know what to do next.

"Hello, are you new?"

My heart jumped as the forty-something, pretty blond spoke to me. Five sets of eyes shifted to me. It was an eclectic group of people. Their faces all held nice, open expressions.

"Yes." I found the nearest chair in the corner. I would just be observing. I probably wouldn't even be back. They passed me some literature.

"Welcome. We're glad you're here."

I was surprised in that moment how warm and invited I felt. They seemed genuinely happy to see me.

As the meeting started, more people funneled in and chatted amiably with each other. But it started promptly on the hour. They read a nice opening welcome for newcomers. I felt welcomed and experienced an instant sense of peace. I felt like I was in the right place.

There was an encouraging reading and suddenly people were going around the room and sharing. I couldn't help but compare and look for similarities in their stories. Then there was Amy. Amy was a big girl. Younger than me, but wiser. She had a kind face and short brown hair. Tears pooled in her brown eyes as she spoke.

"When I was growing up, my mother was simply not there. You know how some people would say their parents didn't listen, so they were not there mentally, like not focused? I mean, I literally could never find my mom. At any given time, day, or night, I would look for her and when I'd check the garage, the car would be gone. I'd never know where she went. Then she'd get back and not even explain. You know how people have anxiety over losing loved ones or being left? I had anxiety because that was my world twenty-four-seven!

"I found myself in one bad relationship and then another and another... I was so afraid to be alone anymore. I did everything – so many stupid, shameful things to keep the boyfriends around. I got a credit card and bought expensive shoes, clothes, and meals for them. One time I bought someone a car! I was so desperate to keep the person I was with I'd try to buy love.

"When mom died, I didn't feel anything but exhaustion! I was so tired of trying to make relationships work, I sort of collapsed. I realized how alone I was. I refused to think about my relationship with my mom or *lack* of relationship with her. I told myself I didn't care and that's why I didn't cry.

"When I came here, I realized that she had abandoned me. I was afraid, without even realizing it, of others leaving me too. Which is why I ran after them so hard. It took one more relationship fail after I started coming to this group to really make me see what I was doing. That relationship nearly killed me. When it was over, I was so broken and devastated to be alone yet *again*. I finally understood that I thought I was trying to fix bad relationships, but I was really coping—unsuccessfully with my mom's abandonment. I wouldn't have seen that without y'all. Thank you for helping me through that process. We all know it wasn't pretty when I finally did start crying!" Amy blew her nose loudly and smiled a little.

My heart was beating so fast. It was like Amy knew me. So much of her story was like mine! The meeting continued. I decided not to talk today. After the meeting, several people approached me, greeted me, and encouraged me to come back. I managed to walk out with Amy.

"Thank you so much for sharing your story." I felt shy. Was I so unaccustomed to making new friends? "I felt like you were describing my life."

Amy smiled at me. "We all have similar stories. I hope you'll come back."

Before I could turn toward my car, she called to me.

"Paige. Your name's Paige, right?"

I nodded.

"You up for coffee tomorrow? My day's booked up today but tomorrow I'm free if you are?" Amy pulled out an oversized pair of sunglasses and jammed them on her face. Then she pulled her hair back into a ponytail using a rubber band around her wrist.

"Sure." I smiled and we exchanged numbers. I was tired of being alone too. The isolation I felt had started way before my mom's death. My life with her had been very lonely.

I left the meeting and found a few places of interest in

town to visit before I made my way back to the house. The first place was the gym. I stopped in and twenty minutes later, I had a membership. More importantly, I had access to showers.

Next, I noticed a gun shop. I parked the car and sat in the parking lot looking at the shop. Before I could lose my nerve, I got out of the car and walked in. The shop was quiet. It looked like only two people were working. I approached the counter boldly. I tried to look confident.

"I'd like to buy a gun, please."

The man behind the counter had short hair and a goatee. Were his eyes judging me?

"Driver's license, please."

I pulled out my license and laid it on the counter.

"Is this address current?" he asked. His voice was decidedly southern. His name tag said "Peter."

"No." I didn't exactly have an address anymore.

"In that case, I'll need a piece of mail with your new address on it."

My heart sank for a second. Suddenly inspired, I ran out to my car. I excitedly produced the letter that Margaret had sent me.

Peter eyed the letter skeptically. "It's supposed to be more official. Like an electric bill or government document."

"I just moved in!" I whined a little.

"Tell ya what, I'm going to accept this, but you need to promise to bring in something more official later on when you have more mail." Peter winked.

"Deal!" I was so relieved.

"Do you know what gun you want?"

"No, what would you recommend?" I asked.

"Glock 43x. It would fit your hand best." He grabbed a gun from under the counter and placed it in front of me, pointing the opposite direction.

I picked it up. My hand shook a little. "It's not... loaded, right?"

"No, it's not. Finger off the trigger. And never point the gun at any target you aren't ready to shoot." Peter pushed the gun from where I had it pointed at his chest.

I could feel my cheeks flush pink. "Sorry," I felt mortified. "I'll take it."

"Four-hundred and fifty dollars for the gun. One-hundred and fifty for conceal and carry classes. Then there's the matter of bullets. How often do you shoot?"

I reached into my wallet. "Not often." I tried to stay casual. "Is the class required?"

Peter paused as if trying to decide what to say next. "No, in Missouri you can carry without it. But it's a good class to take for inexperienced shooters."

"Of course," I agreed. I was a little embarrassed that my inexperience was so obvious.

"Class is this Saturday. It's a full day. Can I get you registered?"

"Yes."

"Okay, fill this out." Peter slid the application across the counter.

When I finished the paperwork, I was surprised when he pulled the gun away.

"We're backed up right now. It'll take three to four hours to check your background. Anything we should be worried about?"

I shook my head. "Maybe when I come back, can you show me some basics?"

To my surprise, Peter smiled. It changed his whole demeanor. He had seemed so rough, but his smile was so big, I could see a tooth missing in the back of his mouth.

"Yep," he agreed.

"Okay, I'll be back."

I went back to the gym. I didn't work out. Instead, I took a nice hot shower. I felt like I hadn't showered in days. As the water washed over my body, I felt my anxieties wash down the drain. Then a thought came to my mind. *What am I doing here?* I think the answer was *running away.* I knew what I needed to do.

"Mom," I whispered. "I'm not strong enough to find your killer. What if he finds me first and kills me, too?" There was no answer. Was I praying to my mom now? It seemed like I should reach out to something greater than me, but what?

The answer eluded me as I turned off the shower, used a clean gym towel, and put my clothes back on. I spotted the hair dryer. As I blow-dried my hair, I reflected on how much I missed modern luxuries, even though I had been at the old house less than a day. Water and electricity would be nice at the house. But I decided I'd take it one day at a time.

I had about an hour before I needed to go pick up my gun. I drove to the gun shop parking lot and sat in my car to wait. I flipped back through my phone pictures. I came across the picture I took of my mom's murder suspects. I couldn't seem to look away. I pulled out a pen and found a piece of paper in the glove compartment. I wrote a list.

Ray Lennon

Ashley Triegger

Matt Cline

Margaret Terry

They all had one thing in common. They were all at the funeral. Is that why Stephen pressured me to have a dumb funeral? Was he just looking for murder suspects? Attending a funeral hardly made a person a suspect. But I knew in my heart it must be so. Even my name was on that board. I snickered to myself as I added Stephen's name to the list. There. He was at the funeral too.

I immediately drew a line through Margaret Terry. No matter how awful she was, I didn't think a mother would kill her own daughter. I wrote notes about what I knew. My mind had played "picture in my memory," so I could remember what everyone looked like and what they wore on the day of the funeral.

Ray Lennon had dark hair with salt and pepper grays sprinkled throughout it. He was handsome and distinguished. His face was serious. He had a dark expression. There were a few wrinkles on his face but those were the only sign of his age. Otherwise, he appeared strong with broad shoulders. He'd worn a nice black suit jacket and button-down shirt with jeans. He'd sat in the back row and was there on time but left before the funeral ended. I wrote questions. *Who is he? Why did he come to the funeral? Why did he leave before it was over?*

Ashley Trieggar, mom's best friend, had been wearing a light pink dress that was clearly too small. Could she not afford a new one? Or maybe she was one of those people who thought size mattered. Come to think of it, it was tight but pushed her cleavage up and seemed snug in a way that was flattering. She was slim and tall. She had long blond hair that she wore in a low ponytail. Her fingernails were neon pink and looked like they were newly manicured. Ashley didn't care that mascara streamed down her face as she cried. She was messy. Or was she the kind of dramatic person who liked to draw attention to herself? Maybe she wore her messed up mascara like a badge that showed she loved my mom the most. She sat in the middle of the church and hugged the aisle seat. Her phone number! I remembered she gave me her phone number and I had put it in the pocket of my black slacks. I'd have to look for them when I got back to the house. I wrote a note. *Call Ashley Trieggar and ask her questions.*

Matt Cline, mom's boyfriend, was a gray-haired gentleman who had a kind face. His eyes were sad. He had tears in his eyes when he spoke. He was a heavier guy with a stout frame. His eyes were brown and compassionate. But there was something missing with this picture. I wrote a note. *If he was mom's boyfriend, why had I never heard anything about him?*

~~Margaret Terry~~ (I had crossed through her name). Mother, grandmother; she didn't even know mom was alive until she wasn't anymore. Margaret was short, petite, and looked like mom. She was perfectly dressed in just the right black dress and shoes. She wasn't as concerned about what her emotions showed. Her eyes showed an occasional glint of anger. She was attractive and seemed to care a great deal about appearances. Anyone could clearly see this in the way she wore her hair, like she had just come from the salon, perfectly colored dark brown. She's a shorter, thicker version of mom with slight wrinkles around her eyes and lips.

Would never kill her own daughter. I stopped writing and re-read my words, trying to convince myself. My hand was shaking as I continued writing.

Stephen Wilton, my ex-boyfriend, police officer, close "friend" of the family, liar. I shuddered at the thought. Why did he have to pretend to care about me?

Rap rap rap!

I jumped and screamed, instantly on guard. Peter, the gun guy, stood grinning outside my window. I could see his missing tooth in the back of his mouth. I rolled my window down.

"Gun's ready."

I got out of my car and followed him into the store.

"Your background came back earlier than normal. Clean as a whistle." Peter eyed me suspiciously. "It's the clean ones you gotta worry about."

My eyes widened.

"Just kiddin'." He laughed again. When he smiled, he seemed kiddish, almost my age. Then the smile faded and he got serious fast.

He put the gun on the counter. He grabbed some bullets and a gun magazine. He put the bullets in the magazine and clicked it into the gun. "This gun is now loaded. Do you know what to do?"

I didn't. I shook my head.

"Alright. I'm on lunch. Just happened to see you in your car. See that room back there?"

Dear God, was he going to lure me into a dark back room with a gun? My forehead beaded up, a sure sign of anxiety.

"There's a shooting range back there. I'm going to show you how to hold a gun properly, how to line up the sights, and then you're gonna shoot."

"But, I…"

He cut me off. "Missouri's a state where you can carry without a conceal and carry license. But I don't recommend it. Which is why I'm gonna show you how to use this before you leave. Nate?" he yelled to someone I didn't know was there. "I'm on lunch. I'll be shootin'…"

He grabbed a pair of large ear protection muffs and clear eyewear. "Put these on. Eyes and ears. Don't ever forget to wear these."

I put them on. I was about to learn how to shoot a gun. I followed him through two doors that closed us into a small room for a moment, and then to a shooting range with seven lanes. He took me to the far left lane. With the ear protection on it was hard to hear, but we were the only ones on the range. I'd have to experience the sound of multiple guns shooting at the same time on a different day. For now, I watched and modeled everything he taught me to do.

Until it came time for me to shoot. My palms were sweating. I could see my own hand shaking, an outward sign of my inward nervousness. My heart dropped to my stomach and I howled as I made the cardinal mistake of letting my thumb slip in the the way of the trigger right as I pulled it back. I cracked my thumbnail and within seconds, there was blood. I quickly put the gun down. I had no desire to pick it back up. Peter held up one finger and disappeared for a few minutes. He came back and handed me a Band-Aid. As I wrapped it around my thumb, I listened through my earmuffs as he shouted to me.

"I know that scared you, but you're okay. You'll never forget where to place your fingers on that grip, will ya? You're gonna have to try again."

I shook my head and felt tears in my eyes.

"I can't let you leave here with a loaded gun, not knowing how to shoot it okay? That's more dangerous than no gun. You can do this. Pick up the gun, don't shoot, just show me your grip."

Against my will, I obeyed and picked up the gun.

Peter tweaked my hand positioning a bit and gave me the thumbs up.

I took a deep breath, lined up the sites as he showed me, and pulled the trigger. I hit the target. But off to the left. I tried again. Again, I was off.

"Again. Don't worry where you hit, just practice pullin' that trigger."

I did. I pulled it eight more times before my gun stopped shooting. Peter took the gun from my hand and showed me how to drop the magazine. Then he showed me how to reload the clip. He loaded the first bullet, then I had to do the rest, which hurt my fingers. I had to push hard for the bullets to fit just right in the magazine.

Peter seemed to notice my struggle. "Your hands need to build up strength. You aren't used to using them that way."

He showed me how to put the magazine back in the gun to reload it. It was all so foreign to me and my hands felt small and clumsy. I felt discouraged in one minute and victorious in the next. It was an exhausting process. Finally, someone knocked on the door.

"I've gotta get back to work," Peter told me.

I was glad to stop. My hands were sore, and I had a lot of

work ahead of me to get comfortable with this thing. I gathered my bullets, clip, and gun and followed him out of the room.

"How do I carry this thing?" I wondered out loud.

"Oh, right," Peter scurried around the store. "You need a holster." He came back with a holster and demonstrated how to put it on.

I couldn't imagine ever carrying a gun on my person and told him so. But I bought the holster. Peter turned out to be quite the salesman. I walked out with a purse to hold my gun, two extra clips, and several boxes of bullets, and eye muffs, which Peter showed me were combined eye and ear protection. On a whim, I had him throw in a few targets to shoot at. My mind was already wondering if there was somewhere around the small cabin where I could practice shooting. I was almost out the door when I turned back.

"Do you know someone around here who can mow really tall grass?" I asked.

Peter smiled widely. "As a matter of fact, my dad does." He pulled out a small post-it and wrote a number on it with a name and handed it to me.

"Thanks," I left the store feeling overwhelmed. Somewhere in the midst of that, another feeling emerged.

Pride.

Maybe if I could protect myself, I'd be okay.

I'd just gotten buckled and began to drive when my phone rang.

"Hello?" I put my phone on speaker as I navigated the car onto the road.

"Hello. Is this Paige Deffer?" The woman's voice on the other end was brisk and sure.

"Yes."

"Paige, my name is Susan and I'm with Liberty Mutual."

I tried to interrupt her. I didn't want insurance right now.

"This isn't a solicitation call, Paige. I'm not asking you to buy insurance. I understand your mother passed away recently. I'm calling you because she had life insurance. Quite a bit and it all goes to you."

"Oh." I didn't know. "How much is quite a bit?"

"Two-hundred and fifty thousand dollars."

I was stunned. "Wow. That's mine? What do I need to do?"

"We need a few things from you first. You'll have to go online and enter a claim. Do you have access to a computer?"

I looked down at my phone. "Yep," I said.

"Okay," she said and rattled off a website. "Go online and fill out a claim. Next, we'll need to see a death certificate."

"Well, I'm not exactly in Arkansas right now."

"No worries. You can take a picture with your phone and send it through our secure portal."

"Okay, once I do all that, where do you send the check?"

"It can take between thirty and sixty days. I'll just need the address of where to send it to as well."

I told her my new address. I had the death certificate with me. Oddly enough, it was in my glove compartment. I didn't know where else to put it. When I hung up the phone, I turned my car into the driveway. I filled out the form on my phone and took a picture of the death certificate. I suppose I should have been excited. Two-hundred and fifty thousand dollars was a lot of money in my world. But right now, I was doing well just to get through the day. I couldn't shake the feeling that I might not be there to pick up the check in thirty to sixty days.

I manually opened the garage and pulled in. I noticed another letter wedged into my front door. It was the letter from the bank. *Well, that was fast. Good*, I thought. I'll take that back to Peter at the gun shop.

19

PAIGE

"You did NOT!" I exclaimed and found myself laughing for the first time in what felt like years. Amy sat across from me. She was funny and happy. We sat in a little country diner. My back was to the door. The coffee was the best I'd ever had, and I needed it today. I didn't sleep well last night. I kept thinking I'd see another vision of mom and I didn't know if I should be scared or excited. Despite the fact that I now owned a gun, I was painfully aware of every creak and moan I heard. The gun made me feel no safer. I was running out of time. I couldn't shake the feeling.

"What about you? Ex-boyfriend skeletons in your trunk?" Amy had the slightest accent. There was just a way she put emphasis on the word *trunk* that made it sound like she was tripping over it. She was casual in her jeans, t-shirt, and flipflops. Her hair was pulled into a messy bun.

"No, no skeletons. Just a guy I left behind. Boring story, really. He wasn't the right one."

"Was he ugly?" Amy made a face.

I laughed again. "No. Good looking."

"Mean?"

"No. Kind. Maybe a little impatient at times, but mostly thoughtful."

"Oh man," she said, breaking into a big smile. "If I had a dime for every good-looking, kind, thoughtful boyfriend *I* dumped...well, I'd be... *broke* actually." She crossed her eyes and laughed. Then she took a big sip of her coffee.

"Okay, okay. Truth? He was a liar. I caught him in a lie, and I just couldn't get past it."

"Good for you. So, he's what brought you to the group?"

"I don't think so. I think it was my mom. She just passed away a few weeks ago." I was skirting the truth and I knew it. I'm a terrible liar. *Careful*, my mind warned me. I knew I couldn't get too comfortable. I felt sweat bead up on my forehead.

Amy must have sensed my discomfort and changed the subject. "I'm sorry about your mom," Amy's eyes were sympathetic and caring. "Let's talk about something else. What's your thing?"

"My thing?" I asked. I was blank again.

"You know. What do you do for fun? What are you into?"

I felt myself panicking. I was blank. I didn't have a "thing." Why didn't I have a thing? "I guess I don't really do anything for fun."

Amy frowned at me for a minute.

I paused. In that moment, I chose honesty and it felt freeing. "I think I'm trying to figure out who I am now that mom's gone. I always just hovered around her to make sure she was okay. I guess my thing was taking care of my mom. Now that she's gone..." I laid my hands on the table face up.

Amy's face cleared up. "Okay, yeah. I get that. I so get that!"

Suddenly, I could feel eyes on me. The hairs on the back of my neck stood up. The same way I felt when the door to the house had flung open and mom had come to visit me the other night. Could I be developing a sense that connected with my intuition? Regardless, I could feel, rather than see, dark piercing eyes locked on me that seemed to burn into my skull. I wondered if the person had just slipped in and sat at a table near the door. Until then, I was under the impression that the diner was empty.

"I'm going to get more coffee." I got up quickly. Amy looked surprised. I supposed I was abrupt. I casually scanned the diner as I went to the counter. As I got up, a man stood up, turned his back to me, and walked out the door. He was in the front of the diner and I was in the back. There was something familiar about him.

"Can I get more coffee?" I left my cup on the counter and followed the man out the door.

"We'll bring it to your table... ma'am?" The waitress yelled after me. I kept walking.

The man was walking fast down the sidewalk. "Sir!" I yelled. What had gotten into me? He walked even faster and started to jog. Why didn't he want to talk to me? I stood staring down the street as he hustled away. Something wasn't right. I felt chilled in the middle of the warm summer afternoon. That man knew me. I was pretty sure I knew him too. I turned back to the diner. When I returned, Amy was staring at the door with her head cocked to the side. She had risen slightly out of her chair like she was trying to decide if she was supposed to follow me.

When I got back to the table, Amy looked stunned. "Are you okay?"

"Yes. I'm so sorry. That was so rude. I thought I knew that man. Turns out, I didn't."

"If I had a dime for every random guy I chased down the street…"

I laughed, thankful that she let it drop.

When we said good-bye, I was glad to go. Amy didn't appear to be offended by my behavior and it all ended well. But my mind could not recover from that incident. I regretted not running after that man.

I came home to a large tractor mowing the tall grass around the house. My brain worked on overdrive. I didn't call anyone. How did anyone know I lived here? Had Peter sent his father?

I parked my car in the garage and came back out. The man saw me and turned off the tractor. He hopped down, amazingly quick for a man of such a large size, and came over.

"Hi, there!" he greeted and offered his large hand. He stood an entire foot taller than me. He was red-faced. The ballcap that sat on what I assume was a bald head did little to keep the sun off his face.

I took his hand. It was sweaty and gross. I resisted the urge to wipe my palm on my shirt.

"Jud Blackwell. Neighbor. I live down the street. Didn't know anyone moved in here until today." He took off his ballcap and wiped the sweat from his bald head.

That's all I needed, neighbor gossip. "Yeah, I haven't been here long."

"Well, you're mighty brave, young lady. You *do* know what happened here…?"

"Yes, I'm aware." I smiled politely.

"Damn shame what happened to Jason Mynart. He was a good man. No one deserves to go like that," he shook his head and looked down at the ground.

"You knew them? The people who lived here?"

"Yeah, I did. I'm Fire Chief 'round here and I was first on the scene after it happened. You can't unsee that shit."

"Did they ever find who did it?"

Jud snorted. "The wife. Apparently, she snapped. People say she went batshit crazy. Jason had twenty-six stab wounds. Twenty-six! Man, she must have hated him! Never saw it comin'. Guess lots of things go on behind closed doors no one ever sees."

"Was she convicted?" I challenged, feeling my temperature rising. I felt defensive of my mom.

"No, she ran off. No one ever found her. Or if they did, they disappeared too."

"Disappeared too?" I stared at him in horror.

"Yes, ma'am. A few people thought they had a jump on her over the years, not one of them came back."

"How many people?"

"A few. One of them was a good friend of mine. She was on the police force down here. Got a lead that Krysta, the wife, might be in Arkansas of all places. Anyway, my friend went to find her and never came back. She's missing. No one's seen her since."

I nodded, thinking about the woman that mom had worked with the bar. She went missing too. Was there a connection?

"I'm sorry. Don't mean to scare you. But you knew this when you bought the house, right?"

"Yeah, right. I guess I just didn't know the full story."

"Well, who really knows for sure, anyway? You know how stories get bigger and bigger over the years. Anyway, I was mowing my yard and I thought I'd do yours as a welcome gift."

"Wow, thanks! That's too kind." My mind was still reeling. "It sure is hot out here. I think I'll go grab a water. You want one?"

"Got any beer?" Jud asked.

I shook my head.

"In this weather, I stay on a strict cold beer diet. Thanks anyway." Jud turned and got back on the tractor.

"Thanks again," I called.

Jud touched the tip of his ballcap and started the tractor back up.

Once inside the house, I doubled over. I was going to be sick. Why was I working so hard to give mom the benefit of the doubt? Maybe her murderer killed her in self-defense? I took deep breaths. I was sweating profusely. I wiped my forehead. I grabbed a room temperature water and downed it. I opened the front and back doors. I felt an instant breeze come through the house. I tried the windows again. Just like the other day, I could not open them.

I could hear the tractor moving further away. I peeked out the front door. He seemed to be driving away, toward the street. I guessed he was done. I went out and waved a final "thank you." He paused the tractor.

"Your 'For Sale' sign is still up," he shouted. Then he waved and continued on down the road.

I wasted no time. I grabbed my loaded gun, the bullets, eye muffs, and the target outline of a human from the car. I went out the back door.

I scanned the open backyard and could see a clearing in the woods. Remembering Peter's words, *Know your target and what's beyond it*, I looked for a place to set up. It would be pretty imperfect with the wind picking up, but I decided to hang it from a low branch on a tree that stuck out in front of a small clearing in the woods. I went inside and came back out with a belt. I put the belt through a hole I ripped in the paper target that held the outline of a human torso, tied it around the tree limb, and stood back. I'd have to work on better placement of that later. But for now, I needed to practice drawing my gun from the holster I had on my jean shorts.

Peter told me to clear my clothing out of the way, draw the gun with my finger off the trigger, and yell "Stop!" From the looks of my yard, no one would hear me for miles. I could hear the vague hum of the tractor, but it sounded like it was way down the street now.

"Stop!" I yelled. I couldn't get my gun out of the holster. Dear God, I was going to shoot myself and no one would ever find me.

I had to really pull to get the gun out. I practiced putting it back in and taking it out again. Three more times and I felt a bit more confident.

Now, I pointed my gun toward my target. I reminded myself how to grip the gun. The stinging blood blister on my thumb was a reminder of what could happen with the wrong positioning.

I closed one eye to see through the sight. I squeezed the trigger, and the gun went off. I gasped. Two things happened. One, I felt terrified. Two, I had hit the target. But that was it. No one came running to see what had happened or why a gun went off. The unsettling realization was that I was utterly and truly alone and out of earshot of any neighbor. All the more reason to learn how to use this gun.

I tightened my grip and my resolve. What good is a gun if you never use it? I fired more rounds. When it was empty, I dropped the mag the way Peter taught me and refilled it. In fact, I refilled both mags. I shot them both. I refilled them again. By that time, my hands and arms were tired, sweat was pouring off me, and I could already feel the pink sting on my cheeks. How long had I been out here? I holstered my gun and put the backup mag in my back pocket.

I changed my focus. Now what about those windows? I was determined to get them opened.

I walked around to the side of the house and stopped short at the room that would've belonged to my parents. I stared hard at the window. What was I missing? This did not look right. Was the window backwards? Who had built this house? Who builds a house with windows facing outward?

I gasped as a sudden thought occurred to me. With outward facing windows, could someone have easily opened them and crawled in to kill my dad and attempt to kill my mom? What if this proved somehow that mom didn't kill him after all?

"They're backwards," a deep voice sounded behind me.

I screamed loudly and pulled my gun. "STOP!" I yelled as I turned.

It was Stephen. The smirk on his face turned instantly to shock. His blue eyes were wide with surprise. He put his hands up slowly and walked towards me.

"Stop! I said stop!" My hands were shaking but I kept the gun steady.

Stephen kept inching forward. "Put the gun down, Paige. It's me, Stephen." He talked slowly as if speaking to a mentally challenged criminal.

My already pink face flushed at the thought. *I'm* the criminal? "What are you doing here, Stephen? How did you find me?"

"Put the gun down so we can talk."

"I don't want to talk to you. I don't trust you."

"I understand." Stephen was only a foot away now. He stood a head taller than me and was now staring down at me.

I backed up. I bumped into the house. Before I could blink, Stephen had my gun and he was inches from my face. "Hello, Paige." He was no longer smirking. His face held something like admiration or respect. I couldn't tell which. I could smell his breath; he was that close to me. It smelled like cinnamon gum. That, mixed with his cologne, brought back strong memories of when we first met. He searched my face and then stared into my eyes.

"We need to talk," he said.

"Okay," I tried to act unaffected by his presence. My body betrayed me. How could I miss someone and dislike them so intensely all at the same time?

"Where can we go?" he asked.

"Inside. It's hot. I don't have air or electricity yet. And there's really nowhere to sit."

"Well, let's open these windows."

We did. Turns out, the whole house was built with inside out windows.

Once inside, Stephen handed my gun back. Before I could take it, he tightened his grip. "You pull it on me again, I keep it. You can't pull a gun on an officer."

"How about on an ex-boyfriend?"

Stephen flinched and loosened his grip on the gun. I holstered it.

"We've made some progress on your mom's case." Stephen leaned against the wall. "Thought you should know."

"And?" I stood in the middle of the living room.

"We've concluded your mom was involved in the murders of at least two people, Alyssa Sky and Scott Nelson. One murder remains inconclusive."

"Mike Polanski. The guy who fell over the cliff?" My breath caught in my chest. "But I saw…"

"Hypnosis sessions are inadmissible in court. Your testimony comes from the memory of a five-year-old child. Though it's likely yours are correct, we can't conclude that in a court of law."

I felt irritated by this. I didn't like this side of Stephen. There was a confidence about him that almost seemed arrogant.

"Huh," I said and crossed my arms.

"There's something else, Paige. The toxicology report came back."

"I don't know what that is."

"Really? Don't you watch crime shows?" Stephen sighed. "It's a lab test to see if there are any substances in her bloodstream. We did an autopsy on your mom before she was cremated, remember? The report came back with a blood alcohol level of point three percent."

"Is that a lot?" I wasn't ever much of a drinker.

"Paige. It explains everything. It explains why your mom

functioned but never remembered anything. She was an alcoholic experiencing blackouts. It's so simple. But even I missed it."

"Hey!" I felt offended by this but couldn't understand why.

"It's not a jab, Paige. I'm trained in this stuff, but I didn't see it. How could you see it?" His eyes got soft and he pushed off the wall. Before I could order him to stay where he was, he was inches from my face again. His eyes were soft and his hand found the back of my neck. "I just got emotionally involved."

"I…" before I could finish my sentence, his lips were on mine. He was kissing me in a way he never had before, and I liked it. I kissed him back. My brain ordered me to stop and throw him out. My hands disobeyed. They found his wild, curly hair. All distance closed between us. My body pressed against his. He lifted me as I wrapped my legs around him. Suddenly, I was against the wall while he held me in place, kissing me. I threw my tank top off. He made a noise I'd never heard him make before. It was low and guttural. My bra was next and I threw it on the floor. Stephen spun me around and gently threw me on the air mattress. The journal I had been reading slid onto the floor.

"What's that?" Stephen asked.

"Nothing, it was just my mom's." I quickly dismissed it.

He took his shirt off. His abs were defined, his chest and arms tan and muscular. Why had we never done this before?

"Paige?"

"I want you." I shocked myself. "Please."

Stephen shimmied my jean shorts off, then his own. He lowered his body on top of mine and looked into my eyes. "I love you. I always have. From the minute I met you."

I wanted to believe him and for that moment I chose to. "I know," I whispered.

I felt my panties slide off and I could feel skin against mine. I had no expectations. I had never had such an experience before. He kissed me with more passion than I'd ever felt from him and left a trail of kisses that led down my body to my navel. He paused before slowly moving lower. His tongue found a spot on my body and I arched and moaned in a way I'd never heard myself sound. He laughed softly and I liked the sound. When I was so wet I thought I couldn't stand another minute, his body covered mine and our bodies met in a way I never knew was possible.

Time flew by but stopped all at once. His hands were all over my body, guiding me until I felt a release so sweet and agonizing at the same time, I couldn't help but scream. Minutes later, he heaved and moaned loudly. Both of us collapsed in a tangled naked heap of skin, legs, arms, breasts, and chest, all meshed together. As we cuddled, both satisfied, my eyelids got heavy and I fell asleep.

20

RAY

Ray was lurking around the corner of Margaret's home when her little white and brown shih tzu started barking and came tearing around the house. Margaret followed the dog with a look of bewilderment on her face. Clearly, she let the dog out to potty as she did every afternoon. The dog might actually bite him, he thought with bemusement.

He'd been waiting for her. He leaned casually on the side of her white two-story colonial-style home. He knew things, he watched, and he waited. He knew her routine. Even though she had no neighbors around for miles, his car sat in a vantage point where he could observe. Night was setting in. It was that time before dark when things start to look hazy, right after sunset.

"Evening, Margaret." Ray stepped out from the corner of her house. Margaret screamed. Her hair was a little flat and she had no makeup on. Her flat slip-on tennis shoes made her seem even shorter than she really was. Her eyes narrowed and she put her hands on her hips.

"What are *you* doing here?" Margaret spat the words out like she had a bad taste in her mouth. "We have no business, you and I." Despite herself, Margaret put her hand to the back of her head and attempted to pouf her hair. She was the most casual he'd ever seen her. She was wearing jeans and a t-shirt. He was surprised she owned such attire.

Ray chuckled. He was rather casual himself in a workout shirt with the sleeves cut off and shorts. He seemed to have more gray hair popping up every time he looked in the mirror. This time of summer found him with a tan which made him a shade darker.

"You're right. We didn't. Now we do." His casual tone turned serious. "Why did I see your granddaughter in town, Margaret?"

"She's here? In Missouri? Are you sure?" Margaret's eyes were wide with pretend surprise. She stared at him.

Ray's eyes took on a hard edge and he quickly covered the ground between them. "I think you know she's here. In fact, I think you set this all up. What's your game, woman?"

Margaret flinched. "Fine," she said. She rolled her eyes and dropped the act. "There's money in that house still and she's going to lead me to it."

"Money?" Ray laughed, revealing his perfectly straight, white teeth. "No. If there was, I would've found it by now. And you know I was looking. I have hundreds of thousands of dollars in medical debt and a dead wife to show for it. No thanks to your daughter and that thief of a son-in-law you had."

"What are you planning?" Margaret tried to remain casual.

"Well, dear Margaret. I'm going to have to kill that granddaughter of yours. I didn't get to kill Krysta. Someone in that family has to pay for what Jason did to me. Besides, she's probably just like her mother. Rotten, the whole generation of you. Should I kill you instead?"

"Stop being so dramatic, Ray. You wouldn't kill a person. You don't have it in you."

Ray stared at Margaret and she stared back.

Finally, she flipped her hands up.

"Fine. Kill her. See if I care. You're right, she seems to be as rotten as her mother was. But let me find that money first."

"You know half that money is mine, if you do find any."

"I do."

"Then we split it fifty-fifty and I get to kill the girl."

Margaret held out her hand and Ray shook it.

"Deal," Margaret said.

21

PAIGE

Stephen was still here. I hadn't dreamt it. Had I expected him to sneak out in the middle of the night with my mother's journal? My mother's journal! Why hadn't I read everything in there yet? It probably held the answers we were looking for. I slipped out of bed and pulled on a pair of jean shorts and a comfortable t-shirt. I slid my feet into a pair of flip-flops, grabbed my gun, and put my holster on. I picked up the journal and went out the door. Stephen was still sleeping.

I hit the gym. My usual time and place just to shower, of course.

"Hello, Paige. How are you today?" Missy, the front desk receptionist greeted. She was young, maybe eighteen, and thin with long strawberry blond hair and brown expressive eyes. She was always upbeat and seemed to live in workout clothes.

"Good, Missy. How are you?" I responded.

"Good. I think it's going to be a great day!" She smiled her most winning smile. I wondered if she was always so positive.

After a nice, hot shower and clean, fresh hair, I went to the gun range. I used to hesitate when I'd go because I was afraid of shooting the gun. But these days, I just did it. I was glad I didn't feel fear anymore.

"Mornin,' Ms. Paige." Peter called out.

"Good morning, Peter." I juggled my bullets and eye muffs and attempted to open the door to the range.

Peter jumped to my aide. "Let me get that door."

"I got it," I had already finagled it open.

I fired several clips until my hands were sore and then I quit. That was always the best stopping point for me. I waved good-bye to Peter. Next stop, a meeting. But I was early today. I sat out in my car and pulled out mom's journal.

July 23, 1996

Canada is cold. Life is lonely here. I'm starting to feel as big as a house. They say I'm about seven months, but I know I'm closer to six. I'm just big. I've had lots of time to think. I miss Jason every day. I can't figure out why I killed him. I wish I knew. Was it because I finally had enough of the way he'd tilt his head sideways and narrow his eyes when he thought I was lying to him? I hated that. Mostly, because he was almost always right. But I'd never admit that to him. God, how I wish now I would've admitted that to him. Maybe he'd be alive now. I tried talking to this huge baby I'm going to have. That makes me feel lonely, too, because she can't talk back to me. I wonder all the time if she'll turn out like me. Wicked, like my mom always said I was. Well, if mom could see me now. She'd really think I was wicked. Knocked up with no father in the picture… She'd be right. She was always right. Oh, no. Note to self, DON'T let her near Paige. EVER. Paige. That's the name I decided for this baby. Krysta and Paige. It's you and me against the world, kiddo. Here's hoping you'll be better than me.

I started to turn the page when a sudden noise startled me out of my reading.

Bam bam bam bam!

I screamed and looked up to see Amy laughing hysterically. She'd banged on the hood of my car. She waved me in, so I put down the journal and walked into the meeting side-by-side with her.

The meeting was good. Probably one of the best yet. The topic was on forgiveness. I supposed I needed to forgive Stephen for lying to me. But by the end of the meeting, I realized I needed to keep the focus on me. There was plenty I needed to forgive myself for. I was learning every day about some new resentment I held against myself. Why did I hold myself to this huge, impossible standard and then berate myself for it later on?

I asked Amy that same question when we had lunch after the meeting.

"We all do that," Amy said. "I put my expectations of what I could—*should*—be able to accomplish way too high and when I don't hit that, I believe I'm stupid or incompetent."

"Yes! Exactly. How do you fix that?" I asked. I never knew what a burden it was to deal with but now that I knew, I wanted it gone.

"Time. You might have to work with someone to get to the bottom of where that comes from."

"Like a trigger?"

"Perhaps. Like something from your childhood, maybe."

As usual, it was a great and fun conversation, but I had things to do. I took a quick trip to the grocery store. As I was loading my groceries, my phone rang. I picked it up on the second ring, half expecting it to be Stephen. Maybe I shouldn't have left him like that.

"Hello?"

"Paige? This is Dr. Burnett."

"Oh! Hello! How are you?"

"Fine, Paige. How are you?"

"Good."

There was a slight pause. "It may be odd that I'm calling when we don't have an appointment scheduled. Is this a good time?"

"Sure!"

"Well, I wanted to let you know that I've been doing more research regarding your mom's condition. I might have found something."

"Oh?"

"There's a psychological state called dissociative fugue. It's such a rare state that I almost didn't remember it. But I got out the DSM-5 and found it."

"DSM-5?" I asked wondering if this was a term I should know.

"Sorry, it's short for Diagnostic and Statistical Manual of Mental Disorders and it's the book we reference for mental disorders."

"Oh, okay," I responded.

"It affects less than one percent of people. A person might find themselves somewhere and not have any recollection of how they got there. They seem to lose all awareness of who they are and where they are for large periods of time. It could even last weeks or months. Did your mother drink at all?"

"Apparently." I heard the sarcasm in my voice and hurried to erase it. I didn't want Dr. Burnett to think it was aimed at her. "Yes. I mean, I had no idea, but her toxicology report showed a high percentage of alcohol in her bloodstream when she..." my voice trailed.

"So, that can aggravate the situation, make it worse. We believe this dissociation is a defense against trauma that has happened at some point in their lives. They may be mentally or physically escaping a threatening environment. These people might attempt to physically leave the environment they are in.

Some say it's like sleepwalking. Did your mom have a bad childhood or an abusive marriage?"

I was quiet for a moment and then answered honestly. "I'm finding I didn't really know much about my mom. I found a journal. I'm learning more, and yes, I do think she experienced some pretty hard things."

"Well, I know you are working through her death. Feel free to reach out if you'd like to continue visits. I can do long-distance phone conversations."

"Thank you, I will. Dr. Burnett, before you go, is there a way for you to send me the notes from the last hypnosis session?"

"Sure. I can email them to you if you want to share your email address?"

"Yes," I agreed. I rattled off my email address, thanked her, and hung up the phone. I pushed my cart to the shopping corral and got in my car. My head was spinning a bit. There was still so much I didn't know. I couldn't help but feel it was my fault for not asking more questions. As I pulled out of the parking lot, I thought, *Would mom still be alive today had I invested the time and courage to just ask her about her life?*

My phone made a notification noise, and I was sure it was Dr. Burnett sending those notes. I pulled off into a gas station. As I put gas into my car, I sat and read the notes.

Hypnosis Session: Deffer, Paige
May 24, 2019

(Dr. Burnett) Tell me where you are right now, Paige?

Mom and I were "cabin camping" as we called it. We were finally celebrating my high school graduation. It was mom's idea. After she decided not to show up for graduation, claiming, once again, to "not know anything about it." I'd grown accustomed to the excuses and the no-shows over the years. In fact, I half expected mom to forget about *this* trip.

For the first time in my life, I was genuinely enjoying mom's company. Hiking and talking while grilling hot dogs over a fire and enjoying breakfast bars and coffee in the morning. We were having such a good time, we decided to stay an extra day. We were swimming in the campground pool and laying out, lazily relaxing in the sun. Mom and I were naturally thin, so we always felt comfortable in our bikinis. We laid out, trying to soak up sun on every inch of our exposed skin.

Paige? Mom propped herself up on one elbow to look at me. *There's something I want to ask you…*

(Dr. Burnett) Was this uncharacteristic for your mom to show interest in your life?

Very uncommon. I remember I tried to open one eye and had to put a hand up to shield the sun.

What's that, mom? I asked.

Since you first decided to be at vet, you talked about going to Mizzou…

And? I didn't like where this question was going.

Why did you decide to go to the University of Arkansas?

Why not? University of Arkansas is an exceptionally good school, too. I tried not to answer snappily.

Was it a money thing? Are you afraid we couldn't afford for you to go to Mizzou?

No. I paused a long time.

(Dr. Burnett) Were you telling her the truth?

Yes and no.

(Dr. Burnett) What was the truth?

I needed to stay close to her to make sure she was gonna be okay... I didn't tell her that I'd had a full scholarship to either school. I had a choice.

(Dr. Burnett) What did you tell her?

I'm not sure I'm ready to go that far right now. Mizzou is four and a half hours. University of Arkansas is a half hour, I told her.

I just want to be sure you didn't give up your dream and that it was somehow my fault. I hated that pained look on Mom's face. Her face was thin, and she had this pointed chin. It quivered a little bit in that moment.

(Dr. Burnett) Did you reassure her?

Yes.

(Dr. Burnett) How?

Don't worry, mom. I stuffed down the resentment I felt

that we were just now having this conversation. It was a little late now.

Besides, I met someone. I really like him.

Ah, yes. Did you say his name is Stephen? Mom asked for the third time since I told her.

I sighed. *Yes, Stephen.* I was too excited to feel annoyed at mom's forgetfulness.

Well, I can't wait to meet him, Mom said.

You already have, I thought to myself.

(Dr. Burnett) Why aren't you honest with your mother?

I didn't want to go into detail because it involved reminding mom of all those things we didn't acknowledge.

(Dr. Burnett) Then what?

The day ended. With a slight pink hue to my nose and shoulders, I crawled into my cot in the cabin. It had been a good and relaxing day. I slept hard that night. So hard, in fact, I had no idea if mom got up and went out.

(Dr. Burnett) But you think she might have?

Yes.

(Dr. Burnett) Why?

The next morning, mom was up before me. She woke me up with a cup of hot coffee.

They're closing the park because a random hiker went missing last night. They're looking for him now. They're asking all guests to leave.

(Dr. Burnett) What did you say?

I stared at her. Fear crept into my heart. I'd just woken up and was holding the steaming cup of coffee, trying to process mom's words. I watched as mom quickly started shoving her belongings in the duffle bag she had brought. I couldn't help but remember the time I was five and forced to shove my favorite things into trash bags so we could escape in the middle of the night.

(Dr. Burnett) What did you say?

Mom?

Mom paused and looked at me.

Are we in some trouble here? I held my breath and for a minute no one spoke. It was the bravest I'd ever been and the most uncomfortable.

She laughed a little and continued packing. *Of course not. But we do need to go. So, drink up, dear.*

(Dr. Burnett) But you knew deep in your soul that she was lying?

I chose to believe her. Like a good, dutiful daughter, I drank my coffee and started packing my stuff as well.

It wasn't until I was putting my bag in the car that I saw it.

(Dr. Burnett) Saw what?

A shoe in the trunk. But not my shoe. Not mom's shoe. It was a man's shoe. I should've been scared. But I wasn't. No chills this time, no drops to the pit of my stomach, no fear. In fact, I felt nothing at all. Had I grown numb to these instances over the years? Without even thinking, I opened my suitcase and stuffed the shoe inside just in case some nosy trooper decided to look in the trunk. I didn't even take time to formulate a theory on why mom was doing this. In that moment, I just accepted it. And I wondered vaguely what that said about me. I wondered if a hiker was dead because I kept hiding evidence. Did that mean, in some way, that I'd killed the hiker?

The gas nozzle clicked off indicating that my tank was full. It surprised me that I had been so focused on these notes, I almost forgot I was pumping gas. I finished the task and drove home. I pulled my car into the driveway. I definitely had a lot to think about. As I parked, I saw Stephen sitting on the front porch steps with his hands folded across his chest. Why did he look so mad?

22

PAIGE

"Hi," I tried to keep my voice neutral and light.

"Hi, yourself," Stephen said. Though his face was serious, his voice sounded light and flirty. Was it an act?

I sat down next to him. I felt relieved that he didn't try to kiss me. I wasn't so sure I was ready to be back together.

"Paige?" Stephen was staring off past the trees. "What are we doing here?"

"I'm not sure I want to talk about us, Stephen…"

He interrupted me. "No, I mean *you*. What are *you* doing here?"

"Here?" I asked confused.

"Here. Why are you at this house? You don't own this house, Paige. Who does?"

"Oh. Well, I kind of do. It was my parents' home."

"It was?" His incredulous tone indicated that this clearly was news to him.

"Ohmigosh! You might not know about my dad. He was murdered. Right here in this house. No one ever bought the house in all these years on account of that, so it has sat vacant all this time."

"Until now?"

"Right."

"Because you went to the bank and bought it?"

"Well, no. Not yet."

"Is that why there's no electricity or water?"

"Yeah."

"So, I'm confused, Paige," Stephen was speaking slowly. I couldn't tell if he was thinking about what he said carefully before he said it or trying to be sure I understood him. "I need to understand how you got into the house, how you're showering, eating, and flushing the toilet...?"

I laughed a little and shrugged my shoulders. "Oh, easy. It's like camping. I'm taking showers at the gym, I eat at restaurants, I buy water and pour it down the toilet to get it to flush, and it really wasn't hard to get into the house."

"You broke in?"

"I mean, I guess you could call it that. I plan to buy it. I like it out here. I feel close to mom. Connected. Maybe even to both of them."

"Paige. It's illegal for you to be here. I'm an officer of the law. Do you get what a weird position that puts me in?"

"I don't see it that way at all," I sighed. This was my parents' home. They are dead, which means it should now be mine. "Well, if it makes you feel better, I'm waiting for my mom's insurance money. When that comes, I'm going to buy this place officially."

"But I swore an oath and I have an ethical responsibility to do the right thing," Stephen pushed.

"In Arkansas," I argued.

"What?" he asked.

"You swore an oath in Arkansas. Do you even have jurisdiction here?" I felt a little proud of myself that the thought came to me.

"Not technically," Stephen admitted. "There's something else, Paige. I followed you today."

"See?" I threw my hands in the air. "That's why we aren't together. You can't just let me be who I want to be. *Why* would you follow me?"

"It's why I'm here. I've actually been assigned to watch over you. Bodyguard, if you will. My lieutenant gave me special permission. Me working on your case used to be a conflict of interest."

"Do you have an ethical responsibility to tell your boss about sleeping with me last night?" I interrupted him, feeling angry and knew I was lashing out. But he didn't have a right to comment on the choice of where I lived.

"As you keep reminding me, we aren't together anymore. So there's no conflict, and here I am." Stephen shrugged. "You were right when you came to the station. You could be in danger. Depending on the motive of your mom's killer, you could be next."

"But I'm safe now. No one knows I'm here. No one will find me."

"I found you."

"So?"

"Paige. It only took me a month to find you. I was actively looking. It's only a matter of time before the murderer finds you as well."

I stared hard at him. Did he say a *month*? I remembered the vision of my mother the stormy night when I arrived. Maybe I *was* in danger. I felt chills raise on my arm. Why did I think I could run away from it all? I remembered the man in the coffee shop. Why did he seem so familiar? I didn't see his face, but I could almost place his body type. In my memory, I think he was wearing different clothes. I shook my head trying to remember.

"Stephen, we probably need to collaborate. Share notes. I

might have some things to tell you about my mom that will fill in the gaps and help figure out who murdered her."

It was Stephen's turn to stare. He might have known I was trying to take the focus off me. "Tell you what. Not that I approve of this," he swept his hand around the porch where we sat, "but let me make some phone calls. I might be able to set this up as a safe house and keep us here, temporarily, off the radar. No one knows you're here?"

His offer seemed contingent on the answer being negative. I was not leaving this house. I lied. "No one."

"Okay, let me work some magic. I need surveillance cameras set up, we need some supplies, and I might need one of those gym memberships," Stephen winked at me but then he got serious. "Paige, do you feel up to this?"

"Yes, but…" I wasn't sure how to say it.

"What's up?" he asked.

"It's about our sleeping arrangement."

"Oh, should I go get my own air mattress and sleep in a different room?"

I felt suddenly shy and silly. "Please. Only, you can't sleep in my parents' room."

"Deal."

After a quick trip to get supplies, one more gym membership, and a pizza, we were back. Stephen installed the battery-operated cameras at every corner of the house along with motion lights. The cameras were set up to alert his phone if anyone stepped in view of the cameras.

"It isn't perfect, but it'll have to do for now," he said.

We set up a card table in the dining area and threw a few beanbags in the room. In a matter of days, this card table would be piled with clues and handwritten notes. Despite everything I was learning, it felt nice to not be alone. I felt safe and protected. At least for the moment. But I couldn't shake the feeling that the safety would not last long.

23

RAY

He watched through binoculars from his place deep in the woods.

"Fools!" he said aloud.

She wasn't alone. This might not be as easy as he'd thought. When he found out where she was, his heart was overjoyed. Maybe he'd gut her the way her father was gutted, in the same room, same number of stab wounds, and he'd pretend she was Krysta. Girl was a dead ringer for her mother.

Regret stabbed his chest and he had to breathe deep to calm himself. Oh how he'd wanted to kill that woman. That awful, wretched woman who'd stolen the last minutes of his life with his darling wife.

He tried not to remember that night. Why could he not forget it? When he got home, his precious Allison was dead. She had been in pain. While he was passed out, like the damn drunk fool he was, Allison had passed in the night. He didn't deserve to live without her. He was a no-good unfaithful husband and God had taken Allison from him as a result.

It was Krysta, that godless witch, who had tempted him, got him drunk, seduced him, and lived her life none the wiser.

Krysta deserved her death, and he wasn't sorry she was gone. But this daughter of hers was an exact replica, a carbon copy, and he was going to pretend she was Krysta as he killed her slowly. Only now, he needed to get this guy out of the picture. He needed a new plan.

Before, he could've gotten in and out undetected. Now there were cameras and motion sensors and lights. It would take some planning. Surely this guy would leave her alone some time. And when he did, Ray would go for the kill, literally. He'd take control quickly and quietly. He'd stab her the first time with such precision, she wouldn't even have time to scream.

24

PAIGE

"It's the damnedest thing!" Stephen walked around my parents' room bewildered. "There's not a drop of a blood stain anywhere." It was morning and Stephen wanted to start at the beginning. The beginning of mom's story, I guess. "Why would your mom kill your dad?"

"Even she didn't know. She was having her blackouts back then too." I was pretty somber and matter-of-fact about that.

Stephen turned to me. "Okay, the neighbor said they got along well, and no one saw it coming. But the police are sure it was her. I wonder if they found evidence? Hmm..." he mused aloud, "I wonder if I could get the case files. Wait, how do you know she was having blackouts?"

"It's in her journal."

"She had a journal?" Stephen looked astounded and irritated at the same time.

"Yes, but there's only one entry so far that mentions my dad's murder. The first one. She didn't remember what happened. She thought she did it." I went to the other room and produced the plain, nondescript writing journal. Stephen tried to grab it.

"Not so fast. This is all I have left of my mother. I would rather be the first one to read it."

"You haven't read it yet? What if it has clues, Paige?" Stephen tried to take it from me again.

"No. It's mine and I'll read it in my time. I'll let you know if I find anything that helps."

Stephen ran his hands through his hair in frustration. "We're going to run out of time here, Paige."

"Right, speaking of time, I have to go." I grabbed my keys and turned to leave.

"Now? Where are you going?" Stephen seemed outraged as he crossed his arms over his chest.

"I have things to do." I was purposely vague.

"You realize that I have to go with you. Bodyguard, remember?"

"I don't know if you realized this, Stephen, but I'm pretty good with a gun now. I can even hit most targets I shoot at close to my aim."

"Close?"

"Close enough." Truth was, no matter how much I shot, I couldn't quite hit the center of the target and I was beyond figuring out why.

"Well, we don't want to be late for... whatever you're doing. Let's go."

Dread filled my soul. These were the elements in my life I had found that were just for me. I was finally figuring out what made me happy and I had no desire to have him ride along. On the other hand, if I was in danger, an armed guard did sound comforting.

Stephen trailed me to the car. I turned so quick, he almost walked into me.

"Fine. You can go. But I'll drive. I say when we get there and when we leave. You don't get to comment on anything I do. This is my life and I like it fine just the way it is."

Stephen stared into my eyes with surprise and then humor. Was he going to laugh at me?

I narrowed my eyes, daring him to try it.

"I think I like this Paige." He lowered his face closer to mine and stopped inches from my face. "Kissing you is not on your agenda for today?" He pulled back at the last minute.

Dear God, I had wanted him to kiss me. But he was right, it was not on the agenda.

We went to the gym first.

"Hello, Paige. How are you today?" Missy was as perky and friendly as ever. Her long strawberry-blond hair was pulled into a ponytail. She was wearing workout leggings and a matching sports bra with no shirt. She didn't have an ounce of fat on her eighteen-year-old body. I had to admit, she pulled off the look.

"Good, Missy. How are you?" I asked her. I could never quite match her energy.

"Good. I've been meaning to ask you… you've been coming here for over a month. Aren't you ever gonna *actually* work out?" She wagged a finger at me.

I forced a laugh. I felt like I might pass out. Why was everyone saying that? A *month*? "Missy, this is Stephen. He'll be my shadow for a while."

"Pleasure to meet you," Stephen charmed her with a wink and stuck out a hand. "I'm Paige's boyfriend."

The hell you are, I thought, but opted for silence.

While I was in the shower, Dr. Burnett's words came back to me. *A person might find themselves somewhere and not have any recollection of how they got there. They seem to lose all awareness of who they are and where they are for long periods of time. It could even last weeks or months.* Today, not even a nice, hot shower and clean, fresh hair, could get me out of the funk that was starting to develop.

Next on the agenda, the gun range.

Stephen and I stepped inside.

"Mornin' Ms. Paige." Peter greeted me with that wide grin of his. His eyes were full of question as he looked at Stephen.

"Good morning, Peter. This is Stephen," I said over my shoulder before I grabbed Stephen a pair of eyemuffs.

"Nice to meet you," Peter said. He put a sign-in sheet in front of Stephen.

"I'm Paige's boyfriend," Stephen informed him.

"Well, that settles a bet we had goin' round here." Peter clapped his hands together triumphantly. "Me and Nate thought there was no way someone like Paige was single!" Peter laughed and shook his head.

I waited until Stephen was out in a lane and firing his gun before I doubled back.

"Forgot to sign in," I said to Peter as I laughed lightly, hearing how fake it sounded.

"It's no big deal, Ms. Paige. We know who you are. You come in here same time every day."

"Right," I casually thumbed through the sign-in sheet where he had put the full pages at the back. Peter was occupied with his phone. I counted about twenty pages with my name on them before he looked up. "Somethin' the matter?"

"Nope. It's fine," I lied. "I just lose track of my days. I was trying to remember exactly how long I've been coming here."

"Well," Peter stared off into space. "The last conceal and carry class was about a month ago. It was a few days before that... so, little over a month."

"Is that all?" I was going to be sick. "It seems like just yesterday." I took a deep breath and faked a kind smile. "I better get in there. Show him up."

Peter snorted. "As if. You're a terrible shot, Paige. You're gettin' better but you just can't quite hit your target."

"Thanks, Peter. Tell me something I don't know."

True to form, I hit just left of every target I shot for. After a half hour, I brought my target in and clucked my tongue as I looked at it. I could feel Stephen peeking around his lane.

"I don't want to hear it," I had to shout to be heard.

"Are you right eye dominant or left eye dominant?" He shouted back.

"Well, I'm right-handed so I'm going to say right eye dominant?"

"That doesn't necessarily determine it. Make a diamond with your hands."

I secured my gun on the tray in front of me. I made a diamond.

"Now, focus on a spot in front of you. Close one eye then the other. Which eye is closed when the spot is still in the middle of the diamond?"

"Right."

"Okay, you're left eye dominant. So, you can try to strengthen your right eye – read a book with your left eye closed – that sort of thing. Or shoot using your left eye and know that because you're right-handed, you'll always be a little off."

"Huh," I muttered. Seems like Peter could have taught me that one. But maybe he did and I didn't remember. "Thanks, Stephen. I'll remember that."

I fired a few more rounds, until my hands were sore, and I quit. We returned his eyemuffs and I waved good-bye to Peter.

"You need to stop telling people you're my boyfriend," I told Stephen when we got in the car. I was starting to feel downright grouchy.

"Would you rather I tell them I'm an armed guard?"

I sighed. The next stop was going to be tricky. I was going to my support group.

"Stephen, I'd rather you not go with me to the next stop."

"Paige, we've been over this…"

"Fine." I cut him off. "Dr. Burnett suggested I go to a support group before I left Arkansas."

"What kind of support group?"

"It's for people who had bad childhoods and developed unhealthy coping skills in life such as co-dependency."

"Oh." Stephen didn't say anything for a minute. "Can I come in? As your guest? I won't say anything. I just want to understand."

I thought about it for a moment. "I suppose so. But maybe you could sit…"

"Somewhere else?" he finished for me. "Sure. No problem."

I pulled into the parking lot. "We're early." I pulled out mom's journal and began to read.

October 5, 1996

Paige cries all the time. She really is the worst baby! I'm so tired. They say to sleep when the baby sleeps. Who is "they?" Don't they know my money is going to run out soon? I should've known better than to leave half of it under the floorboard. Whoever buys our house will get a nice surprise some day. I guess it'll be a payoff for buying a house where a murder took place. It's hidden pretty good. Jason always made sure of that. Most people put money in banks. Not that man! Paranoid as could be, that one. The point is, I'm going to have to go to work at some point and I can't get used to sleeping through the day, can I? I've read every baby book I can get my hands on and I can't get her to quiet down. Paige, what am I doing wrong? I'm not a good mother. I'm so sorry you're stuck with me.

Even that was a rotten entry. I slammed the book shut and Stephen eyed me quizzically but said nothing. I felt like he was studying me, like he was trying to learn a new language. *Good luck with that, Stephen, I'm trying to learn my new language, too.* I hopped out of the car and headed into group.

25

PAIGE

"Dr. Burnett, thank you for taking my call," I was in my car, in the dark garage because I needed privacy from Stephen. This was the only place where I could find it these days.

"Of course. I hope you are well?"

"I'm not so sure. I have some more questions about my mom... and maybe me."

"Sure. I have you scheduled for an hour."

"Well, it appears that I've lost time."

"Lost time?"

"Yes, I thought I'd been here three days, but I've been here over a month."

"Let me see..." Dr. Burnett was shuffling papers around on the other end. "Ah, yes, you left right after our last session. Which was about a month and five days ago."

"I don't remember being gone that long," I almost whispered it into the phone. I was sitting in my car, by myself, and yet, I couldn't seem to say those words aloud.

"Tell me more."

"I remember three days. The people in town say I've been

doing the same thing for the past month. They know me. They know things about me. As if... it's true."

"Why does this bother you?"

"Because I'm afraid. What if... I'm just like her? What if I have the same disorder she had?"

"Hmm, it is possible that the condition is genetically linked. But more likely, it's brought on by the trauma of losing your mom in such a violent way. Have you been sleeping a lot?"

"I don't think so. No more than usual."

"Why don't you keep a diary? Then you can track when you appear to be losing time?"

I thought about my mom's journal. Was that why *she* was keeping one?

"What else is happening?" asked Dr. Burnett.

"I guess that's it..." I trailed off.

"I'm curious, how are you processing all the guilt you feel from your childhood?"

"Guilt?" I had no recollection of this.

"Did you have a chance to read through your hypnosis session?"

"Yes, but I don't remember that!"

"In one memory you expressed, your mom was arguing with a man on the mountain. A fire started..."

"Yes, I remember that memory."

"You said you started the fire. You also said you were the reason that man died. You said you killed him."

I gasped. Where did I put those notes? *The glovebox,* I suddenly remembered. I had zero recollection of that. "I said that?" I didn't feel any guilt right now at all.

"Yes, maybe I could give you a homework assignment to read through those memories and re-read your words. Are you in a safe space where you could do that?"

"Safe space?" I asked. *Sure, if you consider hiding away in my car in a dark garage to have privacy a safe space.*

"I mean, mentally." Dr. Burnett clarified. "Are you in a good, mental head space to go through those notes?"

I opened the glove compartment and the notes came tumbling out.

"Yes, I think so," I said, though I wasn't actually sure.

"Great. There might be more we could talk about and I don't want to cut us short if you have anything else? Have you been able to process your grief over your mom's death yet?"

Yes, one night mom's ghost came to me and I felt how much I missed her, so I finally cried... while sitting in the rain...in a mud puddle.

"Yes, I finally cried about it."

"Great! Is there anything else you want to talk about?"

I said no and got off the phone. I grabbed my notes but paused on the date. I didn't remember having two sessions that week. I sighed and started reading.

Hypnosis Session: Deffer, Paige
May 13, 2019

(Dr. Burnett) Paige, can you tell me about the incident on Hilltop Bar?

It was late. I was supposed to be in bed. But I heard my mama get up to leave and I didn't want her to.

(Dr. Burnett) How old were you?

Umm... four or five years old.

(Dr. Burnett) What happened next?

Mama? I asked. *Where are you goin'?*

Paige? What are you doing out of bed, darling? Mama asked.

I don't want you to go, I whined at her.

She sighed and picked me up, jammies and all, and put me in the car. I dozed off for a while but woke up when the car stopped.

Now you stay here, Paige. You don't need to get out of the car. Just go back to sleep, mama said. She got out of the car.

I didn't listen. I followed her.

We were parked at the top of a hill and I could see for miles. The moon was bright in the sky and I could see the full trees on the hills.

(Dr. Burnett) What else, Paige? What else do you see?

Well, there's a small building off to the corner of the hill. I learned later that it was Hilltop Bar.

(Dr. Burnett) Did your mom go in there, Paige?

Yes.

(Dr. Burnett) Did you follow her in?

Yes.

(Dr. Burnett) Who was in the bar?

Just me, mama, and a man. I remember the wood was light brown and it was so little inside. I don't know if mama saw me come in with her. I stood behind her.

The man seemed scary to me. Then they started fighting.

(Dr. Burnett) Do you remember what they were saying?

No. I just remember angry voices. I'd never heard mama so angry before.

(Dr. Burnett) Did they hit each other?

No. But then something happened.

(Dr. Burnett) What happened?

I killed the man.

(Dr. Burnett) You killed him?

Yes. I could smell smoke. *Mama?* I tugged at mom's pant leg. I had to look up to see mama.

Not now, Paige. Mama's voice was tense and strained. I knew she wasn't angry at me. But I also knew better than to try again. The room was getting warm and smoky. Their voices were getting louder. I turned and ran outside. I ran hard and fast in the direction of the car. I could hear mama's voice, but I didn't stop.

(Dr. Burnett) Did you have anything to do with the fire?

I don't know. I just feel like it was my fault.

(Dr. Burnett) But you don't know for sure?

No.

(Dr. Burnett) So you were running?

Yes, I was running toward the car.

Paige? Mama sounded frantic.

I turned and looked over my shoulder. It was just in time to see mama push the man. He was flying through the air, over the cliff! Then mama turned and yelled my name. I hid by the car. I was afraid.

(Dr. Burnett) What were you afraid of? Your mama?

Yes, it looked like she pushed the man off the cliff! I got behind the car and squatted down. I peeked around the car but couldn't see much. I can still hear the scream of the man whose body flew through the air and was suddenly falling off a cliff. His voice sounded farther and farther away as he fell.

(Dr. Burnett) Where was your mama?

Paige? She called for me.

This time when I peeked out from my hands covering my eyes, I could see mama walking away from the shack with flames to her back. Large, angry, red and orange flames were coming out of the shack... I can still hear the sound the glass made as the windows broke.

(Dr. Burnett) I still don't understand why you think you killed the man. Did you push him before you ran to the car?

No.

(Dr. Burnett) Explain how you killed him?

I wasn't supposed to be there. I was supposed to be in bed, asleep. Because I woke up and got out of bed, the man died.

(Dr. Burnett) Paige, I'm remembering that you told me about the nightmares you had about a fire? Do you think they are connected to this experience?

I always had nightmares about fires. All the time when I was little. I dreamt there were fires in the house. I dreamt there were fires outside. I even dreamt there was a fire preventing me from getting to mama. I always woke up screaming, all the time.

(Dr. Burnett) What would your mom do?

If she was there, she would comfort me.

(Dr. Burnett) But she never explained why you had the dreams?

No.

26

PAIGE

"Hello?" Ashley Trieggar answered the phone, drawing out her syllables with a thick southern twang. I was standing in the living room on my cell phone pacing the room. I couldn't figure out why I felt so nervous.

"Hello, Ashley?"

"Yes, ma'am," Ashley answered cheerfully.

"This is Paige Deffer."

"Krysta's daughter! Ohmigosh, honey, how are you?" her voice was laced with sympathy.

"I'm okay, thank you."

"I'm just so... sad..." Ashley sniffed and sounded like she might start crying.

"I know," I paused, "is this an okay time?" It just now occurred to me to ask.

"Yes, absolutely, whatever you need."

"I was wondering if I could ask you some questions?"

"Yes, hang on."

I could hear her tell someone she was going to go outside.

"Okay, I'm here."

"Did you see my mom the day she…" my voice broke. Why was it so hard to say that word?

"I did, actually. I'm gonna tell you everything 'cause you deserve to know." She lowered her voice. "And I feel guilty. I didn't tell that cop anything. I just don't trust them!"

"I understand why. What happened?"

"Well, your mom, God rest her soul, got a call one day from a man named Ray. About a week or two before… you know. From that day on, she was different. She was always such a quiet and serious person, but after that call, she seemed…" she paused, probably searching for the right word, "lighter. She was laughing and happy. So, I asked her about it."

"What did she say?" I found myself gripping the phone tightly and hanging on to every word.

"Ray was someone from her past. He was going to clear her name, whatever *that* meant. It's all she would say. She might have said she'd be able to go home again… yes, I think she said that, too."

"Huh. Did they ever meet?"

"Sure did. The night she went missin.' He came in here. I was working. He was a really handsome guy. They talked for 'bout a half hour when Matt showed up."

"Matt?" I asked.

"Her boyfriend. Oh, I forget she kept you two separate." Ashley *tsked* her tongue disapprovingly.

"What happened next?" I was standing up and started pacing again.

"Well, Matt was mad. Furious, even. Caused a big scene. Called your mom names. I guess he was jealous. Said this disappearing act she does was all a game. Said he saw right through her."

I felt my stomach tighten. "Was he always like that? Was he abusive?"

"Heavens, no! I'd never seen him like that before. He was

always the nicest guy. He's lived around here over twenty years, and nobody ever had a bad thing to say about him."

"Until that night?"

"Yeah, he really snapped. Krysta tried to explain. Then she apologized to Ray and left with Matt. That was the last time I saw her." Ashley started sniffling.

"Maybe the last time anyone saw her," I mused aloud. "What did Ray do?"

"He just sat there. Ordered another beer, drank it, paid the bill, and left. I saw him at the funeral. He sat in the very back. But he left before I could talk to him. Really mysterious guy, that one."

"Matt was at the funeral too. I remember. He seemed nice. Maybe mom just really pushed him over the edge that night?" I recognized the flimsy excuses I was attempting to make, but it sounded like Matt might have been the last one to see her alive.

"I don't know. I just wish…" her voice trailed off. "I wish I'd done something. Anything. You know, told her not to leave with Matt. Stood up to Matt or told him to calm down before they left."

"Ashley, none of that is your fault. Mom was a grown woman. She made her own choices. Right or wrong. I hope you find peace in that." I found myself discovering the truth as the words came out of my mouth. I'd had the same moments of guilt and regret. If only I had gotten closer to her. If only I had made her include me in that other part of her life, maybe I could have saved her. If only I had cared enough to ask questions about her life, she wouldn't have felt the need to sneak around in this alternate existence. *There's too many if onlies*, I thought.

"Thank you, Paige. I needed to hear that. You're a lot like her, you know. She was very wise."

I thanked her back and hung up the phone. Was she? Was mom really wise? I guess I'd never know.

I didn't have to relay the conversation to Stephen. He'd been listening on some contraption I'd never heard of. When I hung up, he got on his phone. He walked into another room, but I could still hear him on the phone with another officer.

"We have first-hand testimony that puts Matt Cline in the bar and leaving with Krysta Deffer the night of her murder. He lied about his alibi. We need to bring him in for questioning on suspicion of murder," he paused for a minute, listening to the other end. "Mmm-hmm, yes. Thanks," he said and hung up the phone.

"What if Ashley doesn't want to testify?" I wondered, feeling quite sure she would not want to.

"We'll subpoena her. She'll have no choice."

"In the meantime?" I asked.

"We'll get a warrant to search Matt's home and car. There will be evidence, there's always evidence. We just have to find it. Then we can put him away."

I should have felt relieved, but I didn't. I couldn't put my finger on it, but something just felt off. What were we missing?

27

PAIGE

I could hear Stephen snoring lightly in the next room. I had put up a strict "no more physical contact" rule in place and at the moment, he was respecting my wishes.

I grabbed my flashlight and crept into my parents' old room. I quietly closed the door and shined my flashlight into the dark room. I waited until my eyes adjusted to the light as it broke into the dark. I started in the bathroom. I was disappointed. I really couldn't see in between the wooden slats on the floor. I don't know why I thought I'd be able to. I kept crawling around with the flashlight in one hand. I had gone through the entire room but could not see anything that might lead to an opening in the floorboards. I was wearing a tank top and a pair of cotton shorts with an elastic band so my knees were feeling raw.

Next, I tried the closet. No secret trap doors there. I sat on the floor of the closet slightly discouraged. I laid down on the floor and shined my flashlight at the ceiling. Nothing there. I flipped the flashlight around and imagined it was a strobe light. *Really, Paige, you must get sleep. You might be going a little crazy right now*. Well, there were plenty of other places to look.

"Where's the money he left, mom?" I whispered to no one

in particular. I stopped flipping the light and turned on my side. I stared at the wall. The wall! Was I looking in the wrong place? I got on my knees and slowly started spanning the wall. What was I even looking for? A discolored piece of the wall? It was always so obvious in the movies. This was very anti-climactic, and I was starting to feel sleepy.

When I felt like I had explored every square inch of the wall in the closet, I turned to the main bedroom. That was a little too overwhelming. I went back to the bathroom. I shined the light in the mirror. The light went out suddenly, but not before I made out a slight outline of a person standing behind me. I screeched and dropped the flashlight. I was standing in the pitch darkness and I could feel a presence behind me. I froze. For a half a minute, I could not breathe.

"Stephen?" I whispered. I stood still, frozen in the darkness.

Danger… The slightest whisp of the word found my ears.

"Mom?" I whispered.

Darkness was my reply.

I dropped to the floor and felt for the flashlight. Where had it gone? I felt and moved, felt and moved. When I found it, it had rolled down into… something. There seemed to be a small dip in the floor with a steel mesh grate of sorts behind the toilet. I grabbed the flashlight and picked it back up. The light turned on and I could see a grate that seemed to be jammed into the wall and floorboard. The glare from the flashlight shining on the metal grate hit my eyes. I turned off the flashlight and let my eyes adjust to the dark.

There was definitely something down there. I just couldn't quite make it out. I tried to jam my fingers into the grate without luck. I'd have to come back in the morning. I got to my feet and turned the flashlight on. I looked up. A human form was standing in the bathroom doorway.

I screamed and dropped the light again.

"What are you doing?" Stephen asked.

"I..." I tried to think of an answer but couldn't. "I wasn't feeling well. I thought I might be sick. I'm okay now. No need for alarm. Sorry to wake you." I tried to walk past him but he gently grabbed my arm. We stood in the dark in the doorway. My eyes had adjusted back to the dark.

"Are you sick?" Worry lined Stephen's tone.

I shook my head. I put my hands out to keep him where he was. Instead, they found his broad, muscular chest.

His body filled in the distance between us. "I want to kiss you," his voice was low.

"I... want..."

His mouth was on mine before I could stop him, and I found myself kissing him back.

My back was against the doorframe. My eyes opened just in time to see it. The shadow of a tall man crossed outside the bathroom window where the moon was shining in, illuminating the curtain and casting a square shape on the bathroom floor. I gasped at the same time Stephen's phone started vibrating in the pocket of his sleep pants.

"Get down!" he hissed and I immediately ducked. He pulled his gun.

I didn't have time to think about why he had a phone and a gun in his pajama pants but then I realized he was wearing jean shorts. Was he always prepared?

The motion sensor light was on now. Clearly something, or someone, had set it off.

"I saw a shadow." I whispered and pointed to the window.

"Stay here!" Stephen moved to the window and flattened himself to the wall. He discreetly moved the curtain. He now had both hands on the gun which was pointed up at the ceiling. He took a knee when he passed by me. "Do not move. Stay here. I'm going to check the perimeter."

"But, I..."

"Don't move. I'll be back."

I watched him leave, feeling helpless. My mind moved on quickly, but I made myself stay still. My purse was in the living room with my gun in it. My cell phone was on my air mattress in the same room. A lot of good either did me right now! I rolled my eyes in disgust and tried to stay still. The silence was deafening. Then I heard footsteps. Were they Stephen's or an intruder?

"Hey!" Stephen's voice was loud. "Stop!"

I could hear fast feet running outside now that seemed to retreat and get quieter as they moved farther and faster. A single gunshot sounded. I froze. Time slowed down. I screamed in horror, but no sound came out. I tried to move, to crawl to the living room. To get my gun, or my phone, or both. Who shot whom? What if I was next?

I willed myself to move. Finally, my right hand and left knee moved. Then left hand and right knee. It was painfully slow, but I crawled into the living room on my raw knees and pulled my gun from my purse. I was reaching for my cell phone when the front door flew open. I pointed my gun. Stephen walked through the door and quickly locked it.

"What happened?" I asked.

Stephen held up a finger and dropped to the floor beside me.

"Are you hurt?" I tried again.

He shook his head negative and pulled out his phone. "I shot my gun in the air as a warning. Whoever was here was fast and knew the woods. Ran off before I could see him. I could sure hear him, though." Stephen played the camera backward until he saw what he was looking for. The outline of a man lurked on the corner of the house, right outside the room where I had been looking for the money! The man had managed to keep his face concealed. The camera only showed the outline of his body.

I gasped as my mind and brain connected similarities. "It's

the guy from the coffee shop!" I whispered. "Did he follow me home?"

"Guy from the coffee shop? Paige, what are you not telling me? You need to fill in the gaps. Anything that seems insignificant is not. Even down to what you were looking for as you crawled around on the floor."

So, he didn't believe me. "I promise I'll tell you in the morning."

"The morning might be too late." Stephen crossed his hands over his chest.

"Fine. I had coffee a few days ago," I paused, confused. It might have been weeks, I supposed. "There was someone there. Watching me. When I tried to confront him…"

"You tried to confront him?" Stephen interrupted sounding incredulous.

"Yes, well, he got up and walked out of the coffee shop quickly. I followed him."

"You followed him? Why would you – "

"Okay, you have to stop interrupting. When I followed him, he sped up and eventually started running. I never saw him again… until now. That's the man."

"Hmm," Stephen thought for a minute. He pulled out his phone. It was a picture of the man from the funeral. "Could it have been him?"

"Yes, I think it could've been."

"That's Ray Lennon. The guy that sat at the back of the funeral. The one Ashley referenced. Your mom knew him. Paige, it's not safe for us to stay here. He could come back."

Now I crossed my arms over my chest. "I'm not leaving. In fact, this house is mine. You can't make me leave."

"If you won't respect an authority of the law, I'll have to take you in and arrest you."

"Trust me, Stephen. I know what I'm doing. This place holds the answers. I just need more time. I think I found something that could explain everything. But right now, I need to sleep." *Did he really have the authority to arrest me here?* I wondered. I didn't think so.

"Sleep? How could you sleep at a time like this?"

I shrugged. "I don't know. I just feel like I could sleep."

"Fine, I'll stay up and keep watch."

"You should! You've been asleep for hours! It's my turn!" Too bad it was dark. I was smirking at his sullen silence. I had won this round. I crawled onto my air mattress and instantly fell asleep.

28

RAY

Ray ran for what might have been miles. Adrenaline propelled him forward. He was quite in shape for his age, thanks to his regimen. Everything he did revolved around self-defense and fighting. This fact, and the daily running, allowed him to easily get away from someone who was probably half his age. Regardless, sprinting through the woods at top speed while random branches hit his face was not what he would call fun.

When he stopped, he felt the energy leave his body with a whoosh. He doubled over and began gasping for air. Even the best runner couldn't sprint that long. Several things about tonight had caught him off guard. If he was honest, that was an understatement. When had they installed the motion-sensor lights?

Who was in that house, exactly, he wondered. The girl, he knew, but only through Margaret, his brief encounter with her at the funeral, and seeing her across the coffee shop. He thought the man had been with her at the funeral, but he couldn't be certain. The girl he could handle. The man, well, the man was at least half his age, in better condition, and he knew his way around firearms.

Ray was still confused how they had caught him prowling around in the middle of the night. It wasn't the first time Ray had been to the house, but it was the first time since they had taken up residence. He'd seen the equipment go in from afar, but he assumed it was all alarms to keep intruders out. Why hadn't he expected motion-sensing lights? The two of them in that house got in the way of his plans. How was he going to do another sweep of the house to find that money with them there?

Unless he killed the two of them. Ironically, in the exact same house her father had died. He chuckled to himself. Did it really matter to Margaret the order of events? He could kill them and then tear the floorboards apart if necessary to find that money she seemed so sure was there. Or maybe he could forget the deal altogether? Once the daughter, Paige, was dead, he could rest in peace next to his darling wife. Her soul would finally be vindicated, and he could stand to face her in eternity.

He walked the rest of the way back to his property. It took an hour. But he knew this path well. Truth be told, he was feeling a little nostalgic. This reminded him of nights when he would walk home from the Mynart's instead of driving to clear his head when he'd been drinking with them. He had been friends with the Mynart's long before he went into business with Jason. Long before Allison got sick. And long before they stole his money.

Tonight, he decided this path was safer than being spotted or heard in a car. Now that he knew what he was dealing with, he could formulate a new plan. The next time he attempted to get into that house, he would. He had no doubt about that.

29

PAIGE

I awoke the next morning to a loud, obnoxious banging on the front door. I was so tired from the craziness of the night before that I didn't get up immediately. Maybe whoever it was would go away if I ignored him or her.

No such luck. The banging continued. I got up, steadied myself on my feet, and put some pants on. I put my gun holster on my jeans and made sure my untucked shirt covered it. I opened the door. Jud Blackwell stood on the other side. I kept the door cracked.

"Everything alright, ma'am? I thought I heard gunshot last night. Sometimes I hear you practice shootin' during the day but a gunshot at night around here is awful suspicious."

I stared at Jud, not comprehending. He stared back. His eyes were a dull gray and his large frame filled the doorway. His big belly doubled over his jeans and his shirt was tucked into his belt. Jud, as I had experienced, was probably the biggest gossip of this neighborhood. Is that what you call a country area?

"Yes, sorry to wake you. A deer tripped the motion sensor and woke us up."

"Us?"

I sighed. I really was the worst liar. I had meant to close the topic. "My boyfriend, Stephen, is in from the city, visiting. He fired a shot in the air to scare the deer off so he wouldn't keep triggering the motion sensor."

"Oh." Jud nodded, seeming to process, but continued to stand there. "As long as you're okay."

I flashed him a winning smile. "We're great, Jud, thank you for checking on us. Mighty neighborly of you." I tried to shut the door.

"Paige?" Jud seemed to be contemplating saying something else but changed his mind. "There's a party at Pickleman Park this Saturday. Did you get the invite?"

"No, I didn't know." I was blank again. Was he hoping I'd invite him in?

"Well, consider yourself invited. Saturday at six, bring a covered dish or bag of chips or somethin.' You can meet some folks from around here."

"Saturday at six at Pickleman Park. Got it. Thanks, Jud." This time I shut the door. Stephen was going to barrage me with questions this morning. I really wasn't looking forward to that. Come to think of it, none of this was fun. When had my life become so bleak and stressful? I almost laughed out loud when I discovered the answer. It had *always* been bleak and stressful. Truthfully, I didn't know what fun was.

"Who was that?" Stephen asked.

I screamed and jumped a little. Stephen had come into the room with ruffled hair that stuck up a little.

"Stephen! I could've used a little help there!" I wasn't sure why I was so jumpy, but it annoyed me just the same.

He stared at me for a heartbeat. "You called me your boyfriend."

"There was no other logical explanation!"

"Right. Get dressed and gather your things. We've got Matt Cline in custody. I need to go question him."

"While I... what?"

"While you watch. There's a two-way glass and you can see the whole thing. If Matt Cline killed your mother, you have a right to know. It's better this way."

"Better than... what?"

"Better than having to read his words in a police report."

"And if I refuse?" I crossed my arms.

"Don't be difficult, Paige." Stephen looked tired.

I hadn't considered the stress he must be feeling.

"If we're wrong about him, I'd be leaving you here alone and exposed. It's a risk I'm not willing to take."

"I was fine before you got here. I'm fine now."

"Call it cooperating with an investigation then. I caught some man prowling on this property last night. Do you know why?"

"I think I might have a guess."

Stephen stared at me impatiently.

"Fine, I think I found something important. Well, something he might have been looking for. Just give me a minute." I went to the bathroom and found the grate I saw last night. It was stuck tight. I hit it first with my fist but yelped in pain. It didn't budge. Next, I tried to use my fingernails to jiggle it free. Still nothing happened.

"Here." I heard Stephen's voice behind me. He handed me a pocketknife with a corkscrew tool which I hooked to the grate and pulled. The grate budged! I did it two more times and it came free.

"Got it!" I was beyond proud of myself. I reached into the small hole carefully. I retrieved an aged green pouch. It was about four inches tall and bulged at the zipper. Still sitting on the bathroom floor, I opened the zipper. A stack of bills lay neatly inside. From what I could tell, they were all hundreds.

"Paige!" Stephen's shocked voice floated to me. "Where did that come from?" He sounded reverent and a little in awe.

"My dad. He didn't believe in putting money in banks. He hid it here in the house. I wasn't sure where until I read it in mom's journal."

"Paige, I'm not sure I can let you keep that."

"I'm sorry, what?" My eyes narrowed and I glared at him with all the anger I felt trapped in my veins. "This is my money. It's all I have left of my parents. It's not your business, Stephen. Move on!" I heard the icy tone in my words as I shot venom at him. I'd never heard my voice sound that way.

"Actually, that's not entirely true," said a foreign voice from behind him.

Stephen whipped around.

Startled, my eyes swung behind him.

Margaret Terry stood there perfectly dressed in a flowery blouse and matching pink, pleated skinny pants. She wore slip-on loafers. Her makeup was perfectly in place. She surveyed the whole scene.

"Hello, granddaughter. I trust you are well."

"Hi." I climbed awkwardly to my feet, not letting go of the money even for one second. I zipped the pouch closed.

"That money needs to stay in the family," Margaret commanded.

"It is. My family. Family of one." I put the money behind my back and glared at Margaret the same way I glared at Stephen. What had come over me? Why did I feel so strongly that I deserved this money?

"Nothing a good lawyer won't fix. That money is mine. It doesn't belong to you. You didn't even come into the picture until after she left. Your slut of a mother…"

I had pushed past Stephen and was in front of the woman before she uttered another word. I slapped her as hard as I could across the face.

"You will not speak about my mother that way. You're leaving. Get out of my house."

Margaret was holding her cheek, frozen in the position where her head had whipped to the side. Her brown hair was hanging in her face. She straightened slowly. All semblance of civility faded away. Her eyes were dark, blackened in anger.

"That's just it, you little *bitch*. This isn't your house, is it? You're a homeless vagabond who squatted in this house after I told you about it."

"Wrong again. I signed the papers yesterday. I own this home, the property, and everything in it. And I'm asking you to leave my property and never come back."

Stephen moved forward and stood beside me as a united front. If he was surprised to hear the news of my recent purchase, he didn't act like it. Instead, he grabbed Margaret's elbow. She yanked her arm away.

"Margaret," Stephen's voice was stern. "I have handcuffs. I could cuff you and take you out or you can go out on your own. You choose."

Margaret lifted her chin and stomped out in a huff. Before she exited, she turned to me with hate in her eyes. Her voice was quiet and spiteful. "You'll regret this. I will get my way. There's nothing you, or your boyfriend here, can do to stop me."

"That's enough, Margaret. You need to leave." Stephen followed her to her car and watched her drive away.

I knew I would see her again.

Stephen was at my side minutes later. He did not look happy. He grabbed a pair of Converse tennis shoes and put them on. Next, he threw on a short-sleeved button-down shirt over his t-shirt and jeans.

"Get your stuff and get in the car. I'll follow you back to Arkansas and I expect you to go peacefully without any tricks or games. You're making a lot of enemies and you're going to get yourself killed." He spoke with short, clipped syllables, as if talking to a five-year-old.

I knew better than to argue. I slipped my feet into Sperry's. I didn't feel the need to dress up anymore. I was comfortable at the moment and that's all that mattered. I stuffed what I needed into my backpack and put it in my car. I was thankful that I had an hour or so to get my thoughts in order. I immediately shoved the money in my glove compartment and locked it. As long as I had the key, the money was mine. I tried to come up with every possible getaway idea I could on the way, but my brain was tired. There was so much to think about. It was exhausting trying to figure it all out. Or was it just exhausting because we were up late last night? Regardless, I was finding it difficult to focus on driving.

We arrived at the police station in record time. I must have zoned out a bit. Before I knew it, I was looking through one-sided glass. These rooms on TV always looked so cold and sterile. This one had decent chairs. The walls were a nice calm shade of gray. The floors were cherry wood. I watched Stephen enter the room with another detective. Matt Cline sat in handcuffs. Stephen threw a manilla folder down on the table and it made a loud smack. It was a nice touch. Even I jumped a little.

"I'm Detective Wilton," Stephen began. "And this is my partner, Detective Brandt."

"Nice to meet you both." Matt Cline nodded but looked sad. His face sagged a little and he seemed to have aged some, at least from what I remember of him.

"You've been read your rights?" Stephen asked.

Matt nodded solemnly and turned his gaze to the other detective.

"Detective Brandt will take it from here." Stephen crossed his arms and leaned against the wall.

"I need to ask you some questions regarding the murder of

Krysta Deffer, whose actual last name is Mynart. Did you know she wasn't who she said she was?" Brandt began.

Matt cleared his throat. His face registered surprise. "No. I knew she'd been married before. Was that her maiden name or something?"

"No, it was an alias." Brandt's voice was firm. He didn't appear to be buying Matt's nice guy act.

Good! I thought. Anyone who would handle my mom roughly wasn't a nice guy at all.

"An alias?" Again, Matt seemed surprised. "I mean, Krysta was private and all, I just let her be private. I didn't ask her a lot of questions and she didn't talk a lot. Guess that's why we got along so well." He chuckled a little. "I didn't know what to do with those chatty women."

"Mr. Cline, where were you the night of Krysta's murder?" Brandt's question was abrupt. He made it clear he was not here to chit chat.

"Oh. I was at home. There was a *Matlock-a-thon* on TV and I was there, binge watching the show."

"And you didn't leave your home at all?"

Matt was silent for a moment before a small smile formed. "Oh. Well, you must already know the answer to that if you're askin' me again."

"Answer the question, Mr. Cline." Brandt's voice took on a hard tone.

"Okay, fine. I did go out before the show started." Matt admitted.

"Where did you go?"

"Okay, look, I'm going to be honest with you. It wasn't my finest hour and I'm aware that this is going to make me look bad, but I would rather be honest. I went to go find Krysta."

"Why did you go to find her?" Brandt asked.

"Because I got sick of waiting around for her. I knew what

time she was supposed to be off work. We had plans." Matt's voice was getting a little wound up.

"I see. Did you know where she was?"

"Yes."

"How?"

"She'd left her phone at my place and I went through it." Matt looked sheepish and his cheeks turned a light shade of pink.

I leaned forward. This was getting interesting.

"Did you go through her phone often?" Brandt asked Matt.

"No," Matt said, "never. But she'd started acting weird and she wouldn't explain why. I got the feeling..." Matt sighed. "I thought..."

"Go on," Brandt prodded.

"I thought she was cheating on me."

"Did the phone confirm that?

Matt's face turned red. "Maybe. I don't know. I saw these texts from a guy. His name was Ray. Ray Lennon. They were planning to meet. They knew each other. I filled in the blanks. An old high school sweetheart, maybe? I didn't know. The messages talked about the good times they had drinking together at Krysta's house. Seems like he wanted more good times with her. They planned to meet, and I planned to confront them," Matt repeated.

Ray Lennon, I let my mind wander a minute. *That name keeps coming up lately,* I thought. He was at the funeral, he was the guy at the coffee shop, and he was the guy Stephen chased from the backyard. *I wonder if he knows about the money hidden at the house?*

"Confront?" Brandt's fingers made air quotes.

My heart beat fast and I leaned forward to hear the answer. The detective's voice sounded extremely firm.

"Like I said, it wasn't my finest moment." Matt admitted weakly.

"An eyewitness says you raised your voice, called Krysta names, and yanked her out of the bar," Brandt told him.

"I know," Matt put up his palms. "I know how it looks."

"Is that why you lied about your alibi?" Brandt asked.

Matt nodded and his face was flushed.

Stephen stepped forward and put the piece of paper he had in his hand in front of Brandt.

"In your original statement, you said you stayed in for the night. You were waiting for Krysta to get off work and come home. You said she would come over for a few hours after work, but you never knew exactly what time she'd get there…" Brandt was reading off a report.

"Yes," Matt cleared his throat again. "Maybe I do need a lawyer."

"That's up to you, Mr. Cline. What happened after you yanked her out of the bar?" Brandt asked.

"I put her in the car and drove off."

"What do you mean, put her in the car? Did she not go willingly?" Brandt leaned forward challenging him.

Matt shrugged. "It was for her own good. Krysta does this thing sometimes where she blacks out. Like she's not really there. I don't want her to wander off and get hurt, so I guide her and she just sort of goes along."

"I see." Brandt's voice didn't sound like he believed him. "And did she go along with you that night?"

Matt shook his head in the negative. "She was mad as a hornet. She got in the car quietly but the minute we drove off, she started kickin', screechin' and cussin' me. She told me to let her out of the car and I did."

"Where did you drive to?" Brandt asked.

"We made it about to I-40."

"You dropped her off on the side of the road?" Brandt's voice was incredulous.

"Yep. As bad as that sounds, it's what I did."

"Then you just drove off?" asked Brandt. Skepticism laced his tone.

"Yes. No. I rolled down the window and tossed her cell-phone to her. I knew she wouldn't be stranded for long. Probably called that new boyfriend of hers…" Matt shook his head.

"Then what?"

Matt's neck was deep red and splotchy. "Nothing. I drove home. I turned on the *Matlock-a-thon* and fell asleep. She was alive when I left her."

"But that's the *exact* location she was found murdered. I think you missed a few important details, Mr. Cline." Brandt's voice was deadly calm but eerily quiet at the same time.

"Nope." Matt folded his arms. "That's what happened."

"Well, you lied the first time you gave an alibi. Why should I believe you now?"

Matt threw his head backwards and stared at the ceiling. "You find her phone?"

Brandt and Stephen stared at him. It was obvious by the looks on their faces they had not.

"Search my place. Search my car. Search my property. You won't find it. In fact, don't those things have GPS trackers on them so you can find them?"

"Yes, yes they do. Unless it has a dead battery… You better hope we don't find anything!" Stephen said as he left the room in a hurry. Brandt followed him out. I could hear them talking around the corner.

"We need to track that phone. Let's get a team back out to that area. We can have patrol help us comb the area, woods and all. We have to find that phone. The phone could show us who she talked to last and if she called anyone for a ride. Where's that warrant to search Cline's property?" I heard Stephen say.

"I'll go check on it now," replied Brandt.

Stephen popped around the corner and gave me a quick thumbs up. He seemed excited but I wasn't as optimistic. If the phone was there, wouldn't they have already found it? I mean, the phone case was silver which means the sun would've been reflecting off the case.

"The case on it is silver," I called after him.

He whirled around and closed the gap between us quickly. He kissed me suddenly and with excitement. Then he disappeared again.

30

PAIGE

I sat staring at Matt through the double-paned glass, waiting until the officers filed out of the building. In his excitement, Stephen had left me here. I casually let myself into the interrogation room. I found myself in front of Matt Cline.

He looked up at me with surprise in his eyes. I sat on the other side of him and stared. He didn't look like a person my mom would've chosen to date. Mom was thin and pretty. When she smiled, though it wasn't often, it was nice. Her eyes would sparkle and she had slight wrinkles around the corners of her eyes from a lifetime long ago of smiling.

"Were you really mom's boyfriend?" I asked, not trying to conceal the suspicion in my tone.

He nodded sadly.

"Why didn't she ever tell me about you?" I asked directly.

"She wanted to keep us separate," he answered with a shrug. "That's what she said, anyway."

"Don't you think that's strange?" I asked.

"It's what Krysta said she wanted. I tried to give her everything she wanted."

"Everything?" I asked.

"Yes. She was so vulnerable at times. I would've done anything to protect her," he answered.

"Except the night she died," I stated.

"I was angry. Can you imagine living your whole life to make another person happy and then she cheats on you?"

"How did that make you feel?" I asked him.

"I was so angry. It takes a lot to make me angry but that made me hot. Instantly."

"Hot enough to kill her?" I pushed.

He shook his head emphatically. "I didn't kill her. I shouldn't have left her on the side of the road that night. But I didn't kill her. I've run that night through my head a million times. Wishing for a different outcome. The one time I didn't protect her and she's dead now because of it."

"I'm still having a hard time wrapping my mind around her not telling me about you." I crossed my arms over my chest.

Matt slumped down a little more. "I didn't think much about it until I saw you at the funeral. I realized I must not have meant that much to her." His eyes clouded with tears.

I actually felt empathy.

"Imagine if you lived your whole life to make someone happy, safe, and protected, and you realized after she's gone that you meant nothing to her."

His words squeezed my heart. I knew exactly how he felt. I couldn't help myself. I reached across the table and patted his hand.

"I know," I said. "Mom had a way of making you feel like that."

31

PAIGE

I didn't take time to consider if Stephen wanted me to stay put at the police station or not. I was done talking to Matt Cline. It didn't appear that he had killed mom. I simply took my car keys and left the building. I had a few loose ends to tie up, so I got in my car and started driving. I found myself back at my old apartment I had shared with my mother.

My key still worked. I don't know why I thought it might not. I had left in such a hurry, I was afraid the landlord had burned my stuff or sold it to pay off the rent I must owe. Instead, I found all of our stuff bagged up into trash bags in the middle of the living room floor. I stared at the trash bags, remembering the moment when mom and I fled in the night, remembering the time when I fled and went out the window not too long ago to get out of town as fast as possible. And now, I was leaving again. This time by my own choice.

I glanced around the apartment. The couches were ratty. They were the same ones we had bought when we first landed here. That was almost twenty years ago. I didn't want them. I could use a bed or two, however. Or at the very least, the frames. Slowly a plan began to form. I took out my phone and called a moving company. They had an opening to come load up tomorrow. I ended the call and noticed a handwritten note on the countertop.

Sorry about your mom, kiddo. Don't worry about the rent. I'll try to hold off getting rid of your stuff until this place is rented. I'm here if you need anything. I'll work with you best I can. - Tom

Tears seeped into my eyes. How kind and unexpected.

I walked around the place, taking an inventory of what would go back to Missouri with me. When I walked into my room, I stopped short. The carpet where I had hidden all the incriminating evidence of my mom's actions was still pulled out of the space where I left it. I'd forgotten I'd given that to Stephen. I hadn't been thinking about the three people I felt sure she had killed. It was easier not to.

Instead, I started thinking about the hypnosis notes I had read. In every reference of these murders, I had ended the story by taking full blame. Not that I had committed the murders exactly, but I had said they were my fault. I sat down on the bed, then lay down, staring at the ceiling. Why did I think they were my fault?

At the Hilltop Bar, I said I might have kicked over a lantern. But I knew I wasn't anywhere near the man who fell over the ledge. I didn't even know my mom worked at a bar when she killed the waitress she worked with. I certainly had no knowledge of the hiker on the trail who disappeared. But Stephen's words came back to me. I was an accomplice to the murders by covering her tracks and by not alerting authorities as it was happening. I had been so afraid to be alone in this world, I had done things that enabled mom to continue her outrageous and terrible actions. Maybe for that reason, I was to blame.

I pulled out mom's journal from my purse and laid down on the bed. I thumbed it open.

December 12, 1998

I saw a man at the grocery store who stared at me a little too long. It was unnerving. With everything in me, I resisted the urge to take Paige and run out of the store. Even here. Even in Canada, I'm terrified someone will recognize me. They probably have me on one of those "America's Most Wanted" shows. It really is just a matter of time, I think. What will become of Paige if they take me in? Will they put her in the foster system? Is the foster system here as bad as it is in America? Or will they find her a nice, non-criminal family to live with? I shudder at the thought. When I first found out I was pregnant, I have to admit, I was horrified. I never wanted to be a single mom. But here I am. And now, I'm horrified at the thought of losing her! Did that man know me? When I was leaving the store, he came up to me and said, "Excuse me, miss…" I whirled my head around and put my hand protectively around Paige. He handed me a pacifier I had dropped on the floor. In all my haste to get away from him, I didn't even notice he was looking at me because he was trying to hand me back a pacifier. I only have two more years left to stay in Canada. Then I'll have to make some choices. Will I ever be able to go home again?

I shut the journal and closed my eyes thinking about the word *home*. I didn't have a home. I wondered if I ever would.

I woke up abruptly to the sound of loud pounding on my door.

I blinked, disoriented, and got up from my bed. It was Stephen. I opened the door, took one look at him, and felt something I'd never felt for him before: compassion. My heart melted over the tired discouragement I saw in his eyes.

"Stephen!" I hugged him, pulling him into the room and closing the door behind him. "You didn't find the cell phone?"

Stephen shook his head. "It's been a long day. We searched

everything. His land, his house, his car... we even searched the location where..." Stephen's voice trailed off.

"Where they found my mom."

Again, Stephen nodded. There were bags under his eyes, and I wondered when the last time was he slept well. His blond hair was a little on the long side right now. Was he taking care of himself?

Spontaneously, I took his hand and led him to my bedroom. "Why don't you sit here and relax?" I went and found another blanket in the bundled-up bags. When I came back, Stephen was passed out on the bed. I quietly took his shoes off and curled up next to him. I, too, was asleep in minutes.

I was dreaming. It was a clear, overcast afternoon turning into evening. Something was wrong. My soul was heavy, and I felt as if I was driving to a place that would drop off into a huge cliff, but I drove forward anyway. Sure enough, when I got there, I barely stopped my car in time before I found myself at the edge of a cliff. My mom stood there, weak and frail, right on the edge. I heard her voice. *Paige, help me...* but it was too late. By the time I got out of the car, she was falling over the edge. I watched her until I could no longer watch.

"Paige, Paige, are you okay?" Stephen was shaking my arm.

I gasped and woke suddenly. I stared at him as tears streamed down my face. "She's gone, Stephen," I cried. "She's really gone."

Stephen wrapped me in his arms and pulled me to his chest. "I know, hon. I'm sorry."

Gently, he kissed my wet cheeks. He kissed my eyes and then he kissed my mouth. Slowly, carefully at first. Then with more urgency and desire. I responded the same way. I wanted this man in the strongest, most irrational way. Before I could analyze, my clothes were on the ground and I was taking his off as quickly as I possibly could. His naked body warmed mine and melded perfectly into me. I no longer felt shy. My hands were on his body, trailing from his chest down until I found what I wanted. With one quick movement, I straddled him. Surprise registered in his eyes.

"Paige...?"

"Shh," I put my hand on his mouth and then kissed it as I sat down on him and began moving my hips. Gently at first, and then harder and harder. Stephen moaned and I gasped in pleasure. Seized by excruciating, nerve-tingling orgasm, I screamed out loud in release as he did the same. And when we were done, I collapsed on top of him.

Stephen smoothed my hair and whispered in my ear, "Paige, I love you."

I paused for less than a heartbeat and said the only thing I could. "I know."

32

PAIGE

The morning found us on opposing sides of the issue of my move back to Missouri. It was official. The movers were coming to haul this stuff off, and after that, I wasn't coming back to Arkansas.

I had found an old favorite sundress that was black with yellow sunflowers on it. It was tight across my chest but fell loosely to my knees. I slipped on a pair of sandals, sighing over my unpolished toenails.

"There's way too much going on, Paige. If we don't get any more evidence against Matt Cline, we'll have no choice but to release him. And there's still the matter of your grandmother." Stephen had showered and put on a fresh pair of jeans and a black v-neck t-shirt.

"Margaret Terry," I interrupted, not bothering to tell Stephen that mom didn't want her to have anything to do with me *ever*.

"Yes, Margaret, and then there's Ray. We need to figure out why he was prowling on your property."

"I have a theory. The money. Margaret knew there was money in that house. Matt Cline said Ray Lennon knew my mother. He must have known about the money too. But I got the money, they didn't, and it's all over." I folded my arms across my chest and resisted the urge to stomp my foot.

"Perhaps, but you don't know that for sure."

"Neither do you."

We glared at each other.

"Paige," Stephen seemed to be considering something. "Do you want to get out of here? Just you and me? Just take a day off this case and be us again, like old times?"

I felt my anger and frustration melt away. I nodded but didn't trust myself to speak. I didn't want to let this go so easily.

But just like that, we were at a breakfast diner. The same one he took me to on our first date. He couldn't wait for lunch or dinner to see me, he had said. He couldn't stop thinking about me and wanted to see me the minute he woke up. I remember it like it was yesterday.

I smiled at him sweetly. He really did love me. I knew that. I felt that. I just couldn't seem to match his feeling. For that, I felt deeply ashamed.

Almost as if sensing the direction of my thoughts, Stephen grabbed my hands. We ordered coffees and the server said she would be back in a minute.

"Paige, it's time to talk. About us." Stephen looked deep into my eyes. "You've been through so much lately, I kept waiting for the *right* time, but it occurred to me that there might never be a *right* time." He cleared his throat. Was he nervous?

"Okay," I said dumbly. I wished I had more to say. Something smart and wise. I racked my brain for words.

"Before your mother was killed, I was going to propose to you."

I interrupted. "Was that a ploy to get closer to me and my mom? I seem to recall at that time, you were living a lie." My tone was filled with bitterness and regret as I remembered the moment when he blindfolded me and took me to the place where Hilltop Bar had burned down. The place where all of this had begun.

"I was living a lie, yes. You have no idea how relieved I was when you figured it out. I apologized. I thought you'd never forgive me. I still don't know. Have you? Can you forgive me for that?"

I shrugged, wanting to hold onto it a little longer but knowing that I had to let it go because I needed him.

"Well, the truth is, Stephen, it's a lot sexier to be a cop..."

"Detective," he corrected me quickly.

"Hello. You two ready to order?" The server's interruption was well-timed. We put in our order and continued the conversation when she left the table.

"Detective is sexier than financial planner. I feel safer with you knowing that you can handle a gun and physically defend me because it's what I need right now. I desperately want to be able to defend myself if the occasion should arise. But you're the only person I have in my life who cares..." I heard my voice crack and was horrified. I took a deep breath and continued. "You're the only person out there who cares if I live or die. So much so that you've pushed yourself into a space where you were not initially wanted. I admire you for that."

"But?" Stephen's eyes were kind and full of knowledge.

"That's just it. There shouldn't be a but in all this."

"But there is," he said sadly.

I nodded. Why was it so hard to articulate the way I was feeling? Did I even know?

"Paige, I have an unfair advantage here. I love you. I knew it when you came home for Christmas break your first year in college. You turned and looked over your shoulder at me, and I knew I loved you then. In fact, I resigned from the case the minute I realized I had real feelings. You were supposed to be a part of the job. My first *real* case. I was to go undercover and infiltrate this mother daughter team who we suspected of murder. I was so excited. I had just made detective. Then I met you; you and your mom. I was so disappointed for my career. I decided you weren't capable of making people disappear.

"I believed my instincts. But I knew others were still on the case. There was some excitement when they discovered that your mom's last name Deffer was an alias. Her real name was Mynart. I didn't know it at the time, that she was connected to your dad's murder. So, you can imagine my surprise when Krysta got murdered. You're so smart, Paige. The only reason it took so long for you to figure out who I really was is because you were busy at college and I was able to work my normal job without you ever knowing."

"That's just it. I don't know myself at all. I don't know if I'm smart. I don't know what I like and dislike. I have no clue who I really am because my whole life revolved around my mom. Where was she? What was she doing? What if she got on a bus and went two states away? I was always watching her. I had no time for me."

"I think I understand," Stephen said. "I never told you about my younger brother."

I searched my memory. The one who died? "I think you mentioned him?"

"Yes. My brother, his name was Greg, he was your classic troublemaker. Always in the principal's office. If anyone was getting bullied, it was often by him. He was charismatic and handsome, and people followed him. I never understood his charm and why he had it, but I didn't. His junior year, he was hanging out with his clique of bullies at a skate park. He pushed the wrong kid too far too fast. The kid pulled out a gun and shot him in the face. Just like that, my brother was gone. I blamed myself. Why didn't I watch him better? Why didn't I care enough to follow him around and keep him out of trouble?

I watched as this kid, this murderer, went to juvenile hall. Then I watched years later when he got out on good behavior. For that reason, I became a cop. In Greg's memory, I planned to put bad guys with guns and tempers behind bars. It's what I'm trying to do now."

"I'm sorry about your brother." My eyes teared up as I listened. I truly knew the pain of losing someone close to me. "But all my efforts didn't keep her alive. My mom was a grown woman and could make her own choices."

"And my brother made his. I know that now, but for years, I was tortured with the guilt of what I didn't do for him."

The food arrived and we ate in silence. It was comfortable but only because the conversation had veered away from the discussion of our relationship. I didn't know why I couldn't bring myself to just be honest. Whatever Stephen was to me, I knew it was not strong enough to last a lifetime.

33

PAIGE

That afternoon found the moving truck all loaded up. It turned out I didn't have nearly enough stuff to fill it, and it took the movers less than an hour to load all my things. I looked at the empty apartment one last time. This had been my home for the majority of my life. Yet, I never considered it my *true* home. In my heart, at my core, I knew I had always been Canadian. I swallowed all my sentimental feelings and said good-bye to my mother's home.

Next came the good-bye that meant more in my heart than Stephen even knew.

"Paige, as soon as I finish my workday, I'll be there. Right behind you."

"I know," I said. But I knew in that moment that I was saying good-bye to us. No matter what happened from here on out, it would be me and this world, not me and Stephen.

"Now, don't go get yourself into trouble, okay? What's on your agenda today?" he had asked.

I guessed that Stephen was feeling slightly more confident because he was convinced Matt Cline was the murderer. When Stephen had gotten the call that Matt was out on bail, he mentioned Matt wouldn't dare try anything because he knew they were watching him. They had Ashley's testimony which would lock him up for good. That, plus the lie he admitted to and his lack of alibi had it looking pretty bad for Mr. Cline. Law enforcement officers were keeping strict tabs on him.

I squinted against the sunlight. "Oh, I'm gonna pop in to see Dr. Burnett in person one last time and probably hit the road. No real reason to stay around." I smiled at Stephen.

Stephen nodded. He was in a happy state today. "Good. I should only be an hour or two behind you."

I let him kiss me good-bye. Then I watched as the moving truck pulled out. Stephen pulled his car behind the moving truck. I waited a few minutes before I hopped into my own car. I was not going to see Dr. Burnett.

I flipped through mom's journal to the end. I felt slight guilt, like I was reading the end of the book before I was supposed to. But this was important. It was time for me to figure out what happened to mom and this was my last shot to do so.

The last entry was not dated. It was just a hastily scribbled note that seemed to slant down into lines that did not stay straight.

He called. He finally called! After all these years of me hoping and praying, he called. I don't know how he found me. But he's the one person who can tell me what happened that night. I know I shouldn't get my hopes up. I most likely killed his best friend. Jason and Ray were gambling buddies. They'd be gone for entire weekends! At first, I hated it! Then, Jason would come back with stacks of cash. Those boys were getting rich quick... Then I had this thought. What if...? What if I didn't kill Jason? Ray is the one person who would tell me the truth. I remember the hours we would spend after Jason would call it quits and go to bed. We'd sit up talking about Allison. Poor Allison. We always thought she'd pull through the cancer, but she didn't. She had good years, then good days, then good moments until she was gone. I always felt a special connection to Ray. I could trust him. I felt it deep in my soul. I had to consider that maybe my feelings ran deeper than I expected a few years after Paige was born. I swear her little two-year-old face had a resemblance to him. It's the eyes, I think. Then I decided I was seeing things. And maybe I had feelings I hadn't acknowledged. For years, I wondered what I would do if he found me. I guess now I'll find out. We are meeting Friday!

I put the journal away and started driving. Maybe Ray wasn't the enemy. Maybe there was a logical explanation for why I saw him at the coffee shop and on the property... okay, so that was a stretch. Was he still looking for money too, after all these years? Surely, he would've had the opportunity to get into that house before now. Especially if he and dad had been friends. Wouldn't he know where my dad had left his money? What if Margaret was half right? What if the money wasn't mine? If it wasn't mine, and it wasn't hers, was it Ray's?

Before too long, I was on I-40. I'd heard enough discussion about where my mother was found that I knew the exact spot. I was going to find that cell phone. The police hadn't found it the day they found her body. Not on her body, not on the ground, nowhere. But it had to be there.

I slowed my car to a creep and then parked just off the side of the highway. I took a deep breath and got out of the car. This was it. The place where my mom's murdered body was found. It seemed peaceful and quiet. I scanned every inch of ground I could see before the woods got thicker and went steeply downhill.

I sat on the ground, *crisscross applesauce*, I'd said as a kid. I looked at the sky.

"Mom?" I whispered and watched the trees sway gently. But

all stayed quiet. I laid back on the ground and let my knees come up, feet right under my bottom. I waited. Still nothing.

"Okay, well it was worth a shot. Wish you'd show us where that cell phone went."

I hopped up and turned toward the car. That's when I saw her. At first, I saw a flurry of leaves that had fallen to the ground. They swirled upward, high into the trees. They merged and whisped into a human form...

"Mom!" I breathed out, relieved.

Danger... I heard the wind whisper the word and could see the outline of my mom in the leaves.

"Why, mom? Why am I in danger?" I asked aloud.

Noooo.... The winds picked up and the sound formed the words she seemed to be moaning. *Nooooo!* There was urgency in her voice now. *Paige, no!*

Suddenly, all was quiet. It was still. The leaves dropped as quickly as they had picked up. Mom was gone. My arms held chills and my hopes were dashed with deep disappointment.

"Come back," I wailed. "Why do you keep leaving me?" Tears rushed from my eyes with such force, I could not see momentarily. I cried until I had nothing left. Then I stood up and just looked at the place where she was. I felt another emotion crowd out the sadness and self-pity— anger.

"What a waste!" I said angrily. I got into the car and I drove. I made a mental note to reach out to Ray. He had to have the answers. Why had he reached out to mom? Why was he following me? Mom trusted him once upon a time. That was good enough for me.

34

PAIGE

The movers were sitting outside when I got to the house in Missouri. *Odd, I gave them the key*. I had bought new doorknobs to change them out after the movers left. I had plans for this little house and it started with adding more security. I hopped out of my car.

"What's up, guys? You're not done yet?"

I hadn't really looked at the two guys in detail before now. One was big and broad with a good-sized gut. His name was Bill. The other guy was the polar opposite. He was tall and thin and was sweating profusely. His name was Rob.

"Haven't started yet," said Rob. He wiped sweat from his forehead and squinted at me.

I stared back at him baffled. "Did the key not work?"

Rob shrugged. "It worked."

"Well, what's the problem?"

"Your house," this time Bill spoke. "You probably need to see this for yourself."

"Oh?" I whirled around and entered the house. Or what was left of the house. My mouth fell open. I was shocked and, for a moment, my eyes refused to tell my brain what I was seeing. Then my brain tried to comfort me and tell me it wasn't real.

Someone had taken a sledgehammer to the entire house. There were holes all over the floor, in the walls, and even some holes in the ceiling. Whoever had done this had been thorough. They must have found what they were looking for. That, or they had been horribly disappointed. No matter what the case was, my home was ruined. Unlivable, even. I sank down on the only part of the floor where I couldn't see straight through to the foundation.

On one hand, it was just a small house that held keys to forgotten memories and a past that might never open back up. On the other hand, this had become my home. Mine! The first place I could call my own. It didn't matter that the bank negotiated an amazing deal with me because the house had sat vacant so long and no one would buy it. The house was mine.

I wasn't out a ton of money and the land alone was worth double what I paid for the house, but it was the sheer principle of the matter. I felt the anger rising up again. First someone killed mom. Then someone vandalized and ruined my home. Were the two connected? I thought not. I wanted to kick my legs and scream. Maybe I would have if I hadn't felt the presence of the movers in the doorway, watching me. Why couldn't everyone just let me live my life?

"Ma'am?" Rob cleared his throat.

"Yeah." I looked up, looked at the demolition one more time, and walked out of the house.

"Go ahead and unload as much of this as you can in the garage." I knew there wasn't much. I was pretty sure it would fit. I pulled out my phone and dialed 911. I reported the crime. Next, I called Stephen. He was on his way but had just left.

I hung up and checked my watch, a plan forming in my mind. What day had Jud invited me to the neighborhood party? I thought about the conversation. Saturday night. Today was

Saturday. I tried to remember where he'd said. I pulled out my phone and texted Amy. It took minutes for her to reply.

Amy: *Hey, I'm here already. Want me to come pick you up?*

Me: *No, thanks. Can you send the address though? I'll GPS it.*

Amy: *Cool. See you soon.*

The movers were done. I paid them and they left. As they were leaving, a squad car pulled up.

"Hi, I'm Officer Huntington, Brighton Police Force. Responding to a call."

"Yes," I wasn't sure what to say. Up until now, I'd only had Stephen to protect me.

"Are you okay?"

"Yes. But my place isn't."

Officer Huntington was heavyset and her dark hair was pulled into a bun at the back of her head. Her brown eyes were astute, and she seemed on high alert.

"This is your place?"

"Yes, I bought it a week ago."

"I see. Well, let's have a look."

I showed her the way in.

When we stepped through the door, Officer Huntington gasped. I watched her slowly walk through the house, dodging massive holes in the floor. She took out her phone. "May I?" She asked.

I nodded.

She took pictures of the damage with her phone. She paused mid-way through her walk around. "Do you have any idea who might have done this?"

I nodded my head. "Margaret Terry."

The officer stared at me and furrowed her brow. "Why do you think it was her?"

"It may sound strange. There was a theory that there was money – cash – hidden in these walls from the previous owners."

"How do you know that?"

I sighed. Why was I always so honest? "Margaret told me so herself. She said it belonged to her, that it should stay in her family." I was starting to feel like it was a mistake involving another authority, but Stephen was just too far away.

"I'm actually on my way out but I thought it would be important to report this vandalism."

Officer Huntington nodded. "You did the right thing."

"Thanks." I followed the officer out. I almost bumped into her when she stopped suddenly and turned around.

"How do you know Margaret?"

I gulped. I really had been hoping to avoid that question. It was the piece of information that gave more of the story than I originally wanted to tell. But I was terrible at lying.

"She's my grandmother."

Officer Huntington said, "Well, now. That's a different story. I think I need to ask you some more questions."

35

PAIGE

After what seemed like an hour but was really twenty minutes, I was on my way. I didn't have much more information that was helpful. Based off my testimony and relaying the anger Margaret had shown, it seemed pretty obvious who vandalized the house. At least, that's what Officer Huntington said.

I texted Stephen the address of the party and drove down the street.

When I followed the address to the neighborhood party, I was sure I was in the wrong place. A barn sat in an open field. *This is Pickleman Park?* I wondered. I turned down the long gravel drive that seemed to go for a mile. The closer I got to the barn, the more party indicators I could see. I heard a thumping music beat, I could see a few people milling around the back corner of the barn smoking, and then I saw a few cars parked on the other side of the barn. The closer I got, the more cars I saw. The barn was open on one side and I could see what looked like over a hundred people inside eating, drinking, and talking. Fairy lights hung around the barn and a band was playing on a stage that had been set up for the occasion.

As I watched the partygoers, I was aware of how wrongly I

was dressed for this party. I observed from the car that most women had on some variation of jean skirts with fancy blousy tops and cowboy boots – some that were ankle boots, and some were mid-calf boots. The men wore jeans and nice button-down shirts, also with cowboy boots. Some wore hats.

I looked down at the sandals on my feet. The soles were thin and leather straps wrapped around my foot and ankle. My capri jeans were tightly fitted. In fact, I had begun to think maybe I was gaining weight lately. I wore a plain white t-shirt half tucked into the front of my jeans. My hair was in a plain ponytail. I quickly took it out and fluffed it. It hit midway down my back. It really was getting too long. I found a tube of mascara in my purse. I put some on, wishing my eyelashes were longer. I glanced around my car and noticed a long neck-lace dangling from the stick shift, which wasn't uncommon for me. I always liked the idea of necklaces but never made it through the day with one on. I threw it over my head to dress up my outfit and opened the car door.

Amy met me right as I walked into the barn. I said hello as my eyes scanned the barn. I questioned why I was here. I knew I was actually hoping to find Ray. I couldn't shake the feeling that he had some of the answers. What were the actual chances that because he lived around here when mom and dad did that he'd never moved? He had been creeping on my property, but it didn't mean he would be here at this party. But a part of me hoped he would be. I needed to talk to him. He held all the answers.

Amy and I made the rounds. Surprisingly, I saw many people I already knew. Several people from my recovery group were there. Peter the gun-guy was there. My eyes kept scanning the room. No sign of Margaret. *Good*, I thought with satisfac-tion. I hoped they had locked her up. But to my dismay and sinking heart, Ray was nowhere to be seen either.

As I mingled with people, I was painfully aware of each

minute slipping away from me. I began to feel panicked. I was running out of time.

"Excuse me," I said to the group of people chatting around me. I wandered toward the stage. The music had stopped. The band must have been taking a break. People were talking and the volume of voices had risen to a dull roar. Before I could allow the fluttering butterflies to talk my brain out of action, I located the microphone and stepped up onto the stage. *Dear God!* I had never done anything like this before.

Right about when I thought I would pass out, I saw Stephen step through the doorway. He was looking pretty frazzled and confused when he spotted me on stage. He stuck out with his tennis shoes and ballcap. But I was glad to see him just the same.

I took a deep breath, "Good evening, everyone. I'm Paige Deffer." The microphone whined loudly, and I walked a few feet. It stopped. I definitely had all their attention. "I've met some of you," I said. I didn't dare look around the room to locate and nod at people. I was not that advanced. "For everyone else, I'm looking forward to meeting you as well. I'm living in the old Mynart house." I paused for effect.

There was a collective gasp from the crowd, as I assumed there would be.

"That's right, the old place finally found an owner," I acknowledged.

"I hear the place is haunted!" someone yelled. A nervous twitter lightly sprinkled the crowd.

"It just might be." I winked. Where was this coming from? Sheer desperation to find Ray? "In fact, this ghost," my fingers made air quotes when I said ghost, "has been prowling around my property." The crowd went silent. I looked around and saw people drop their eyes. The discomfort level in the room skyrocketed and every person felt it. Only one man in the corner of the room held my gaze. It was Ray! He was most definitely the man from the diner and the funeral. My pulse quickened and I tried to catch Stephen's eye, but he was too busy surveying the crowd. He was looking for guilty faces of men who fit the profile.

"So, this is just a friendly reminder that the property is not vacant anymore. I welcome all front door visitors. And if we have a neighborhood watch party, sign me up," I laughed a little, but it fell flat. My eyes flicked back to the corner, but Ray was gone. I felt surprised and instantly disappointed.

"In the meantime, thank you to those of you who have already welcomed me so kindly!"

Someone clapped and it caught on. I forgot to put down the microphone and the cord jerked my arm just before I hit the stairs. Then, I put the mic down and left the stage on wobbly legs. *What* had I been thinking?

Stephen quickly found me. "Good job," he said. "How do you feel?"

I searched his face for sarcasm but saw none. "Not awesome, and *not* empowered." I looked through the crowd for Ray. "He was here!"

"Who was?" Stephen asked.

"Ray, the man from the diner, the prowler. He was in the back corner, then he was gone."

"Well, let's mingle a little and meet back. Do not leave here without me, please. And don't talk to that man without me either."

"Yes, sir!" I thought about saluting him, but he was already gone. I felt a little relieved that he'd made it back. I searched for a few minutes before the room seemed so stuffy and congested, I stepped out for fresh air.

Once outside, I took several deep breaths and looked up. The stars were muted tonight under a slightly clouded sky. The moon was barely visible against the dark blue sky that peeked around the clouds. A cool breeze brushed over me. I felt a strange twinge in my spirit as I stared at this sky. Was it possible, just a little possible, that God created these natural wonders? As I looked up, a sprinkle of water hit my face. I brushed it, surprised. I hadn't expected it.

"Looks like rain," a deep voice sounded behind me.

I screamed and turned. Ray stood leaning against the barn, watching me. I could tell he was tall, even while leaning. He was lean and muscular, in shape for his age.

"Oh! You scared me!" I was suddenly nervous. Should I get Stephen? Then I remembered my mom's words. She trusted Ray. Maybe I could too.

"Sorry about that," he pushed off the building, moving easily when I turned around. He was standing in front of me with a strange expression on his face. Despite his ease and confidence, he looked a little shaken. "Man, you look just like your mama."

"She once told me I have my daddy's eyes," I blurted out the first thing that came to my mind.

"Well," he stared long enough to almost be rude. "Jason had brown eyes, yours are green."

"Weird," I said.

"Yes," he said slowly, "weird."

"There you are!" Stephen seemed to pop out of nowhere. He immediately extended his hand to Ray. "I'm Stephen."

Ray clasped his hand. "Ray." He still hadn't taken his eyes off my face. "Was just telling Paige here how much she looks like her mama."

"Her *late* mother," Stephen said. "But you would know that because you were at the funeral."

"Yes," Ray admitted. His eyes flicked to Stephen. "Damn shame about Krysta. I hope you find her murderer." He turned back to me. "And I hope you find whatever answers you're looking for in that house of yours. Those walls hold the memory of a pretty gruesome night. I'm a little surprised you want to be there." He didn't appear to want an answer as he turned to go.

"Please, wait. Ray, you were my dad's best friend. If it's not too difficult, would you be willing to talk to me about what happened some time?"

"Or at the very least, what you were doing on her property the other night," Stephen said coldly as he took a step closer.

Ray tilted his head up to look at the stars for a second. He looked back down, looked at Stephen, then at me and shrugged. "Maybe some time." And with that, he walked away.

I stared after him dumbly. I felt frustration and anger converging. I clenched my fists. I turned to ask Stephen if he could make Ray talk to us.

Stephen held up one finger. He was looking at his phone. There was a tension in his shoulders and an intensity on his face so strong, I closed my mouth and waited.

"Paige," Stephen finished his text message and shoved his phone into his back pocket. "There's been a development. We have to go."

"Go? Go where? My place isn't even livable…"

"We need to get on the road back to Arkansas. Matt Cline's body was just discovered. Looks like a suicide. There's a note but we can't be sure."

"What would that mean for this case?" I asked. I knew Stephen had been hoping to pin this murder on Matt Cline.

"I don't know yet," Stephen answered. "I don't have any answers. But I need you to swear to me that you stay with me until I do have answers, no matter what?"

I nodded. I didn't dare disagree.

"This is where things are going to get a little crazy and I can't have you fall through the cracks right now. Can you agree with that? Just for now, no questions, no disappearances?"

I nodded again. I felt a little scared.

Stephen got in his car and I got in mine. It was a long and fearful drive back to Arkansas. It felt especially long since it was the second trip in one day.

But then, all the drives back and forth were starting to look the same.

36

RAY

"She's your daughter, Ray, you can't kill her." Margaret began talking before she made it up the front stairs of his porch the next morning.

Ray had just gotten home from his boxing session and was still in his workout gear, looking at the newspaper while he sat on the front porch. He lowered the paper and glared at her. He really disliked this woman. He always had.

"Did you enjoy your night?" Ray was maddeningly calm. He pretended to be surprised by a thought. "You didn't just come straight here from jail, did you?"

Margaret shot him a dirty look. Her flat hair and yesterday's makeup crusted on her face confirmed his words. She reached into her bag, took out a hairbrush, and shook it at him.

Ray sighed and reluctantly put the paper aside, giving her his full attention.

"This is Paige's hairbrush. I fished it out of her purse during a coffee date. So, I have Paige's DNA. Then I took a cup you were drinking out of at the coffee shop in town a few weeks ago. I have your DNA too. Anyway, the lab says it's a match.

What do you have to say for yourself? I should have expected such a thing from my slut daughter. But *you?*"

Ray sighed. "I know she is, Margaret. I figured that out as well. Is that why you've come, to convince me she's my daughter? What's your point?" Ray challenged her.

Margaret opened and shut her mouth. She seemed a little deflated. "You knew?"

"Yep," Ray was smug. Of course, he didn't know beyond a shadow of a doubt, but he wasn't going to give her the satisfaction of one-upping him.

"You always acted like you were so devoted to your dying wife. All the while you were sneaking over, shacking up with my daughter, and taking advantage of poor Jason? Right under his own nose!"

"Hey," Ray's voice was cold as steel, and he slowly stood up. He towered over her. "You will watch your mouth when you're on my property. It happened one time. We were both drunk. How the hell was I supposed to know she'd get pregnant? I loved Allison." Ray's voice softened. "Love Allison. But you're right about one thing. Krysta was a filthy, vile woman and every blood relative of hers is the same."

Margaret backed down one step.

"Anyway, that little sledgehammer stunt of yours get you what you wanted?" he asked.

Margaret shrugged. She pouted a little. "Not really. I found one more roll of bills in the bedroom floorboards but nothing over a couple hundred dollars."

"So, we're even then. You got what you want so you go about your life and I go about mine?"

Margaret nodded. She looked like she might say something else, but she thought better of it. She walked down the rest of the steps and turned back when she was in the yard.

"Are you still going to kill her, Ray?"

Ray stared at Margaret with a smirk on his face.

"Kill who, Margaret?"

"Your daughter, Paige."

"Why on earth would I do that?" he asked with all innocence conjured into his voice.

Margaret sighed, seemingly relieved.

Ray watched her go, wondering why him killing Paige would bother Margaret Terry. In fact, he wondered if he was focusing on the wrong person. Maybe Margaret's name needed to be added to his list. She was, after all, the one who made Krysta the way she ended up. A black-out drunk who had no clue what she was doing when under the influence.

37

MARGARET

Margaret smirked as she walked to her car. What Ray didn't know is that Margaret had discovered something else when she'd used the sledgehammer. It was the knife. She'd found the knife from that night all those years ago, complete with crusted blood. She assumed there would be fingerprints.

She had inadvertently hit a metal grate in the bedroom with the sledgehammer, causing it to pop off onto the floor. There, in the gaping hole where the grate used to be, lay the knife. She didn't know how the police hadn't checked in there all those years ago.

She reached into her purse for her keys and fished around. Her hand brushed the wad of cash she'd found in the house. She'd lied about that too. It was a pouch of money, similar to the one Paige was holding when she busted in on their party, and it held one-hundred-thousand dollars. She found her keys. They were right next to the knife she had carefully put into a quart-size zip-up bag, which she kept close by her side. She had no clue what she would do with it, but she knew she was going to have to move fast.

38

PAIGE

The police station was alive with activity. I was beginning to hate this place. I hated the feeling of being dragged around like a doll. I hated the cold, methodical way the officers looked at people like statistics, constantly summing them up. I hated that my whole life had become stuck in this world of looking for answers so I could live my future life in safety.

Stephen asked me to stay put. For once, I agreed. Truthfully, I didn't know where else to go. I could see him in the room where I first discovered where he worked, my mother's crime board, and the suspects on it. *If anyone could solve this case, it would be me*, I thought arrogantly. I crept closer. They looked like they were suiting up for a big mission. I knew they were really just going to confirm it was Matt Cline's body and look for clues. They already had a suicide note. A picture of it had been sent to someone's phone. They had printed it and had blown it up. The letters were so big, I could see them from where I stood.

Dear Krysta,

I failed you. Since you've been gone, in your death, I still couldn't do right by you. I'm sorry. I knew more about you than you knew. We both know I didn't kill you. I was awful mad that night. But even then, I didn't want to kill you. It hurt me to see you were with another man. When I saw that, I knew my life was over. I didn't know you'd turn up dead. But I just knew we'd never be the same. I realized that night that I couldn't live without you. And I realized you couldn't care less if I was in your life. I knew about the murders. You talked in your sleep. You said you killed three people. You'd told me just enough about your life that I understood why. You'd kill to keep those secrets of yours buried. One day, you might have realized I knew them and killed me too. But the thought of being without you was so unbearable, I just pretended not to know. But now they got me pinned for your murder. I can't die in prison. It's not how I want to go. In fact, I don't want to go on at all. So, I'm done. Maybe we can be together in the afterlife. Or maybe there's a special place in hell for me goin' out this way. It's a chance I'm willing to take.

I'll love you forever, Matt

Tears streamed down my face. Not because I was sad to see Matt go. But because his words could have been my words. I knew about the murders too. I pretended not to. I just wanted my mom, my only relative who loved me, to stay around. But it didn't work. I couldn't control it. None of it. I couldn't control her. I couldn't control her fate. I couldn't control how alone I would inevitably be in this world. Now, I stood clinging to a person who was utterly not right for me in the same way, for the same reason. Because without him, there was absolutely no one in the world to care about what happened to me.

I must have been sniffling or crying loudly because Stephen

and the other officers turned at the same time. Stephen rushed toward me.

"Paige, hon, you can't…"

"Be in here." I finished his sentence. "Well, I don't know where I'm supposed to be!" My voice was loud, but I didn't care. In fact, it felt good. Eyes of other officers looked up. The room hushed for seconds. In that moment, I had control back. Even if only for that moment.

"How many officers does it take to solve one woman's murder?" I looked around the room, satisfied to see them all listening. I turned back to Stephen. "Get this thing solved, would you? I'm done."

I turned and spun on my heel, vaguely realizing I had echoed the words of Matt's suicide note. As I stomped off to the ladies' room, the realization did not sit well with me.

39

PAIGE

Someone was pounding on the ladies' room door. I gasped at the sound. Where was I? I opened my eyes. I was on the floor. I could see the sinks above me. Had I passed out? There were several stalls, had I locked the door?

"Paige, come out. Please. We're leaving and I need to talk to you."

"Leave me alone," I said quietly.

"If you don't come out, I'm coming in."

I got off the floor in a hurry. Why had I passed out? How much time had passed? I looked in the mirror and gasped. Mascara had smudged under my eyes and a single lone streak had made it down my cheek. I splashed water on my face and wiped it all off with a paper towel. I'd forgotten I'd even put it on. Next, I took the ponytail holder from my pocket and threw my hair back into a messy bun. I pushed the door open.

Stephen's hair was rumpled up and he looked distraught. He was immediately at my side. He hugged me. The ballcap from before was nowhere to be seen. His blond curls looked a little smashed down.

"Paige, I'm sorry. I keep forgetting how hard this must be for you."

I nodded but didn't speak.

Stephen sighed deeply. "I need to ask you to come with me."

"Where?"

"I have to go to the scene. You can stay in the car. I don't want you to see Matt. You won't ever forget when you see that stuff. But you have to stay with me. We've got a killer on the loose."

I looked at him surprised. "You don't think Matt was…"

Stephen shook his head. "We're not ruling it a suicide until we investigate it. But you're not safe."

"Okay," I had no fight left in me. I followed him to his car and got in. We drove in silence, but it occurred to me that this might be the most productive use of my time.

We arrived at the Cline home. I looked around. It was a nice little homestead. He looked to be on five-plus acres of land. It was plenty of house for just one person. It had a nice, inviting look to it. I could see a few other officers had beaten us to the scene.

When the car stopped, I flung open my door. "I'm going in," I declared and walked off in a hurry so Stephen couldn't stop me.

Stephen loped easily and caught up to me.

"I don't want to hear it, Stephen. I'm going in."

He blocked my path. "You can't. It's illegal to enter a crime scene without authorization." His voice was firm. "This is my career. Please respect that. Wait in the car. Everything in this house could be evidence and we can't destroy it or contaminate it."

I nodded. I understood the gravity. I had no desire to go near the body, I just wanted to find one clue. At least, that's what I told myself. I pretended to go back to the car but waited until everyone was inside.

I slowly and curiously walked to the house. I had no idea it would be so easy to slip inside. Officers were marking off the floor with tape, and dusting for what I assumed were fingerprints. They were so busy with the dead body, I walked right in.

I was not prepared for what I saw when I walked through the door. Matt had killed himself in the living room. The gun lay on the floor as if it had slid out of his hand when it went limp. His body was slumped and hunched over to the side. I saw the intense amount of blood splattered all over the wall with droplets splayed on the wall around it. I couldn't make myself look at Matt. Poor Matt. Poor me. We were one and the same. Two people desperate to live the type of life that my mother would agree to be a part of. I left the room.

My eyes looked around the kitchen, the next room I'd come to. He was a neat and orderly man. Everything seemed to have its place. I scanned the floor, the cabinets, and the ceiling. Nothing seemed amiss. I found his bedroom. It seemed odd to be here, in such a personal space. Except, it was so clean. Like he had staged it for an open house. Then it hit me. He had planned all of this and he didn't want anyone to have to clean up after him. He put everything in order and took control of the way he died. Maybe the two nights he spent in jail were enough to tell him this was not how he wanted to live out his years.

I went back to the kitchen. What was I missing? I looked around again. Then I saw it. It was a tiny, white piece of paper that looked like it had been torn off a bill. It seemed to have fluttered to the ground and gone unseen. There was writing on it. I bent to pick it up.

"Don't touch it," said a voice behind me. It was Stephen. I jerked my hand away like it had been burned.

"I'm sorry." I truly was. I'd already forgotten his warning about not contaminating the crime scene.

Stephen motioned for someone on the team and another officer showed up. First, he took at picture of the paper and the location. Then he picked it up with his gloved hands and put it in a plastic bag. I could see the words scrawled on the note as it settled in the plastic bag.

Millie's Diner
Thursday, 2 pm

What Thursday? I could see Stephen thinking the same thing. Apparently, we were finished because we all trooped back to our cars. Stephen, at the moment, was refusing to talk to me. I had just sat down and was buckling the seat belt when Stephen's phone rang.

"Yeah? Hmm. Interesting. Keep her there would you? I'm on my way." He hung up.

"Who was that?" I asked. I could tell he was angry.

"Your grand... Margaret Terry just showed up at the station. She says she has evidence."

"Evidence from what?" I wondered.

"Your father's murder."

40

PAIGE

"It's about time!"

I heard Margaret's voice before I saw her. I'd recognize it anywhere. It grated on my nerves. I had no desire to see this woman right now. Yet here she was looking like she just left the beauty salon. Every hair was smoothed in place and she wore crisp blue ankle slacks and a white blouse with tiny blue flowers all over it.

I checked my phone time. It was 8:37 p.m. Why did it feel so much later?

"Margaret?" Stephen asked. "How can we help you?"

Margaret put her hand in her purse but paused. "Can we talk somewhere private? Without *her* lingering around?"

"Are you afraid I'm going to bring up the wrecking job you did on my home?" I snapped. "I hope it was worth it. Did you find what you were looking for?"

"That and more. That's why I'm here. You know, when I mentioned your parents' house to you, I never dreamed you'd plant yourself there permanently. Tell me, do you enjoy walking down the exact path your mother did?"

"Go to hell, Margaret," I spat out with contempt. My eyes narrowed hatefully.

"You are wicked, Paige, just like your mom was, and one day the whole world will see you for who you are."

Stephen stepped forward. "Okay, ladies, that's enough. Margaret, why are you here? It's a long drive from Missouri."

"If I give you this information, I need to know I'll be protected." Margaret looked doubtful for the first time.

"Come with me, Margaret. I'll need to bring in another detective because I'm not actually lead on this case." Stephen grabbed someone and the three walked toward a conference room.

Margaret turned and gave me a superior look and followed Stephen into the room.

I held up my hands and backed away. I was done talking to her anyway. I knew full well that I could sit on the other side of the double-sided glass and hear what she had to say but I had no desire. I assumed Stephen would tell me what I needed to know. I found a recliner in a random corner of the room. I don't know why I hadn't seen it before. It was soft and comfortable. It took two minutes for me to fall fast asleep.

When I woke up, sunlight was streaming into the station. I blinked and squinted at the sun. Where was I? I was disoriented for a few minutes before it all came rushing back. I gasped suddenly and jerked awake. Did I sleep here all night? I groaned aloud.

Stephen showed up at that moment with coffee. "Morning." He seemed excited.

"Morning," I said suspiciously. I took the coffee and took a sip. It was made exactly how I liked it. I didn't know how he liked his coffee. It struck me as I took another sip that he knew me way better than I knew him. It gave me a moment of profound sadness. That thought defined one of the biggest problems with our relationship.

"Sleep okay?" He asked.

"Umm," I sat up a little. My neck and back were cramped up, but I did feel rested. I stood and found a place to set down my cup. I stretched.

"Okay, you ready?" Stephen asked.

"Ready for what?" I felt a little dread in my stomach.

"We're going to have breakfast."

"Oh, well breakfast sounds great! But let me stop by the ladies' room first." I left Stephen standing there and walked into the bathroom.

I looked at myself in the mirror. Then I took a deep breath and washed my face in cold water. It was no shower, but it would have to do. When I was finished, I dabbed my face dry with paper towels and left the bathroom. Stephen was waiting with my coffee. I took the cup and followed him to the elevator. "Where are we going?"

"Millie's Diner," Stephen grinned like an excited little boy.

"Ah." We were still on the case.

The car ride was quiet.

Millie's Diner was alive with activity. We found a spot in the corner of the room and waited.

"Now what?" I asked.

"Now, we wait."

The waitress greeted us, bringing cups and silverware to the table. "How are y'all doin'?" She was on the plump side with short brown hair. When she smiled, she had dimples and I thought she was quite pretty.

"Good," Stephen said with an excited smile.

I smiled politely.

"Coffee?" she asked.

I shook my head, having just finished a cup earlier.

"Sure," Stephen smiled at her. "Susan?" He was reading her name tag.

"Yep, Susan. That's me." She smiled sadly at him. "Sorry,

I'm just a little off this morning. I'm Susan and I'll be helping y'all today." She found a spot of food on her Mille's Diner t-shirt just above the 'M' and brushed at it, momentarily distracted.

"Thanks, Susan. Do you normally work the morning shift?" Stephen asked.

"Every morning and through the day. I start at eight in the morning and go to three in the afternoon."

Stephen put his badge on the table. "Do you work Thursdays?"

"Every one of them for as long as I can remember."

"What time does your shift end? I'd like to ask you some questions."

"Oh." Susan looked immediately concerned. "About what?"

"Do you know this man?" Stephen showed a picture of Matt to her from his phone.

Susan dropped the coffee cup. It hit the floor with a loud clash. The diner fell silent and all eyes were on her as she bent to pick up the broken pieces of the coffee cup.

"I take that as a yes?" Stephen asked when she had everything picked up and the volume and activities returned to normal.

"Yeah, I mean, not really, but he's been in the diner. I'll take a break here in an hour. Breakfast crowd dies down then. Can you eat breakfast and wait around?"

Stephen nodded.

I watched her leave, then leaned forward. "What did Margaret tell you?" I asked.

"Tell me?" Stephen was puzzled.

"Last night. What made her come all this way?" I pushed.

"It's more like what she gave us. When she wrecked your home, she found something," Stephen answered.

"What did she find?" I felt like Stephen was being purposely vague.

He sighed and lowered his voice. "A knife. Presumedly the knife that killed your dad – Jason Mynart. We sent it to the lab to check for fingerprints."

"Wow!" I sat back and thought about the implications of that. "We could determine who killed my dad."

Stephen nodded.

"When will they know?" I asked.

"Could be as quick as a few hours," Stephen stated.

The hour went by fast. The diner thinned out. The breakfast crowd was gone. Susan sat down in a chair at the table.

"He sat right here… I think it was a couple weeks ago. He was with another man. I heard their conversation."

"They were talking right in front of you?"

Susan shook her head. "Ya'll don't know, but this corner is actually the loudest table acoustically in the room."

"Is that possible?" I asked.

Susan smirked. "Yes, everyone who wants to have private conversations sit right here in the corner. But sound travels most here. You should hear some of the conversations I over-hear! The guys were alone in the room."

"I'm surprised you remember him," Stephen mused.

"Oh, I never forget a face," Susan replied.

"Same! That's me, too." I nodded.

"So that means you probably remember the man he was with?"

She nodded. "He was average height. Salt and pepper gray hair. Kinda had stubble on his face but he looked like the type who preferred to be clean cut. Nice clothes. Good looking. Intimidating. Made you think he was better than you."

Stephen pulled out his phone again and scrolled through his pictures. He showed Susan a photo of Ray. "Is this him?"

Susan nodded emphatically. "Yes, that's the guy!"

"Do you remember if it was on a Thursday?" Stephen asked.

Susan sat back and thought. "Hmm, I really couldn't tell

you that. It was a while ago, like I said. You know, it's so weird you two are asking about this because I saw on the news this morning that the first guy – they said his name was Matt – committed suicide yesterday?" She whispered the last two words and ended as if she was asking a question.

Stephen nodded in confirmation. "Do you remember what they talked about?"

Susan sighed. "I couldn't forget it. The handsome guy thanked the Matt guy for killing some girl named Krysta. Matt said he didn't and handsome guy—"

"His name is Ray," Stephen interrupted. He seemed annoyed by the handsome guy reference.

"Okay, Ray said something like, 'One of us killed her and it wasn't me. I wanted to. So, thank you.' Matt looked real scared and confused. He didn't say he *didn't* kill her, but he didn't say he *did* either. I was more concerned about the guy who said he wanted to kill her but didn't. What's up with *that*?"

Stephen looked at the ceiling, thinking. "Can you remember anything else?"

Susan shook her head. "I'm sorry. That's all I remember."

Stephen handed her his card and encouraged her to reach out if she remembered anything else. I followed Stephen out to the car. Shadowing Stephen made me feel like I had been dropped into a cop show. But in real life, things moved way too slowly. It was time for me to go back home. In Matt Cline's words, I was just "done."

41

PAIGE

"I'm leaving." I stood with my arms folded. I was not taking no for an answer.

We were back at the station, but I was done with this place. I had secretly been browsing on my phone during breakfast and had found a nice hotel with availability. I wanted to take a shower and sleep. Stephen wouldn't find me. It was just over the border of Missouri. I would make a reservation under a false name. I had cash. I needed some time to myself. I just wanted a good night's sleep. The room had a jacuzzi tub, which was the biggest perk.

"I have to keep you safe," Stephen's tone held an edge of finality to it.

"You're running out of suspects, Stephen." I pointed to the room where the pictures of the suspects were still on the board. My voice was quiet. I felt sorry for him. This was his job and life, not mine. I was done playing cops and robbers for now.

"Running out of suspects..." Stephen repeated, his mind churning. He walked to the room and I followed as if my brain was on autopilot.

Stephen studied the board and mumbled quietly. "Ashley Trieggar…" He was talking to himself. "She answered questions for you but wouldn't answer any for us. She said as much on the phone with you. That's suspicious, right? We should bring her back in." He snapped his fingers and turned back around.

"You do that, but remember she has an alibi." I tried not to yawn. Something about sleeping in a chair was not the equivalent to a good night's sleep in a real bed.

"Her… and Ray." Stephen was still talking to himself.

"Ray?" I asked. "The waitress said Ray told Matt he didn't do it. Can't we just rule him out already?"

Stephen whirled around. "He's our best suspect right now. In fact, I'm eighty percent sure he's our guy. I don't care what he says. Maybe he was just trying to pin it on Matt to see if he had an alibi or how much of a fight he'd put up if he tried that."

"It wasn't Ray. He was my mom's friend."

"What on earth would make you think that?" Stephen asked accusingly.

"Mom's journal."

Stephen's jaw clenched. "I told you I need that journal. You're withholding evidence every day you don't turn it in."

"I am not withholding anything!"

"You have one day to produce the journal, or you'll spend your nights in a jail cell with a twin bed in it."

"You'd prefer that wouldn't you?" I asked. "To have me locked up. Well, you're out of luck, I left it at the house," I lied. That journal was the last piece of my mother I had left.

"Then you have twelve hours to get to the house and back, don't you?"

"Sure!" I said and spun toward the elevators. "I'll just do that!" I called behind me.

I got on the elevator satisfied that for once he didn't follow me. I wasn't going back yet. In fact, with my wrecked home, I didn't have anything to go back to at the moment. I drove to the hotel and checked in.

Once inside my hotel room, I took a long, hot shower and wrapped myself in the comfortable robe I found hanging in the wardrobe. Then I pulled out mom's journal. If I was going to have to give it up, I might as well read the rest of it. I turned back to the page before the day she disappeared.

May 11, 2019

Paige seems so angry these days. I don't know why. I can't get a straight answer. I'm sure it's me. I'm just not the type of mother she deserves. I check out far too often. I know this but it's not new. I've always been that way and Paige knows. So, it can't be that. I wonder if something is going on with her right now that she just isn't ready to talk about? A couple nights ago, she and I were having dinner and she just exploded. She slammed down her fork and stared at me with HATRED in her eyes. She yelled at me. "Do you EVER listen to anything I say?" Then she threw down her fork and left the room in a huff. She's always been such a good kid, and everyone has bad days. But later that night, I had passed out on the couch, I was so tired! I woke up and Paige was just standing there staring at me. I've never said this about my daughter in my life, and I wouldn't repeat it. But it was... strange. She just stared at me with no emotion. When she saw that my eyes were open, she quickly said, "You need to go to bed, mom." And that was it. It was weird for her. I hope she's okay.

I didn't remember the reference. I didn't want to remember the reference. Suddenly, I was so tired, I walked from the chair to the bed. I sank down into the soft, plush, overstuffed comforter. I was asleep in minutes. I slept so deeply, it felt like I slept for days.

42

STEPHEN

Stephen ran his hand through his hair for the tenth time that day. Paige was officially a missing person. He was running on caffeine and protein bars. There were permanent bags under his blue eyes. He hadn't smiled in days. He couldn't bring himself to say what he was thinking. *What if Paige was dead?*

They'd gotten the report back from the knife and the finger-prints were inconclusive. The knife was now working its way through the DNA lab on account of blood that had dried on the tip. No news yet.

Because Paige was an adult, they couldn't spend department resources looking for her. But that would never stop Stephen. He'd looked everywhere he thought she could be.

At first, he'd looked in all the obvious places like her favorite coffee shops, her therapist's office, and her old apart-ment. But she wasn't in the usual places and no one had seen her. He'd made a trip back to her home in Missouri, but she wasn't there either. No one in the neighborhood had seen her.

The reason he knew no one had seen her is because they had all chipped in their time, resources, and manpower to restore her floors and walls as a surprise. They were all eagerly awaiting her return. Stephen could also monitor the activity around the house on his phone with the cameras they had installed. Aside from the work the neighbors did to fix her house, nothing was happening.

Then Stephen scoured the area in the non-obvious places in town. He began questioning the locals. Had anyone seen this girl? He might as well have put her picture on milk cartons. His methods were every bit as effective. There was no trace of Paige anywhere. That was week one.

Something else that was not happening lately was the case. All leads were growing cold. Stephen knew that statistically, the percent of cases that were solved dropped each day, week, and month they went unsolved. Time was starting to become an issue. He was losing everything. It was all slipping away from him.

43

PAIGE

Blue and red lights were flashing obnoxiously behind me. I'd never ran a red light before so I don't know what I expected.

"License and registration, please," asked a police officer when I rolled down the window. "Where are you coming from?"

I handed over my ID obediently. "The Palace Hotel."

"Where are you going?"

"Home."

"Sit tight," he said. "I'll be right back."

I waited. It seemed to be a long time, so I knew he was running my plates.

As I waited, I thought back over my morning. I'd woken up to a dark room, in an unknown bed, surrounded by too many pillows and a fluffy comforter I hadn't gotten used to sleeping on. The room was quiet and still. It seemed too quiet.

Why am I here? I questioned myself. The day I checked in I had turned off my phone. In the days that followed, I'd read the rest of mom's journal. I'd watched TV. I'd ordered room service. I never wanted to leave. I was comfortable. I had time to myself. I was safe. I was well-rested. I'd only left the room to venture downstairs for a trip or two to the gift shop when I ran out of clothes and basics. I had been able to live with very little considering I lounged around in the big, fluffy robe most of the time. I slept. I don't remember the last time I slept so long or so hard.

I woke up this morning and turned on my cell phone. It was time to leave. I had so many missed calls and texts from Stephen. But I didn't care about that. The text that got me moving was one from Amy.

Amy: *Hello, friend. Comin' home any time soon? I'm not supposed to ruin the surprise but let's just say, you have a pretty nice place to come back to. We miss ya. See ya soon.*

It was time to go home. I couldn't stay in mindless luxury forever. I had a life to live and I needed to get on with it. I had made a decision. I was done looking for clues that would lead to mom's murderer. I no longer cared about that. Mom made choices and lived her life in a way that I always knew would land her in a heap of trouble. Deep down, I knew she would probably end up dead way too young as a result. I'm not sure why any of this shocked me when it happened. I should have been expecting it. I had decided to let mom go. She wasn't coming back, and I'd made my peace with that.

I pulled on a pair of baggy jeans and frowned. Not as baggy as I'd remembered. All that room service might not have been such a good idea. I put on a new "I Love Branson" t-shirt and slid on my shoes. I pulled my long hair into a ponytail and even put on a little mascara. I was going home.

I packed up what few belongings I had and looked around the room. The journal lay nicely on the nightstand where I knew Stephen would find it. I was keeping my promise. It had only been a few days. I knew Stephen would find my trail soon enough. In fact, I'd make it easy to find me.

I had checked out of the hotel and found my car. When I'd left, traffic seemed a little heavy, so it was difficult to find an intersection that wasn't as traveled. But I made sure to look both ways as I ran a red light when I drove through the small bordering town. Small towns always had police close by waiting for something to do.

The police officer who had pulled me over came back to the car. "Did you know they have an APB out on you?"

"I don't know what that means." I was trying to be polite, but this really was starting to take too long.

"Apparently, you're a missing person," he said. "Extends past the Arkansas border."

I tried not to roll my eyes when the officer announced that. Must Stephen *always* overreact?

"Can they do that? For adults? I mean, I know exactly where I am. What if I just don't want to be found?" I smiled at him, trying to lighten the intensity of the moment.

"Are you in any danger, ma'am?" he asked.

"No, sir. Looks like you found me and I'm just fine." I flashed him another smile.

He looked suspicious. "Give me a few more minutes. I'll have you out of here in no time."

"No problem, officer." But I was starting to get fidgety. My plan might be working a little *too* well. I just wanted to get home.

He was back faster this time and handed my license back to me.

"Have a good day, ma'am." He tipped his hat.

"No ticket?" I was genuinely surprised.

"No, ma'am, just drive safe."

I did drive safe. Home was where I would finally be safe.

44

STEPHEN

Paige had been missing for fifteen days. Stephen had been calling hospitals and following false leads. He was just about to dial another number when his boss, Lieutenant Roger Higgins, stopped in front of his desk. He motioned for Stephen to follow him to his office. Stephen walked on two wooden legs with deep dread in his being. Stephen sat down in a hard chair that had very little cushion.

"Stephen, when is the last time you slept?" Lieutenant Higgins had more grays in his thick eyebrows than when he and Stephen first met and right now, they were furrowed in a seriously stern way.

Stephen didn't answer him. Mostly because he didn't know the answer.

"I'm debating telling you we got two new leads," Lieutenant Higgins said as he made a tent with his fingers.

Stephen sat up excitedly.

"What I should do is tell you I know you've been investigating this case and you have no business being involved in it. You're too close to it and you're exhausted. You're a living example of why we aren't supposed to investigate cases too close to us. There are other officers on this case, you know."

Stephen was horrified at the thought. "Wait, what do you know? How bad is the news?"

"I know you need resolution. So, we're going to proceed. But when this is done, I want your word that you'll take time off and get some R and R."

"Anything. Yes, absolutely. Please, tell me Paige is okay?"

"Her car was spotted leaving The Palace Hotel in Branson, Missouri. A local sheriff ran her plates when she ran a red light. He gave us a call immediately. He let her go without at ticket, but he's been following her ever since. Your call. Do you want him to stop her and bring her in?"

"No," Stephen cleared his throat. "I know where she's going next. What else?"

"Got a DNA match from that knife. It belongs to Ray Lennon, but we also got DNA from Krysta Mynart."

"Huh," Stephen said. He sat back and stared at the wall. "Well, that puts him at the scene of Jason's murder. Could have been a struggle, which would account for blood from both of them. Is it enough to convict him of that murder?"

Lieutenant Higgins nodded affirmatively.

"If he killed Jason Mynart, quite likely he killed Krysta as well," Stephen mused aloud.

"He was in Arkansas the night Krysta was killed," said Lieutenant Higgins.

"And he's been stalking Paige," Stephen finished.

A sudden, horrible thought came into Stephen's mind. "I've gotta go," he said. He stood up without saying goodbye and walked out the door. A few other officers fell in step with him and followed him out the door and into separate cars.

It took a good forty-five minutes to get to the Palace Hotel, which was on the way to Paige's Missouri home. Stephen made a quick stop there on the way in case she had doubled back. He had found the journal. He knew Paige well. If he'd found it, it was because she had wanted him to find it. Was it a sort of peace offering? Was she just done with it? He flipped through it, convinced it was all there until he got to the end. One page was torn out. Still, Stephen tucked it under his arm. The rest of the room was cleaned out.

"I know where she's going," Stephen said. He turned to the officers who'd come with him. "It's yet another long drive back to Missouri. If I need backup, I'll have to call in police there. Different jurisdiction."

As Stephen drove, he took the time to think. Paige wasn't answering her phone. He had been trying to locate her for the past two weeks. He tried to calm his mind and tell himself that Paige would be fine for a few hours at the house by herself. But he had a new theory now and he felt in his gut it must be true. Ray must have killed Paige's dad, Jason. Which made it probable that Ray killed Krysta too, or he was at least involved in it. He'd heard Paige's theory that maybe Krysta was supposed to die that night her husband died, and the murderer finally came for her. Ray, he thought, must have come back to finish the job he had planned more than twenty years ago.

Could the connection to Paige be as simple as her mother and father were killed? Was this a vendetta against the whole family? He needed to warn her. He wondered what the chances were that she would answer her phone this time.

Stephen picked up the phone and dialed her number.

"Hello?" Paige answered on the second ring.

"Paige?" Stephen was astonished.

"Hello, Stephen."

"Hello! Where are you?"

"I'm safe. Thank you for asking."

"Did you go back home?"

"Stephen, I'm fine. You need to let this go. All of it – the case, my mother's murderer, me. Let it all go. I don't care anymore."

"I can't do that, Paige. This is my job. I need to warn you about something. Ray –"

Paige interrupted him. Her voice held a hard edge. "I don't want to hear any more about it, Stephen. I'm done running around looking for clues and trying to figure out whodunnit. I understand this is your job and I won't tell you what to do and what not to do, but I get to choose what I do with my life too. I choose not to care anymore. I'm letting it all go. You should too."

"Paige, listen to me!" Stephen heard his voice raise. He couldn't help it. She wasn't making any sense. She had completely checked out from reality.

"Don't yell at me, Stephen. I swear I'll hang up on you."

"Don't." Stephen took a deep breath and calmed himself. "Don't hang up, Paige. You need to know what we've discovered about Ray."

"Ray? You're still on that? Ray was my mother's friend from back in the day. If he's following me at all, it's not to do me harm, it's to talk to me. Probably about my mother. NOT my mother's murder, like you. He might actually be able to tell me how my mom was back then. And he might even be able to tell me about my dad."

"Paige, please. You're not listening!" Stephen's voice was up again.

"I'm done listening to you!" Paige yelled back this time. He wasn't listening. He refused to listen to her. "It takes two to communicate. You've been talking *at* me for years! Not only am I done with this murder investigation, I'm done with you! Do you hear me? You and I are through. Done. I don't want you in my life anymore. Leave me alone!" Paige continued to yell. "Do not come here either. You are not welcome in my home ever again! I'm done!" Paige hung up the phone.

Stephen cursed loudly and hit the steering wheel. He kept driving. He slammed on his brakes at a stop light. He texted Paige a message he prayed she would see.

Stephen: *Ray killed Jason. We have proof. DON'T let him in. Don't believe his lies. Please be careful!*

The light turned green. He couldn't see if Paige read the text. Stephen pushed the gas pedal down and drove faster.

45

RAY

It was no coincidence that Ray showed up right after Paige stopped yelling inside the house. He assumed she and the boyfriend had just argued. But Ray was feeling pretty done himself. Done with this game of who lives and who dies. Ready to complete his own destiny. He got the impression the girl trusted him. He might never know why. He didn't care. He'd heard her yelling and then everything went quiet. Then he heard silence. This would be his best chance.

Everything about the way he dressed was meant to convey that Paige could trust him. Fall chill was starting to set in, so he wore a zip down jacket vest over a long-sleeved t-shirt, jeans, and boat shoes. He was clean shaven. Nothing he could do about the gray hairs that were coming in more every day.

He fixed his face into a pleasant look and bounded up the front porch. Before he could knock on the front door, it jerked open. Paige was scowling and she had tears on her cheeks. When she saw Ray, she let out a loud scream.

Her sudden appearance caught Ray off guard, as did the unfamiliar feeling that tugged at his heart. She really did look like him. Why had he never admitted it to himself before? She quickly wiped the tears away from her green eyes that mirrored his. She tucked a flyaway hair from her ponytail behind her ear. She was tall like he was.

"I'm sorry," Paige said, "I'm not in the mood for company."

"I can see that." Ray's voice was deep but quiet. "Perhaps I'll come back another time?" In the darkness of the porch, there was a momentary clap of light. It lit up the porch. In that moment, Ray saw fear in Paige's eyes.

She seemed hesitant. Was she trying to make up her mind? He played a hunch and turned, is if to leave.

"No, wait." Paige stopped him. "Sorry. I didn't mean to be rude. It's okay, you can come in." She opened the door wide enough for him to enter.

A loud clap of thunder sounded overhead just as Ray crossed the threshold of her house. Minutes later, lightning struck with a loud smack. Rain suddenly dumped out of the sky.

"Would you like something to drink?" she asked.

"Sure," Ray said. "Water is fine."

Paige shivered and laughed a little. "I got my air conditioning turned on. Ever since, I can't seem to get warm," Paige said as she left the room. That explained the big baggy sweatshirt she wore.

Ray looked around. It appeared Paige was moving back in. There were several full trash bags and a few other trash bags already half emptied. She looked to be unpacking.

Paige came back with two bottles of water just as her phone beeped. It was a text message.

Stephen: *Ray killed Jason. We have proof. DON'T let…*

As the message popped up briefly on the screen, both Paige and Ray glanced down at it. From his vantage point of where she had laid the phone, Ray could see the message.

Paige gasped softly. Her eyes immediately locked with Ray's. It was clear they had both seen the message. Paige casually tried to pick up the phone.

"I wouldn't touch that if I were you." There was an edge in his voice that told her he was used to getting his way immediately.

Paige looked him in the eye and defied him. She grabbed her phone.

In one swift movement, Ray closed the distance between them kicking her phone out of her hand. The phone went flying and hit the wall hard. It broke and landed on the floor with a sickening smack. She yelped loudly.

The kick had caught her off balance. Her hand and arm flung to the side and her body followed. She moved her hand around with pain in her eyes. Before she could retaliate, the back of Ray's hand connected with Paige's face, sending her whole body flying this time. The back of her head hit the wall and she crumbled weakly to the floor. Paige blacked out momentarily.

Ray picked Paige up and moved her to her parent's old bedroom. Just as he finished tying her to a chair in the corner of the room, she blinked her eyes and regained consciousness.

She tried to move. She blinked a few seconds. Ray had tied her hands together behind a chair. He had tied her feet together in similar fashion with twine. Try as she might, she couldn't budge.

Her eyes roamed around the room until they settled on a sight more terrifying than what this room represented.

Ray sat in a chair in the corner of the room across from her. An old-fashioned pistol sat on his lap. He seemed to not have a care in the world.

"Ah," he said conversationally, "there you are. Sorry that twine is so tight, but I can't have you slipping away. It's ironic, isn't it?" Ray began rhetorically. "There you are sitting in the corner of the very room where your mother slept long before you were born. Where she was sleeping the night—"

"You brutally murdered my father?" Paige interrupted angrily. "Why are you doing this?" Paige asked, her voice shaking violently.

Lightning lit the room momentarily.

Ray was smiling. Not a fake smile. Not a smirk. A real, toothy grin, like he was proud of his efforts. "I'll tell you the story. But first, let's have a little fun."

"Fun?" Paige spat the word bitterly, eyeing the gun as Ray picked it up and pointed it at Paige.

Paige's heartbeat seemed to slow, frozen in fear. Adrenaline pumped through her veins. Somehow, her core warmed. Her whole body started shaking.

Ray pointed the gun at her, put his finger on the trigger and pulled it. There was a click but no bang. He looked disappointed.

Paige felt her body numb and her emotions shut down. Her logical brain kicked in.

"What game are you playing here?" Paige heard her words steady and strong.

"The game, young one, is Russian roulette. I have two bullets placed randomly in this gun." He put the gun up to his own temple and pulled the trigger.

Paige gasped and squeezed her eyes shut. But, again, nothing happened.

"Why are you doing this?" Paige found her voice came out a little more forcefully than before.

"Ah, yes, story time. Your mom and Jason were friends to me and my wife, Allison. Then Allison was diagnosed with cancer. I didn't have insurance. I had no plan. Your dad and I were gambling buddies. We were pretty lucky…" Ray smirked. "Well, let's just be honest, shall we? We were scammers, card counters, tell-watchers… We had it down to a science. We made hundreds of thousands of dollars. Jason was holding it because he said he could wash it so we wouldn't get caught. I actually believed him. I was going to use my share to pay Allison's medical bills and get her the best doctors we could afford. There was even this new experimental procedure we were looking into. Which might have worked had it not been for Jason's double cross."

"My dad? He double crossed you?" Paige asked.

"He's not your dad, Paige. You might as well know before you die. Margaret had your DNA tested. Jason was not your father."

Paige felt the blood leave her face. "If he's not, then who...?"

Ray pointed the gun at Paige again and shot. Paige's eyes flinched and involuntarily squeezed shut. She jerked her head. Nothing happened.

"Well, that's easy. I'm surprised you didn't figure it out. That would be me."

Paige gasped loudly. "You're lying!"

"Shocking, I know. But surely, you can see the resemblance?"

Paige stared at him horrified. "So, this is how it all ends for me? Murdered by my own father?" Paige's face seemed to have a revelation. "What were the words the pastor said at mom's funeral? I rise before dawn and cry for help; I have put my hope in your word... Help," she said to no one in particular. Her voice trailed off.

"Making deals with God, Paige? How cliché. Does everyone do that before they die?" Ray laughed bitterly at the thought.

"I don't even know if there *is* a God," Paige whispered more to herself than Ray.

"Your mother was an alcoholic. The blackout drunk kind. The night she seduced me, I came home the next morning and Allison was dead. My dear, sweet, Allison died when I was off with some other man's wife. A woman, who wasn't even *half* the woman Allison was, robbed the last moments I would have had with my wife on this Earth." Ray's face was so low and so sad, Paige wondered for a minute if he might cry. He brought the gun to his head and pulled the trigger. Nothing happened.

Paige exhaled audibly. "You don't have to do this," Paige said.

"What other choice do I have?" Ray laughed bitterly. "Did you want to reconcile and be a family?" His voice oozed with sarcasm.

"No, I just... did you say Jason double crossed you?"

"Yes. As if losing Allison wasn't enough, I went back over for my cut of the money, and it was gone. He said he lost it in a poker game. He played this sad story about having a gambling problem and he was going to get help. I knew he was lying. I just needed to get both of them out of my way to search for it. Jason was neurotic and didn't believe in banks. Not that I blame him. Depositing large stacks of money would've alerted them to our scams."

"I found some money. Here in the house. How much are you in debt? I can help you."

Ray stood up angrily, his eyes wild. "It's not about the money!" He yelled loudly. He lifted the gun at her.

"Drop the gun." Stephen's sudden voice sounded in the doorway. Out of nowhere, Stephen had appeared.

"Stephen, thank God!" Paige said as her hands finally came free of the knots she had been working. Her wrists were raw and bleeding as she cleared her clothes from the gun she wore on her holster around her waist and pulled it.

Ray swiveled his gun in Stephen's direction and pulled the trigger. Stephen flew backwards. A bullet hit him squarely in the chest.

Paige screamed. Stephen's sudden appearance had

distracted Ray from her momentarily. She kept her eyes on Ray who seemed a little surprised his gun had actually fired.

"Stop!" She yelled, pointing the weapon right at Ray's center of mass. Paige fired off five shots at Ray. One missed, one hit his shoulder, but the other three hit him in his chest.

46

PAIGE

As Ray slowly began crumpling to the ground, I shot one more time for good measure. The bullet went right through Ray's temple. Ray slumped against the wall. A smear of blood marred the paint as he fell down to the floor.

I kicked Ray's gun away so he couldn't reach it if he somehow was still alive. I checked Stephen. Blood soaked his chest. Where exactly was all that blood coming from?

I feared the worst. As I felt for his pulse, my fear was confirmed. Stephen's pulse was so light, I felt sure Stephen was dying in front of me.

I looked around for a phone. My phone lay broken in the living room. Stephen's phone lay on the floor inches from where it had flown out of his hand when he was shot. I lunged for it and dialed.

"Nine-one-one, what's your emergency?"

I could not speak.

"Nine-one-one, what's your emergency?"

"They're dead. Both dead," I managed to get out. I quickly rattled off the address, hung up the phone, and put it in my back pocket.

I grabbed the bag that was still packed from the hotel and paused before leaving. The floors were new. The walls had been restored and repainted. The little house had a hodge-podge of trash bags, some that were full and some that were empty, none of which held anything of value to me now. I realized with a twinge of guilt that no matter how much work the neighbors had put into restoring this place to a better condition than before, it would never be my home. I could see into the room where Stephen and Ray lay bleeding. The room was destined for death and nothing good would ever come of it.

The EMT and police would be here soon. I quickly ran out of the house.

I got in my car and hit the gas. I had to leave before anyone could arrive to stop me. I had just killed a man and left another one for dead on the floor. I had a wad of cash, a few changes of clothes, and a passport with the name "Paige Mynart" in my bag. I had decided months ago to embrace my family name.

I was going home. Home to Canada. I was ready to break the pattern of these tragedies that were beginning to form my early adulthood. I could grieve for what my life had become later. For now, I had to get away. To put as much distance between me, my grandmother, Stephen, and memories of mom as possible.

I could hear her voice. The voice that belonged to my grand-mother was floating in my head. The voice that confirmed what I know I had become.

You are wicked, Paige, just like your mom was, and one day the whole world will see you for who you are… Now, I knew it was true. She was right. I had no choice now but to believe her.

I am wicked.

I drove to the airport and bought a plane ticket. When I settled in my seat on the plane, I felt so very tired. I buckled and felt my eyes get tired. My head nodded and my eyes closed.

ADDISON MICHAEL

Before the airline steward began to pantomime the safety precautions, I was fast asleep.

My dreams were a series of dark, horrific nightmares. In one frame, I was a small girl, terrified and walking all over the house calling for my mama who never answered. I was forced to crawl into bed and cry, soaking an empty pillow. In another frame, I was a middle-school child covering my ears as Billy Groot mocked me and sang made-up songs about my "missing mama." She didn't show up to the assembly where I performed a poem I wrote in front of the whole school. In another frame, my mom was not home to protect me when Eric Marple pushed his way through my front door after our first date and forced himself on me.

In another, my mom killed three people, all unsuspecting, innocent people, who didn't deserve to die. She was killing to protect her own secrets. No one could know that she'd killed her husband in such a brutal way. Yet, somehow, people kept figuring out her secret, and she had to kill them.

Another frame turned darker still with Ray. The handsome, yet ominous, man who vowed to kill me and almost succeeded. He was the darkest dream of all. He tried to kill me. My own father tried to kill me. Both my mother and father were murderers.

The last dream was the worst. I followed my mother. I followed her the night she was murdered. I was tired of wondering and worrying what she was up to all the time. I needed to know. I saw her. First with Ray. But I didn't know his name yet. Then she was with Matt. I didn't know him either. She left with him. But a few miles down the road, he pulled over and she got out of the car. He left her there, just standing on the side of the road. I pulled over. I got out of the car. I meant to ask her to get into the car and come home. I had every intention of saving mom from the predicament she was in.

246

But as I looked into her eyes, I snapped. Her green eyes were blank and lifeless. I could smell the alcohol on her breath. I knew in an instant why she functioned in a black out state and I felt so foolish. I just snapped. I slapped her first. I shouted at her. I told her she was a horrible mother, and my life was horrible because of her. I grabbed her shoulders, shook them, and told her to snap out of it. She didn't. My hands moved to her neck. I felt a strange sense of release as I tightened my hands around her neck, tighter and tighter. Suddenly, her body went limp. She fell to the ground. I could see what I'd done, and I panicked. I drove home and crawled into bed and slept until early afternoon. When I awoke that day, I remembered nothing of the night before. I was at peace.

"The captain will now turn on the fasten seatbelt sign as we make our descent into Canada. Welcome. We hope you enjoy your stay."

I opened my eyes, realization dawning. I had been dreaming but remembering simultaneously. I had remembered. In a panic, I took out my phone to take it off airplane mode. It wasn't my phone. My phone was broken in the living room of the tiny cabin.

In my hand, I held a small, silver phone. My hand started shaking. It was my mom's phone. I knew what I would find before I even opened it up and looked. Dread filled my soul. I found the text strand with my name. It wasn't hard. It was at the very top of her texts.

Krysta: *Paige, come get me. Please. Some jerk left me on the side of the road on I-40—you know the shoulder where I pulled off the road when you got sick that one time when you were little?*

Fine time for her to remember something, I thought bitterly. I read my own response.

Me: *I'll be right there.*

"It was me!" I whispered. *I was the one mom called. I was the last one to see her alive.* Tears formed in my eyes and I worked to quiet the hysteria I felt rising in my heart. I took deep breaths in and out, working to calm myself and not alert anyone as I thought about what to do next.

I should turn myself in. I could do that. But I had just made it to Canada. No one had stopped me. I was free and clear. I could easily get lost in the crowd, change my hair color, learn a new language, travel to other countries. No one would ever know. *Calm down, Paige, you've got this. No one knows. They never will.*

I was in Canada. It was just after midnight. I had a new identity and a plan to become this new person. I could put the past behind me and keep moving forward.

The one thing I hadn't counted on and had no plan for was an unexpected pregnancy.

I still remember the strange look I got at the hotel gift shop when I made three separate trips down to the store in the lobby for supplies, which consisted of cheesy tourist t-shirts and pregnancy tests. After the third test, I couldn't deny what my overly exhausted body was telling me must be true.

"I am pregnant," I had said in the bathroom after the third test came back positive. Saying it out loud did not make it feel real.

I never thought about the kind of mother I might be one day because, quite simply, I never wanted to be a mother. Why did nature, or perhaps God, have a different path for me? That's something I didn't think I'd ever understand. I had to shut that down. God doesn't exist for people like me. The wicked. The ones who have a murderer for a mother and a murderer for a father. But I did choose to murder both of them.

Genetically, I am the sum of the genes my parents gave me.

I had no choice. I wonder, knowing that I had killed both my own father and my own mother, will my child turn out the same way? I supposed I had better just accept my fate and the knowledge that she will. Because of course I will have a girl.

There was a chance that she could be noble, honest, and live with integrity like her father, Stephen. Stephen, who only wanted to love and protect me. Stephen, who also ended up dead thanks to me. But more likely, she will be exactly like me.

She will inherit my genes, my metabolism, my hair and eye color, and my disorder. She will become like me, black out for long periods of time and forget important moments of her life. Do terrible, wicked things as my mother did before me.

And one day, she will very likely kill me.

THE END

If you liked *What Comes Before Dawn*, check out book 2 in the series—DAWN THAT BRINGS DEATH.

PROLOGUE
JUD BLACKWELL

Dark red blood pooled underneath the body of Stephen Wilton. EMT, the Brighton Fire Department, and Brighton Police Department were all on the scene approximately ten minutes after a frantic 911 call was placed by an unknown female caller.

"They're both dead," she had pronounced with a finality in her voice that no one could dispute. She gave an address. Then she hung up.

There was no sign of the female, though Jud Blackwell, Fire Chief and dedicated neighbor, thought he knew exactly who had placed that call. Paige Deffer was the newest owner of the "Mynart Murder House" as Jud was starting to dub this place. He hooked his thumbs in his belt loops under his large belly that rested over the top of his jeans. His t-shirt was tucked in tidily. He had hastily thrown on his signature ball cap to hide his balding head. Then he rushed right out to the scene.

It had all started over twenty years ago with Jason Mynart, devoted husband and man of the community. Jason's body had been found with multiple stab wounds and blood dripping off the bed sheets. His wife, Krysta Mynart, had gone missing and all bets were on her as the murderess.

The home sat vacant until less than a year ago when Paige Deffer bought the place and moved in. *Trouble sure follows that gal around*, Jud thought as he surveyed the blood and damage in the exact bedroom where Jason Mynart had been murdered. Here they were some twenty-five years later. The boyfriend, *his name was Stephen*, Jud thought he remembered, was the first body they'd found.

It was hard to maneuver around Stephen's body and the blood that was pouring out of him. There was so much blood. *Was all that from the gunshot wound?* Jud wondered. From the looks of it, Stephen had just stepped through the doorway when he was shot, likely as he'd entered the room. Jud could see a slight smear of blood on the doorframe. Maybe Stephen had hit his head on it after he was shot. The blood was too high to be where a bullet went through, and there was no splintered wood.

Peering into the room at a certain angle, Jud could see the blood smeared down the wall as well as a second body. The slumped lifeless man lying there was Ray Lennon. Ray, he knew well.

"What in the world…?" Jud muttered aloud. What would put Ray Lennon in the same room as Paige's boyfriend? Jud assumed the two had shot each other. Guns lay discarded on the floor and only one person could logically explain what had happened here. Paige Deffer.

Jud clicked his tongue in shame. He had just been in this home repairing floors with his fellow neighbors as a goodwill gesture after some vandal came in and destroyed the wooden floors with a sledgehammer. The floors they had lovingly fixed were now stained once again with blood.

"This house is cursed," Jud announced, breaking the terse silence.

"We have a pulse!" a slender female EMT worker cried out. She had been working on Stephen. The rest of the team flew into action. Excitement and fast movement erupted. The workers applied a pressure bandage to slow blood loss before they carefully moved Stephen to a stretcher.

A lone police officer had managed to finagle his way past Stephen's body and the blood on the floor. He was bent over Ray's body inside the bedroom. When he straightened, Jud caught his eye. The police officer shook his head negatively at Jud.

"No pulse. This one's gone," the officer said.

The EMT crew left in a flurry of activity desperate to get Stephen in the ambulance and en route to the emergency room as quickly as possible. Jud could hear the siren's wail, which faded as they drove further away from the house. The officers sectioned off Ray's body with police tape. They were now calling this house a crime scene.

Jud stepped carefully over the blood and into the bedroom to get a better look at Ray.

"It's Ray Lennon. Lived around here his whole life," Jud said with a frown and looked at Ray's still, dead body. "What the hell happened to you, Ray?"

"Sir, if you don't mind?" A young female police officer gave him a pointed stare and motioned for him to step back. She was polite but firm.

Jud looked up in surprise and saw that he was standing a little too close to the crime scene.

"Sorry, ma'am. Tell ya what? Why don't I head on down to the hospital and see if I can help there?"

At her nod and grunt of approval, Jud turned away. Before he left the room, he took a picture of the crime scene with his phone. Just in case he noticed anything later on that no one else had noticed.

Jud sat heavily in his car and started it. He hit the gas. With any luck, he could get there when the ambulance did. He knew a shorter way.

Sure enough, he arrived at the same time. He could see the EMT unload Stephen and wheel him quickly through the doors. Jud was sure they had been working to stabilize him in the ambulance, but they were still moving pretty fast to get him in to the emergency room. It didn't look good.

Jud went into the emergency room and made himself

comfortable. He knew a bit about Paige Deffer, but he didn't know her boyfriend's last name. Stephen was definitely her boyfriend. Jud had seen him twice. Once when he decided to check up on Paige at her home and another time when the two of them left a neighborhood party together.

He opened his Facebook app and looked for Paige Deffer. She wasn't hard to find. Most young people were mighty proud of their relationships. Sure enough, she had it listed. *In a relationship with Stephen Wilton.*

He picked up his phone and called his buddy at the police station.

"Heya, Will," Jud greeted in his slow, laid-back way. "Say, we got a fella that came in here tonight," Jud paused and listened. "Oh, yeah, right. Of course, you know. Well, you guys get an ID yet?" Jud listened as his friend said they'd found his car parked just off the road down the street from the Mynart house and they were about to run his plates.

Jud chuckled. "No need, my friend. His name is Stephen Wilton. Think you can find his parents or next of kin? His girlfriend is Paige Deffer and she owns the place. Didn't see her there and there was no extra car. Suppose she could have come with the boyfriend." Jud had a terrible thought. "You guys might want to check her property to see if she's laid up somewhere there." He listened once more and then said his goodbyes.

He went to the check-in desk and asked them to tell him if any news came down about Stephen Wilton.

"Hi, Jud," the kind woman at the check-in desk greeted him. "You know I can't break HIPAA law, even if you are the Fire Chief and worked the scene."

"Right, right," Jud frowned. Jud knew from years of living in such a small town, it was only a matter of time before the gossip came out and he preferred to be the one to break it.

"Well, I'll be over here in the waiting room in case anyone needs a statement from me."

She smiled at him, grateful he didn't push her for more information and went back to her triage duties.

Jud found a semi-comfortable chair and closed his eyes, planning to fall asleep. A few years ago, the emergency room got a furniture update. This was the only big, overstuffed chair they left in the room that wasn't hard and plastic. Jud must have fallen fast asleep.

Jud was dreaming a little when he felt someone shake him awake. Disoriented, Jud opened his sleepy eyes and worked to figure out where he was. How long had he been out? He'd guessed a few hours at least.

"Excuse me, sir?" The man was wearing scrubs and an air of authority. It seemed clear he was a doctor. Jud thought he knew all the doctors but he had never met this man.

"Yeah?" Jud asked.

"Sir, are you a relative of Stephen Wilton?" the doctor asked.

Before Jud could answer, a frantic woman bolted up from her chair. The emergency room was small. She must have heard the doctor ask. It was pretty impossible to keep things private here.

"I'm Stephen's mother, Linda." She was thin and pretty with blond hair that waved down to her shoulder blades. She looked like she had cried off some make-up, but she was still fairly put together.

The doctor moved walked away from Jud to address Linda. Jud could hear them speaking in low voices.

"Is he okay? Will he make it?" Linda asked.

"Time will tell. He's lost a lot of blood. He has a collapsed lung which could take weeks, maybe even a month to heal."

She started crying softly. "Is that fixable?"

"Yes, but it will take time," the doctor double-checked his

notes then looked up. "He also has some swelling and bleeding on his brain that needs to be closely monitored. Do you know if he hit his head on something?"

Jud approached quietly. "Jud Blackwell, Fire Chief. I was at the scene earlier," he took a moment to shake both their hands.

Linda was too shaken up to be surprised by his sudden appearance.

"There was a blood smear on the doorframe. Also, the floors were real hardwoods. If he fell without catching himself on the way down, I reckon he could've hit his head pretty hard," Jud admitted, thinking himself clever to have joined the conversation the way he did.

"We're going to put him on a ventilator. He's stable but we need him to recover. He's in a medically induced coma right now."

"Medically induced?" Linda repeated with uncertainty.

The doctor nodded. "For now. I think it's the only way for him to stay still long enough to heal."

"How long do you think it will take?" she asked.

"We don't have an answer to that. It could be a month. It could be six months. A collapsed lung takes time to heal. Swelling in the brain takes time to heal. Then there's the matter of how much blood he's lost. That's a lot less predictable. We've moved him to intensive care if you would like to see him?"

"Yes, please."

Jud heard the doctor tell her to keep the environment as stress-free as possible as they walked back to the hospital room.

ALSO BY ADDISON MICHAEL

A Mynart Mystery Thriller series is ghostly suspense with psychological elements. Tap the links to buy these books today!

Book 2 - *Dawn That Brings Death* - Two men are dead at the Mynart Murder House. Paige, a newly single mom, is hiding in Canada. Will she be able to keep her daughter safe when a new enemy emerges?

Book 3 - *Truth That Dawns* - When Paige's secrets are exposed, she must face the consequences including a serial killer looking for revenge. He'll stop at nothing. Will Paige live to see her daughter again?

Book 4 – *Dawn That Breaks* - Anna is gone. It starts with a deadly car accident that creates too many questions. Will Paige learn the truth about her daughter, Anna, *before* a deadly ghost from her past ends Paige's life?

Book 5 - *What Comes After Dawn* - Soon-to-be father James is on his way to a business meeting when he's kidnapped with no way out. James soon realizes he's being used as a pawn in a game of revenge that may cost him his life.

The Other AJ Hartford - A phantom on a train. A mysterious kidnapping long ago. Can she connect the dots before all her futures disappear forever? Tap the link to buy the book today!

Join the Addison Michael Newsletter and receive the FREE story *How it Began.* Plus, receive alerts for new releases, FREE and ON SALE books, and what's new.

REVIEW REQUEST

If you enjoyed this book, I would be extremely grateful if you would leave a brief review on the store site where you purchased your book or on Goodreads. Your review helps fellow readers know what to expect when they read this book.

~ Addison Michael

ABOUT THE AUTHOR

Addison Michael writes riveting, character-driven stories heavy in suspense with a focus on the intriguing motivations that make a person a murderer.

Addison grew up in a home where rules were not meant to be broken. As such, she was the "goodest" of the "goody two shoes" around. Being the oldest of six siblings forced Addison to lead by example. Her golden reputation solidified well into her thirties.

But every good girl needs to have an outlet. Behind every smile and sweet comment, there is a dark side waiting to emerge. Addison Michael found the outlet for her dark side writing thrillers.

She has an uncanny ability to step outside herself and create believable characters who navigate unbelievable circumstances involving murder, mystery, secrets, and suspense.

Made in United States
North Haven, CT
08 January 2024

47183690R00147